He was afraid. More afraid than he'd ever been in his life.

"Susan!" The darkness swallowed his voice and there was no reply.

"Oh, God." He cut back the boat's engine to minimize the noise. Desperation drove him, but he had to hear and try to see. Other engines rumbled. Other voices called. They raised a spark of hope.

Scanning the water's surface constantly, he zigzagged. A searchlight came on. Coast Guard, he figured. Something tickled down his face. Sweat.

"Help!"

"Susan! Where are you?" He dashed the sweat out of his eyes.

Silent seconds passed. He must have imagined the voice. "Susan?"

Then faintly, "Here. Quick. *Please*."

And he saw her.

STELLA CAMERON

UNDERCURRENTS

MIRA

ISBN 1-55166-495-X

UNDERCURRENTS

Copyright © 1991 by Stella Cameron.

All rights reserved. Except for use in any review, the reproduction or utilization of this work in whole or in part in any form by any electronic, mechanical or other means, now known or hereafter invented, including xerography, photocopying and recording, or in any information storage or retrieval system, is forbidden without the written permission of the publisher, MIRA Books, 225 Duncan Mill Road, Don Mills, Ontario, Canada M3B 3K9.

All characters in this book have no existence outside the imagination of the author and have no relation whatsoever to anyone bearing the same name or names. They are not even distantly inspired by any individual known or unknown to the author, and all incidents are pure invention.

MIRA and the Star Colophon are trademarks used under license and registered in Australia, New Zealand, Philippines, United States Patent and Trademark Office and in other countries.

Printed in U.S.A.

For the crew:

Jerry Cameron, Bob and Colleen Fox,
Jim and Kathy Von Der Linn.

With love and with thanks for
keeping me afloat.

1

"**W**hy do you want to adopt a child?"

Because I want someone to love.

"Ms. Ackroyd?"

Because I've got so much love to give and it shouldn't be wasted.

"Maybe I should phrase the question differently?"

"No, no, Mrs. Brock. I was thinking, that's all." Susan smiled at the caseworker. She must say the right things, the things they wanted to hear. "I want to adopt because I believe every child deserves a good and loving home. I can provide that and there has to be a child out there who needs me." She stopped fingering her skirt and made her hands still in her lap. Any hint of nervousness could be seen as a sign of mental instability. They'd be watching for that.

The woman jotted notes on a yellow pad, her sleek blond hair swinging forward as she worked. Professional. Thirtyish, pretty, petite and confident, impeccable in a gray suit, Mrs. Harriet Brock was a pro at dealing with people.

Why was there so much to write about so little?

Susan stared at the Seattle skyline through the only window in the small office. July sun glinted on the colored glass of a dozen soaring buildings: pink, bronze, a blue to vie with the heavens, and the sinister black beauty of the Columbia Center—or Darth Vader as locals called it. From the streets below, honking and the roar of engines rose to dull the whir of an overhead fan. Susan had almost forgotten it was Friday afternoon. The city was already emptying out for the weekend.

"What made you decide you wanted to adopt a child?"

Susan started and looked into Mrs. Brock's light gray eyes. "Well..." Wasn't this the same question she'd just been asked? Susan wondered, and hadn't she already answered all these questions on the application forms?

No, she must relax and stop expecting traps.

"I've always wanted children. I had two miscarriages—" She paused, blinking rapidly. Crying wouldn't help. "It seems like the right course for me."

"I see."

More writing. What did Mrs. Brock see? That the woman facing her was very different from herself? That Susan Ackroyd felt she was a success because she owned her own small hairdressing salon and had no desire to help decide the fates of others?

"Now—" Mrs. Brock smiled and her eyes softened "—you were married for twelve years."

"Yes."

"Your husband...William...?"

"Bill. Yes. We've been divorced for two years. We—" We what? We stopped loving each other, and when we found out we probably couldn't have children, there didn't seem any point in going on?

"He's a banker?"

"Yes. In Boston."

"But when you moved from Oregon—you did come from Portland?"

"I grew up there."

"You had a happy childhood?"

"Uh...yes. My parents are retired and travel a lot. I have

a younger sister, Libby, who's married and lives in Switzerland. She and Georges are very dear to me.''

"Good. But back to your marriage and the move to Seattle. It was because of your husband's job, wasn't it?''

Susan laced her fingers tightly together. Of course they'd want to know about her marriage. She mustn't be defensive. "Bill was given a branch on San Juan Island, in Friday Harbor. We built a house on Brown Island. That's where I still live." This was all on the forms.

"Will you be able to keep the house?''

Heat rushed into Susan's face, the heat of irritation. "It's mine. I bought Bill out. My business isn't big, but it's successful. Providing for a child will be no problem. Believe me, I wouldn't have attempt—I wouldn't have decided to do this if I didn't know I'd make a good parent. My child will never want for anything, I promise you…'' No, not like that, not pathetic eagerness.

Harriet Brock kept smiling, waiting politely to be sure Susan had finished. "Was your sex life with your husband satisfactory?''

"Why?'' The retort was reflexive. A dull throb of embarrassment heated her face.

The woman blew out a slow breath, riveting her attention on a vase of overblown roses.

Susan pressed the fingers of one hand to a hot cheek. The roses smelled cloying. Drops of water from a careless hand lay between the sagging peach-colored petals of blooms that appeared too heavy for their drooping stems. Perhaps Harriet Brock cut them from her garden and brought them here in an attempt to put her clients at ease, to inject something of a relaxed, homey atmosphere. Her efforts weren't working—not on Susan.

"You do understand that it's essential for us to be sure about anyone we consider for a potential placement?''

"Of course." But her sex life with her ex-husband had nothing to do with her fitness to be a parent.

"We look for well-balanced people—in every regard."

They pried. No, that wasn't fair. They just did the job that had to be done. The thinking behind some questions was bound to elude her. "Our physical relationship was satisfactory." Not strictly true, but Susan couldn't risk more interrogation than necessary.

"Good. What about relationships now, Ms. Ackroyd?"

She obviously meant with other men. "None," Susan said with finality.

"You're thirty-five and attractive. Surely you must have had some, er—"

"No. I've been too busy and I'm not interested." And she didn't want to talk about how she'd like a man to share her life—the right man—but that she didn't expect to meet him.

"Do you think you'd be as interested in a child if you were involved with a man?" There was no change in the woman's serene expression.

Why did she have to go through this? Wasn't wanting a child the most driving force in most women? "Nothing could be as important to me as this is."

"Why did you and your ex-husband divorce?"

Susan lifted her chin and willed her mouth not to tremble. "We grew farther and farther apart until we were two strangers living in the same house. The decision was mutual and we're on good terms."

"The two of you never considered adoption while you were married?" A tiny frown of concentration accompanied the query.

This had some deep meaning. Susan breathed slowly. "The subject came up."

"But as long as you both thought you could have a child of your own, adoption didn't appeal to you?"

"It *always* appealed to me. Bill was…Bill wasn't comfortable with the idea." It was the truth, but she couldn't force the woman to believe her.

"Good, good," Mrs. Brock murmured, and Susan allowed her shoulders to relax. "Would you ever consider reconciliation?"

"No. And he's remarried." Stop, stop, stop.

"Hmm. I do feel we should stress that we prefer one parent to be at home with the child—at least during the first months."

Her throat hurt. "You know I'll be a single parent. I have a business to run, but I have an excellent staff. I can arrange to take some time off."

"Hmm." Mrs. Brock rolled her chair back from her desk and rocked. "You should regard this interview as simply an introductory one. My first responsibility is to the children we place. But I also want to help you avoid disappointment."

Susan's heart bumped. "Disappointment?" Was this it? Would they turn her down without giving her any chance at all?

"Should you decide to pursue this, you must be aware of the obstacles, the facts. Adoption isn't a simple process, even for people who are established in solid marriages. For the single applicant the procedure can be overwhelming. Very few stay the course."

"That's fine," she told Harriet Brock. "I'll be one of the few."

Only for Libby and Georges, Susan thought, would she cross San Juan Island on a Sunday, her mental health day. She should have come looking for Mike Kinnear on Friday. And she would have if her interview with Mrs. Brock hadn't left her in a ferocious mood. Even now she was still seething. The woman had deliberately tried to discourage her!

But all that had to be put aside, at least until Susan had done what she'd come to do. Somehow she was certain she'd need a cool head for this attempt to see the elusive Mr. Kinnear. She'd phoned and left messages for him three times. And so far, he'd ignored her.

One last try. This time in person.

She'd parked beside the narrow road above his property, and now she threaded a reluctant path through a white trellised arbor festooned with baskets of nodding fuchsias in a riot of colors from blood-red tipped with blue to palest pink and white.

Ahead and downhill she saw glimpses of the tiled roof of Michael Kinnear's house surrounded by tall evergreens and, beyond, stretches of sea the color of turquoise satin. In the distance, Vancouver Island rose darkly verdant.

Susan continued on, firmly putting aside the appealing thought of turning around, getting back into her trusty yellow Volkswagen convertible and zipping for home territory. She'd only been here once before, five years ago, and from that day to this hadn't seen Mike Kinnear or his glamorous wife, Frances. Coming in search of them now felt strange.

"Who are you?"

Susan spun around, her hand going to her throat. A diminutive girl stood on the path, her hands stuffed into the pockets of a knee-length cotton vest of frayed and torn denim.

"Hi, I'm Susan Ackroyd. I'm looking for Michael Kinnear."

"Why?" The girl blew a large fluorescent-purple gum

bubble, popped it and chewed, teeth over lower lip, until the mass disappeared into her mouth. She took off a battered brown felt fedora and angled her head to give Susan a better view of her hairstyle. One side of the girl's head was shaved. The initial *A* had been clipped on the scalp. "Why d'you wanna see Mike?"

Susan gathered her composure and moved closer. "That's between Mr. Kinnear and me. I don't suppose you're the person I talked to on the phone?"

An elaborate shrug shifted the ratted tangle of long green hair on the other side of the girl's head. "Don't know what you called about, do I? So I can't say if I ever talked to you."

"I'm the woman who called three times to ask for an interview with Mr. Kinnear. A girl answered. Was that you?"

Another shrug was the only response. A breeze sent the girl's vest flapping behind her skinny body, which was encased in a baggy black T-shirt and skintight black pants. High-top pink sneakers were the finishing touch. Susan tried not to stare at them.

"Well, if you'll excuse me, I'll go to the house and see if he's there."

The miniature scarecrow scurried around her, blocking the way to the house. "He isn't there. He's gone out."

"That's not what the gardener said." She hooked a thumb over her shoulder. "The old man who was pruning roses told me Mr. Kinnear was working on plans in his den."

Laughter transformed the elfin face. "Don't listen to old people. They don't know anything."

What color would the hair be? Blond, Susan decided while she noted the brilliant blue of the girl's eyes, lovely despite badly applied black eye pencil. White lipstick daubed onto the girl's pretty mouth added a clownish air to her appearance. Another case of someone's unwanted child running wild, a child with so much potential—if only she had a parent who showed her some love.

Susan didn't think the Kinnears had had any children. She opened her mouth to ask what the girl was doing here but changed her mind. Probably belonged to a neighbor and wandered untended all day.

Susan tried a smile. "What's your name? I expect it begins with *A*."

"Maybe it does."

So much for attempting to communicate. Already this youngster was moving beyond help. Susan thought of all the children no older than this one who ended up as runaways on the streets of Seattle. The stories were all variations on the same theme: their parents didn't understand them or were too involved with their own lives to notice a cry for help...like ridiculous dress and a sassy mouth.

"Excuse me." She skirted the girl and walked determinedly toward the house.

"I'm Anne," the girl said, catching up and sounding breathless. "He's not here. If you like, I'll tell him you came. I could ask him to call you."

This was definitely the voice from the phone calls. "Like you did before? No thanks." From what Susan remembered, the Kinnears were unlikely humanitarians, but she'd give them the benefit of the doubt. Maybe they'd taken pity on this waif and allowed her the run of their home.

When she visited the Kinnears before, with Bill and her sister Libby and her soon-to-be husband, these beautiful grounds had been cool and dripping on Thanksgiving Day. The house had been full of loud, extremely successful people who were so self-involved that the only voices they'd heard were their own. Mike had been something in finance then. He and his wife had lived in a Seattle condo all week and used the San Juan house on the weekends and holidays. From Libby, Susan had learned that the Kinnears lived here full-time now because Mike had changed careers. He'd become the owner of a boat refurbishing business on the island.

Susan reached a broad fan of curved steps made of pale stones and descended to the edge of an expanse of blue-green lawn edged with billowing masses of flowers. The path skirted this, but she spotted a big blond man working amid a mass of giant dahlias.

"Hello!" She started across the grass, realizing too late that it was soaked from recent watering. Her white sandals sank with each step, but she ignored the damp seeping beneath her bare feet. Matching squelches let her know that Anne was still following.

"Hi." The man had straightened behind the flowers, flexing hefty bronzed shoulders inside a sleeveless and tattered orange T-shirt.

Susan hesitated. Two gardeners. The Kinnears evidently still made a lot of money.

"Can I help you?" He had a deep rumbling voice. A shaggy mane of sun-bleached hair and an unruly beard made it tough to see his features.

"I hope so." This was what happened to so many people who settled in the San Juan Islands as teenagers because the life was easygoing and casual. They turned into middle-aged hippies.

He came into full view, carefully moving the flowers aside, and extended a muddy hand. Susan gingerly put her own into it and received a firm pump...and glanced down. His legs were long, extremely long and heavily muscled beneath faded cutoffs that had reached the point of no-more-to-cut-off. His toes showed through the split seams of ancient brown boat shoes.

When Susan's attention darted back to what she could see of his face, he appeared to be grinning. His clear green eyes definitely held deep humor or... Geez, men were all the same—he thought she was admiring his body.

He *was* grinning. She made her own smile broad while she removed her hand. Maybe he wouldn't notice she'd blushed. "I'm looking for Michael Kinnear."

"You're in luck. At your service." He bowed, then stood with his hands on his hips, the picture of healthy, self-confident charm.

She took a closer look. He couldn't mean...

"Mike, how long before we can go get Fredda? We wanna go to the park."

Susan had forgotten Anne.

"Soon, sweetie." He turned a different smile on the girl, a soft smile that did nice things for his already attractive eyes. "Maybe Miss, er, maybe the lady would like something cold to drink. Iced tea?"

"Aw, Mike..."

"No, thank you," Susan said hurriedly. She felt rooted to the spot. "Are you Mike Kinnear?"

"The same." He took a long stride from the dirt to the grass, and muscle rippled in every visible golden inch.

He couldn't be Kinnear. The man she'd met on that long-past Thanksgiving Day had been a flawlessly dressed and smoothly confident executive. If she remembered correctly, he'd been with a Seattle investment firm. He couldn't have changed this much, regardless of the career switch he'd made.

His smile went on and on, his teeth very white against the deeply tanned skin, until she realized she was staring, openmouthed.

"You look as if you think I'm an impostor."

Susan glanced at Anne, who stared back with frank curiosity.

"Hey." Kinnear ducked his head to peer at Susan. "Do I know you? You're—no, don't tell me. I never forget a face."

Was that why he'd chosen to hide behind a beard, because he didn't want to be remembered? He rolled onto his heels, flexing his thighs while he gazed at the sky and back to Susan.

"I wouldn't have known you," she said weakly, and winced. He'd undoubtedly think she was being critical.

"Yeah, I don't look the way I used to." He jabbed a long finger at her. "You got better-looking, that's what it is. But I've got it. Four, no, five years ago—here—right? Yeah, right. You're...Susan. Susan...Ackroyd!" He flung up his hands as if savoring an important triumph.

She nodded and felt a bubble of laughter rise in her throat. He was apparently guileless, except she knew otherwise. A knife-edged personality lurked inside his warm, fuzzy disguise.

He gave another of his marvelous grins. "You came to the house with your husband—a banker, right?"

She felt a little weak. "Right."

"And your sister, Libby, had just become engaged to a nice Swiss guy named Georges Duclaux."

"You've got quite a memory," she said honestly.

"I know. Georges was a friend of my friend Aaron Conrad. They knew each other from their ski racing days. It was Aaron who invited you all over because he was staying with us."

"Right." Couldn't she say anything but 'right'?

"Mike, when—?"

"Patience, pumpkin." Mike draped an arm around Anne's shoulders.

"I'm sorry to drop in on a Sunday like this," Susan said. "I did try to call several times, but you never got back to me."

He frowned. "I never got the messages. Who did you talk to?"

Susan avoided looking at Anne, but she needn't have tried to protect the girl. "I forgot," Anne said, a defiant thrust to her bottom lip.

Mike took his arm away and plunked his fists on his hips. "You know better than that, sweetie. You're supposed to write those things down." He returned his attention to Susan. "Sorry. You know how kids are. Important stuff on their minds."

Susan eyed him narrowly. Anne needed explaining. "Are you two related?"

"Related?" He laughed. "What do you think? Anne's my daughter. I'd have thought that was obvious."

Not from the girl's appearance. Susan glanced from one to the other and amended that. Maybe Mike's clothes should have clued her in. He was an overgrown version of his daughter, minus the makeup. What must Frances Kinnear think of all this? Would she be the kind of woman who appreciated a daughter using her parents' first names?

"Listen, Anne," Mike said, squeezing the girl's shoulder, "I think Susan has something she wants to discuss with me. Why don't you run inside and give Fredda a call? Tell her we'll be a little late."

"Mike..."

"Do it, sweetie." He interrupted her whine, but his smile never wavered.

Anne glowered at Susan. "She called Lester an old man. And she thinks he's the gardener."

If Susan believed children this young capable of deep jealousy, she'd say Anne didn't like to share her father with anyone—even casually.

He laughed. "The gardener, huh? That was my father, Susan. He hates gardening, but I make him get out for exercise."

Oh, great. She muttered an apology, waiting for Anne to leave.

"If I tell Fredda we'll be late, will you take me into Friday Harbor for those boots I told you I wanted?"

Susan looked from daughter to father, expecting him to be angry. Instead, he patted the green hair and said, "Sure thing. Run along."

"I'm gonna call Mom," Anne said, slanting a glare at Susan. "She's gonna visit soon. She said so."

Visit? What did that mean? "How is your wife?"

"Fine as far as I know." He watched Anne's progress as she backed away and turned to run in the direction of the Tudor-style house with its exposed cross timbers. "Aren't children wonderful?"

"Yes." Susan heard the flatness in her voice. Anne was a cute child, or would be if she were properly looked after. "How old is she?"

"Twelve. A real free spirit. I believe children should do their own thing, don't you?"

She didn't respond. This was another example of how the wrong people ended up with children. People like Mike Kinnear regarded their offspring as toys or pets—playthings to be indulged.

"When I was a kid everything was so rigid. If it hadn't been, maybe I wouldn't have taken so long to do what..." He paused. "Leave 'em alone and they figure out what they need."

She couldn't believe what she was hearing. Keeping her

mouth shut took superhuman effort. "When I was here before, I didn't realize you had a child."

"No." For the first time the sunny expression slipped and a speculative shadow crept into his eyes. "I came pretty close to ruining my chances of being a friend to my own daughter."

She wouldn't pursue that. He ran a hand through his unruly hair, and Susan's mind flitted over their conversation so far. Was she getting the message that the Kinnears were divorced?

Mike breathed deeply and painted the smile on again. "You really did get better-looking."

Susan couldn't help smiling. "Thanks…I think."

"Well…hell, call me Mr. Tact. What I meant was that I remember you with your hair long and pulled back in some sort of thing. I like it short and curly."

Susan restrained the urge to touch her hair. "I'm glad. I like myself better," she added, and felt a swell of pride in being able to sound comfortable with herself.

"It was the blue eyes that fixed it," he went on blithely. "I thought back then that you had the bluest eyes I ever saw on someone with such dark hair. Great combination."

"Thank you." Heat rose in her body, but so did a faint thrill. For whatever reason, Mike Kinnear was attempting to snow her, but she might as well enjoy the experience. It didn't happen too often these days. "How's Aaron Conrad? I never did find out what he does when he's not running his ski resort."

"Aaron's always into something. His outdoor equipment stores keep him busy. He calls from time to time— and visits. He's a silent partner in my business, you know."

"I heard. That's why I tried to get in touch with you. Evidently Aaron told Georges and Libby about it. They're in Hawaii. They'll be coming here and they asked me to talk to you first...about the work you do now."

He raised an eyebrow.

"The work you do with boats. Restoration. That sort of thing." She should have expected that with the change of occupation the man might undergo other changes. People who spent their days in boatyards, knee-deep in varnish and wood shavings, or whatever, were unlikely to work in chalk-stripe suits and silk ties.

Mike had been staring at her. He stirred visibly. "It's hot out here. We can talk on the other side of the house, on the patio. It's cooler close to the water."

Before she could respond he'd taken her elbow and moved them toward the path. Susan was conscious of him at her shoulder. She was average—average height and weight—but he was a very big man, and she felt his strength and bulk...and liked it. She almost laughed. Maybe she was frustrated, after all.

Approaching the back of the house, she heard the sound of distant surf. Mike smelled like the sea, she decided— clean and vaguely salty...and warm. And he was a lousy parent, and she wasn't interested in people like him.

On the patio he flapped a hand toward a white wrought-iron chaise. "I've got to have a cool one. Let me get you something."

"No...well, ice water would be nice." She must learn to take the time needed to be sociable.

In the few minutes that passed before he returned, she settled in the chaise, allowed her eyelids to droop and listened to the sea below the bluff where the house stood. She rarely had time to sit in the sun, and it always made her sleepy.

"Tired?"

Her lids flew open. "Oh, no, just resting."

He stood, looking down, his expression disturbingly somber. Susan had the sensation he'd been there a while and was suddenly very conscious of her thin yellow cotton dress. This had been one of the hottest summers she remembered, and she'd gotten into the habit of wearing as little as possible. He could probably see she wasn't wearing a bra. She resisted the urge to cross her arms.

Mike handed her a glass of water clinking with ice and topped with a thin slice of lemon before flopping into a chair and stretching out his legs. He sighed, popped the tab on a can of beer running with condensation and tipped back his head to drink deeply.

Susan observed, fascinated. Automatically she checked his belly. No flab there, just solid flat muscle.

"Aaah." He breathed contentedly through his nose. The sun glittered on his bleached hair, the tips of his curly lashes and the glimpses of hair that showed through his awful shirt. "Well, Susan Ackroyd. This is nice, but I do get the feeling you've got something on your mind."

And he'd caught her looking him over again. She drank from the glass and set it on the brick patio. "Georges and Libby have been in Hawaii on a combination business and pleasure trip. He and Aaron Conrad are in regular contact, and Aaron suggested Georges should get in touch with you."

Mike regarded her for an instant before tilting his head to swallow more beer. He rested the back of a hand on his mouth while he stared some more. Then he leaned toward her so abruptly that she jumped. "Why? Why does he want to get in touch with me?"

He was too close, but she was loath to try to move away. She felt an odd test of power between them, which seemed ridiculous.

"Georges bought a boat, a seventy-two-foot motor

cruiser, at an auction on Kauai. Evidently it's in good mechanical condition but pretty run-down otherwise. That's where you come in."

"I doubt it."

She blinked, taken aback. "I beg your pardon?"

He dangled the beer can between his knees and swung it back and forth in strong fingers. "Whose boat was it?"

Susan remembered Mike's cool, beautiful and self-involved wife with her mass of carefully windswept-looking blond hair and gorgeous figure. Five years ago Frances and Mike had seemed a matched pair, at least in appearance. Imagining Frances with this compelling but unconventional man would take more inventiveness than Susan possessed.

He made her nervous. Even as he smiled he made her nervous. The thought startled her.

"I asked who the boat—"

"Yes, yes. Georges said it was abandoned by some sort of Middle Eastern royal who skipped Hawaii leaving a pile of debts behind. Evidently it had been bought as a gift for a female friend but never given. That's all I know."

Mike got up and walked to the railing surrounding the patio. A hummingbird hovered at a feeder, its wings like tiny helicopter blades in action. Mike stood very still, watching, smiling. He had a wonderful mouth that even the beard and mustache didn't hide. Susan shifted awkwardly in the chaise, afraid to disturb the moment, afraid of her own reactions.

"Was it auctioned by creditors?" Mike asked, still studying the bird.

"Yes, that's right." She swung her feet to the ground and pulled her full skirt around her legs. "Georges said it was a steal."

"Yeah, sure." He sighed as if pained. "Standard auctioneer crap. They're like buzzards waiting for a gullible mark. I only hope he hasn't bought a complete load of junk.''

Susan bristled and stood. She went to stand beside him. ''My brother-in-law is a highly successful financier. You know that. He isn't the type of man to get sucked in by talk. He would have had a preliminary inspection done. In fact, I know he did because he mentioned it.''

Mike cast her a reflective and disturbing glance before turning to lean back against the railing and cross his ankles. Susan didn't remember being quite this aware of a man in longer than she wanted to think about. Her first assessment couldn't have been more wrong. He wasn't middle-aged. Late thirties perhaps, only a few years older than she was, and stunning, or he would be without the excess hair.

''Do you still live on Brown Island?'' He inclined his head to the south where tiny Brown Island nestled in the outer reaches of Friday Harbor.

''Yes.'' Evidently he remembered a great deal about her. Her heart made a strange little turn. He remembered just about everything that could possibly have been said in that brief conversation five years ago. ''I like it there. But this is a more spectacular spot. Your house is beautiful, and the view.''

''Mmm. I love it. I wouldn't live anywhere else.''

Much as she might like to stand and talk like this, Sunday was her day for running errands and there were other things to be accomplished. ''Georges and Libby expect to wind up their business in Hawaii within a few days, a week at the outside. They'd like to meet with you and discuss having you work on their boat.''

''Mmm.''

"Would you be available toward the end of the week? Thursday, say?"

He turned toward her, frowning. "I really don't think so."

He was odd, elusive behind the charm. "Friday, then? If we could leave the time more or less open, either for the morning or the afternoon, it would be better since their schedule will be uncertain."

"No, Susan. I'm sorry, but that probably won't be possible." His green gaze settled on her mouth, then flickered to her eyes.

She took a deep breath that didn't take her mind off a shivering under her skin. One of late July's torrid breezes caught at her dress, flattening the skirt against her legs. Mike's attention ran to her toes and back, so fleeting it might never have moved from her face, but she felt the impact.

This was getting her nowhere, and sexual tension wasn't something she needed, particularly with a man with whom she could have nothing in common. "Am I to take it that you're completely uninterested in meeting with Georges and Libby?"

He rested an elbow on the railing, digging at his bottom lip with his teeth. "I've never worked on a boat I didn't buy myself. I buy at auction, too, and do the renovations, then sell. Bigger profit margin that way."

"You mean you wouldn't work on a boat someone else bought?"

"I mean I'm choosy." His smile was a little strained now, and he spoke more to the brilliant sky than to Susan.

In Susan's business the customer was the choosy one. She hadn't worked her salon into the most successful of its kind in the San Juans by being "choosy" about who she served. "Well, I've given you the message I was asked to give—"

"I'm also choosy about who buys my boats," Mike continued as if she'd ceased to exist. "My men and I work on one at a time, and when they're finished, they're a work of art. People who raise pedigree dogs don't let them go to just anyone. A good boat takes a hell of a lot longer to put together than a dog."

Or a child. Susan stared, a familiar sick feeling in her stomach. He sounded horribly like a strange twist on Mrs. Brock. Only Mike didn't seem to have nearly the concern about what was best for children as he did for boats.

He'd bowed his head while he watched her, a faint upward tilt at the corners of his mouth. He believed he was right—in everything. "Do you have a problem with what I say—about special things deserving special attention?"

"Well…let me get this straight. You don't work on boats you haven't chosen in the first place and then you don't sell them to people you don't think will make good parents.…owners, I mean."

He wrinkled the bridge of his straight, slightly sharp nose and looked almost shy. That *had* to be an optical illusion. "I guess so."

She took a second more to recover. "So I'll tell Georges you aren't interested?"

"I didn't say that."

"Then what are you saying?"

"Mike!" Anne cannoned from a French window that stood open onto the patio. "We've *got* to go. I mean it's like *so* important. And I want to tell you about Mom. She's in some kind of bind."

Susan turned away and made to leave, wishing she didn't want to stay, didn't want to spend more time with a man who obviously had a very full life already…and she wished she didn't feel so resentful of his having a child he had no idea how to care for.

"Susan." He caught up with her, and for one moment seemed about to touch her. Instead he put his hands in the pockets of his cutoffs. "Look, I doubt very much if there's anything I can do for your sister and her husband, but I'll let you know."

"How long will that take?"

"I can't tell you—"

"Mike!" Anne wailed her father's name.

"I'll be in touch, okay?" He gave Susan a last lingering glance, before he loped back toward Anne.

"Okay," Susan murmured.

2

Tired, Mike slumped on a bench by the waterfront and shut his eyes against the sun. Today had been rough—fraught with wrangling customers, truculent suppliers, and his never-ending worry about just how well he was really doing financially. But he'd left the boatyard early to come into Friday Harbor and ask a few questions about Susan Ackroyd.

Now that he thought about it, he couldn't believe he hadn't seen her in all these years. Not that their paths were that likely to cross. She was a hairdresser who owned the salon on the balcony above a row of shops to his right. He squinted up: The Island Clipper Company. When Frances had still been with him and they'd spent each week at their condo in Seattle, she'd used one of the big salons there. His intelligence network told him Susan had only been in business two years, which meant he'd already been divorced a couple of years when she opened her doors.

He could have waited until later to stake out the shop. Six o'clock had already come and gone, and there had been no sign of her, although customers and staff members had dribbled out since five.

Before him stretched the harbor with Brown Island rising on the right. To his left, the main marina was jammed with boats, millions of dollars of discretionary income bobbing and jostling along the wooden fingers that stretched out from shore. The usual colorful melee jammed the waterfront. He hooked his elbows over the back of the bench and idly studied the familiar line of passengers filing aboard the green-and-white Washington State ferry that had just docked. A steady clanking sounded as cars filed over metal plates and into the vessel's lower hold. Close to the dock wobbly adventurers wove back and forth on rented red mopeds, trying their skills before being turned loose in their ill-fitting white helmets.

Clasping his hands behind his neck, he resumed his vigil over the little shop. Hanging baskets laden with begonias swung above the windows, and brilliant wind socks twirled like giant fishing lures. When Susan put in an appearance—and he hoped that would happen soon—he'd maneuver himself into her path and at least hope she'd buy a "fancy bumping into you" approach. He didn't intend to really examine his motives for being here.

What *did* he think about working on a boat bought by Georges Duclaux? He hadn't seen the guy in years, but he remembered him. Big-shot financier from Geneva. Handsome in that very European way, with the kind of Continental manner women went crazy over. But nice. Mike had to admit that. And Aaron liked him a lot, which was the best recommendation anyone could get as far as Mike was concerned.

The truth was, that whether the guy's boat interested Mike or not, it would be months before he could start work on her. Every member of his five-man crew was busy on another boat—a big schooner— On the other hand, the books didn't look so good, and the only way to make more money was to step up production. He closed his eyes and breathed in the scent from a bed of carnations struggling for survival amid the dust thrown up by passing vehicles.

Susan Ackroyd had been a surprise. He'd taken a few

minutes to recognize her, but only a few. Her new, short curly haircut softened her features, but how could any man forget those eyes? Big and blue…such a dark blue. Her brows followed the same line, fine and feathery, and her lashes were thick.

She was smaller than any other woman who'd ever interested him, but not too small. Was he interested? Maybe. Maybe she was just right and just what he needed. Different, not a classical beauty but…right.

He remembered that when he'd come back to the patio with the drinks on Sunday he'd watched her resting for a moment with her eyes closed. A tight sharpness gripped his insides. When she'd opened her eyes and caught him at it, she hadn't looked as if she minded too much. And he sure hadn't. Her body was all smooth lines and curves, slender and lush in all the appropriate places. He whistled through his teeth, deliberately shifting mental gears.

He'd told her he would think about Georges's proposition. When he said it, he'd been trying to make sure he had an excuse to contact her again. But it could just be that he should give the whole thing more thought.

Susan hadn't been wearing a ring. When he found out her occupation, he'd assumed she took it off for work. But that wasn't it. His informer told him she was divorced and a loner.

He concentrated on Brown Island, accessible only by private boat. Houses hugged the shore, most with private docks. He had to find out exactly where she lived…just in case. An interesting woman like Susan Ackroyd shouldn't spend too much time alone…and neither should a man who was growing tired of his own company.

Susan crossed the salon with the last load of clean towels from the dryer. Jeff, her only male hairdresser, stood by the door, zipping up the leather jackets he wore to ride his motorcycle.

"You about done, Susan?" Jeff let her know in many carefully casual ways that he cared about her safety. A tall, rangy twenty-five-year-old with straight dark hair that he wore slicked back, he was one of the few true artists Susan had encountered in her profession.

She dumped the towels behind the washbasins before she could speak. "Another five and I'll be gone. And you're going to be late to meet Molly, which won't make me popular." Molly was Susan's manicurist, when she wasn't doubling as receptionist. Molly and Jeff were engaged, and Susan frequently found herself praying they wouldn't decide to settle elsewhere once they were married.

Jeff added leather gauntlets to his outfit and slid on a black helmet. He saluted and muttered something unintelligible before he left. Almost immediately he stuck his head back inside, lifting his visor. "Lock this door after me until you leave."

Susan grinned at his departing form. "Yes, Dad." The setting sun shone brightly through the glass, and plenty of people were walking by. With the closed sign in place she had nothing to fear.

Tuesday was the day when she usually went home early, leaving Jeff to close up, but not today. Today she'd switched with him, too unsettled to face her beautiful but empty home across the water.

Out of habit, she checked supplies against her stock book, counting bottles and jars and making notes. Since Sunday, too many unwanted and confused thoughts had been tumbling around in her head. At the center of every one hovered Mike Kinnear. She couldn't get the man out of her mind. For disquieting moments she'd even daydreamed about how it would be if she discovered that he, too, was interested in adopting a child. Really crazy. He already had a daughter and could probably have more biological children whenever he wanted them. Besides, she and Mike Kinnear were total strangers and never destined to be more.

The promised call from the adoption agency to set up her next appointment hadn't come. Unable to stand the wait any longer, she'd called Mrs. Brock, her heart hammering in her throat, only to be told that the woman was out of town and would get in touch when she returned. No, the receptionist wasn't sure when that would be. Sure, Susan could leave a message. And she'd done so, convinced at the same time that the effort was futile. Harriet Brock would proceed at her own pace—her own *slow* pace.

The whole thing would be like this. One big put-off, only Susan wouldn't give up. She set her mouth in a thin line and slapped the book shut. If by no other means than through sheer tenacity, she would eventually have a child of her own. Even as she thought it, a lump of wanting rose in her throat and her eyes prickled. She *would* adopt a child of her own, Susan repeated to herself…if she didn't die of anxiety first. She'd feel better when Libby arrived and they could talk. Surely whatever was troubling Georges would turn out to be nothing.

Libby had called again—still sounding subdued and anxious. The Duclaux' arrival in the San Juans had been put off to Thursday of next week. But that wasn't long. Susan could hardly wait to see her sister, and Georges— and Jean-Claude Duclaux, too. Jean-Claude was Georges's nephew and close business associate. Susan had never met the nephew but Libby spoke of him with great fondness.

Susan smiled. Having company would feel good. At

twenty-nine, Libby was as bubbly as she'd been from childhood. And Libby could always whip Susan into a good mood.

That was good. So far Susan hadn't discussed her adoption plans with her sister, but she expected Libby's approval and could really use a dose of her enthusiasm.

Susan paused, the stock book halfway into a drawer. The unpleasant rolling in her stomach came again, as it had every few hours since Libby's peculiar phone calls had started. Each time Libby's voice had been lowered, urgent. Georges didn't know Libby was using the phone and Susan must never tell him, but Libby was frightened. No, she couldn't explain why because she didn't really know. But Georges felt threatened by something. Libby was sure of it, and whatever threatened him was also a threat to her, Georges's overprotective behavior proved that.

Susan sat behind the reception desk. When they were children, Libby had been the imaginative one, always making up elaborate games that involved skulking through the grounds of the rambling house on the outskirts of Portland, Oregon, where they'd grown up. This latest intrigue was probably just Libby's imagination at work again.

Susan's stomach made another unpleasant revolution. If she was so sure Libby had nothing to worry about, why this pervasive sense of doom?

She got up to close the vertical blinds over the door and made her usual round of the salon, making sure faucets were off and appliances unplugged. Getting home would probably be a good idea. The peaceful trip across the harbor in her trusty old motorboat always calmed her down, and she needed to be at the house in case there were more calls.

Michael Kinnear had been some shock. His pale green

eyes were unforgettable—sometimes distant, sometimes searing...sometimes devastatingly gentle. And when he grinned...he was the type of man who could be dangerous to a vulnerable woman's peace of mind.

Oh, fanciful silent hours. How they played havoc with an unoccupied mind. Finding out from Claire at the bank that Mike was divorced hadn't helped, except to encourage Susan's psyche to declare open season on daydreaming. She could see him now, big-boned, all well-toned muscle. Clearly his work kept him physically fit. Physical. A small animal shimmer of sensuality slipped through her insides, and Susan found her face hot.

When Libby arrived, they'd talk, and this time Susan would try to be open to any suggestions her sister had for a dramatic change in life-style.

Please let Libby be only imagining that there was anything wrong. She made it sound as if there could be danger.

In the small staff room, Susan ran a comb through her hair, changed from her lace-up work shoes to sandals and turned off the radio that had been left blaring.

Rattling. She stood very still. Someone was rattling the shop door handle—trying to turn it. If Jeff had returned, he'd use his own keys. Anyway, she'd heard the engine of his bike when he rode away. No one came here after hours, and with the closed sign in the window anyone would assume the place was empty and leave. Unless they were checking, planning to break in.

She sidled into the salon, keeping against the wall until she could see the door—and the vague shadow of a figure through the blinds. She glanced at the phone. To reach it she'd have to walk within a few feet of the door. The figure moved, seemed to turn away. Was he looking around to see if he'd been noticed?

If she stayed still, he might go away. Or he might jimmy

the lock. She began to sweat. There had been break-ins in the area recently.

This was ridiculous. All she had to do was make a noise and he'd go away. Burglars wanted a fast in-and-out and no trouble.

She burst into song. "Whenever I see…whenever…" Song lyrics never stayed in her head. She whistled, picked up a brush and thumped it against the wall.

"Hey!"

At the bellow from outside, she froze.

"Susan. Open up."

Blood seeped slowly back into her veins. A second later her legs responded to command and she crossed to open the blinds over the door.

Against a backdrop of dazzling late sunshine she was confronted by the intimidating picture of Mike Kinnear frowning at her through the glass.

More seconds passed before he brought his face closer and yelled, "How long are you going to keep me out here?"

Susan went into action. Settling a calm expression in place, she opened the door. He didn't have to know her heart was doing jumping jacks. "I'm sorry. I didn't—" She didn't make a habit of lying. "Frankly, you scared me to death. I thought you were a burglar or something."

He looked momentarily nonplussed, then spread his hands. "Hell, I'm sorry. I should have thought of that. I was…I was in the area and decided I'd, er, drop in. I did knock first. You had music on, so I figured I'd try the door."

Unsure of himself? Nope, she *must* be imagining things.

"Are you going to invite me in?" He rallied visibly, his irrepressible smile firmly back in place.

In his case, at this moment, in her frame of mind, Susan

wasn't at all sure she should have him anywhere near, but she assumed he'd come to talk about Georges and Libby's boat. "Come in," she said, standing aside for him to pass.

He walked to the center of the room, more presentable in faded but clean jeans that accomplished what she would have considered impossible: made his legs look even longer and more powerful. A long-sleeved cotton shirt, gray and white-striped and open at the throat, intensified his tan. He'd combed his hair, and in the salon's subtle lighting he took on a golden glow that turned his extraordinary eyes the color of pale polished jade.

"Nice little place," he said.

"Thank you." All she wanted to do was watch while he literally seemed to fill her "nice little place."

"You've got an eye for color and style. I like that. Most women don't have it."

She laughed. "I've known many women with flair for decorating."

He smiled, deflating her irritation. "I expect you're right. I always react positively to blues and grays—and beautiful wood. I guess you'd say I'm a wood man." He stroked the edge of the reception desk, an antique cherry piece Susan had lovingly sanded and oiled. His broad hand was gentle in its touch. She had the sensation that he felt the grain as a blind person feels braille.

"Did you come to discuss the boat?" she asked, uncertain that was all she hoped for.

"Mmm."

"Good." Glancing around, she saw the only chair that appeared remotely substantial enough for him and dragged it forward from its place near a hairdryer. "Please sit down."

He remained standing and continued smiling. "I thought we could go somewhere for a meal. Might as well make talking more pleasant. I thought we could go over to the Blue Heron.''

Susan's heart flipped. "Um, well, I can't."

The smile jelled a little. He probably wasn't accustomed to women who didn't swoon in their rush to accept an invitation from Mike Kinnear. "Why?" he asked. "Hot date?"

"No!" Damn, why did she have to sound so adamant? "No, I have to get home."

He rested an elbow on the reception desk and regarded her seriously. "Do you know I'm divorced?"

"Yes." There wasn't enough air in the world to fill her lungs.

"I know you are, too. So there's no reason not to have a friendly bite to eat and a drink like civilized people, is there?"

At this moment she could think of one very strong reason. "What about Anne?"

He shrugged. "She's got my father, and Connie...and everything imaginable a child could want."

"Connie?"

"Our housekeeper. What do you say?"

"I'm expecting a call from my parents. They're touring in their motor home and they check in at odd times. And Libby and Georges might call."

"Might? Doesn't sound to me as if you've got anything pressing, unless it's a pressing dislike for me."

"I...no, of course not. Are you sure Anne—?"

"I'm sure. I understand you don't have any children. On days like today I think you're lucky."

Susan's mind became ice clear. "I thought you loved your daughter."

"Oh, I do. But let's just say the old nerves wear a little thin sometimes. Single parenting is no joke."

She made fists at her sides. "Really?"

"Really." He sighed. "I don't do so badly at the job. But this is a case when one child is enough—take it from me."

She had nothing in common with this man—nothing at all and never could.

"What do you say?"

"Thanks for the invitation, but I really must do what I'd decided on. Perhaps we could set up that meeting I asked about—between you and Georges. They've put off their arrival date. They won't be here until Thursday of next week."

"Oh." He pursed his lips, apparently deep in thought. A deep line formed between his brows. "I do better at these things in a relaxed atmosphere."

Susan wasn't fooled. For whatever reason, he was angling to spend time with her. "The atmosphere is relaxed here. And it would save time if we just got this over with."

"No, I don't think so." The upward tilt of his jaw revealed a strong throat. "Look, I've got an idea. I need a few more days to think things through."

"All we need to do is set up a date and time. I won't be involved in anything more. If you need further information, I could tell you what Georges told me. About the boat." There was no doubt he was playing with her. "It's seventy-two feet and—"

"No, no. That's not necessary, not now. Come to my place on Sunday. We're having a barbecue. Nothing fancy, just Lester and Anne and me."

Bemused, Susan squelched the temptation to tell him that what he suggested made little sense to her—as an appropriate setting for a brief, and for her, casual business discussion. "I'm not really the one you should be talking to. Maybe we should just wait until they arrive. When I talked with him on the phone, Georges suggested that since you're busy, you might prefer to work them in at a time that's convenient for you. Anyway, I'm sure a meeting can't be all that difficult to arrange.'' She was sure of nothing except that he confused her.

He grinned again, and the result was exactly what he must intend it to be. Susan couldn't stop her own smile, or the melting of her reserve.

''Okay, fess-up time. I'd like you to come over. Simple as that. Dad always told me honesty was the best policy, so there it is. How about it? I'll feed you and you can keep me company.''

She laughed. He had that effect on her, made her inhibitions wobbly. ''And you'll tell me when you'll be able to see Georges and Libby?''

''Maybe.''

''Then maybe I can't come.''

He sighed and bowed his head. ''I'm still trying to make up my mind how I feel about this, Susan.'' When he looked up, his smile had become wry. ''You probably think I'm being difficult, but I don't mean to be. But—'' the smile became devilish ''—if you come, you could work on me.''

Susan grinned in return but suspected there had been some innuendo in his suggestion. She made her decision. ''Okay. Okay, yes, I'll come.'' It was time she did a few things she simply wanted to do—because she wanted to and for no other reason. In truth, she'd like to see him again, regardless of how futile the exercise would undoubtedly turn out to be.

''Great.'' He stood, hands on hips, radiating satisfaction. ''Do you use the public dock?''

''Excuse me.''

''On Brown Island?''

"Oh, no. I've got my own."

He nodded, squinting into the middle distance. "I'll bring a boat around for you at about four. I don't think you ever told me where your house is."

Susan felt an unaccustomed jolt. She wanted to go, but she didn't want it to feel like a date. "I keep a car here in Friday Harbor. I'll bring my own boat over and drive to your place."

"You don't have to do that. Really, let me come for you."

Her privacy and independence had become more important than she'd previously realized. "I usually stop in here sometime on Sundays. It would be easier if I came to you under my own steam." It would probably be easier if she didn't come at all. "Would about five be all right?"

"Hmm."

Obviously he was coping again with the unfamiliar experience of not having his wishes snapped up.

"Good," Susan said. "I'll look forward to it then." And she'd worry and fume and try to talk herself out of going. She took her purse from beneath the desk and found her keys.

"I'll walk you to your boat," Mike said, evidently taking the hint.

Outside, he surprised her by holding her elbow in an almost courtly fashion. The gesture made it impossible not to walk very close. Mike was a big solid presence at her shoulder, not an unpleasant sensation, but an unnerving one. They were strangers, yet there seemed to be an intimacy between them that made Susan all too aware of being female and in the presence of a very masculine male.

On the wooden steps leading down to the sidewalk, Mike paused and rifled through his pockets. Susan glanced at him until he met her gaze.

"I've got a thing with keys," he said. "Where did I put the darn things?" He rammed his fingers into his front, then back pockets.

Susan couldn't take her eyes from his face. His cheekbones were high, his nose straight. The distinct outline of his mouth showed, even with the beard and mustache she itched to shave off.

"What's wrong?"

She jumped. "Nothing." Keys in hand, he'd probably been looking at her for several seconds while she mentally rearranged him.

A quizzical light remained in his eyes, but he took her elbow once more and led her to the sidewalk, past the Blue Heron restaurant and down to the marina where dinghies and other small craft were moored along floating wooden piers.

Susan approached her Tollycraft, untied the bowline and hopped aboard.

"What were you thinking back there?" he asked.

She shaded her eyes to peer up at him. With the sun behind him his face was in shadow. "I told you. Nothing."

"Remember what my daddy told me about truth?" He sounded as if he was smiling.

Grimacing, deciding she had nothing to lose by being direct, she said, "I was remembering how you looked without the face fungus. Or trying to remember."

His laugh was short, a bark. "Face fungus? Nice."

"Well, you asked."

"And you don't like it, huh?"

"I didn't say that." She turned the key in the ignition, and the engine roared smoothly to life. "Bye," she called, waving as she nosed the boat alongside the pier.

He waved back, standing with his legs braced apart, his hair blowing in the breeze. As she turned to port, her angle on him changed and she could see his face again—somber. The effect stilled her hand on the wheel. Somber, speculative, assessing. Mike Kinnear had slipped into another frame of mind, one she hadn't witnessed before. She wondered what thoughts were coursing through that quick mind.

"Do you know I'm divorced?" he'd asked. Meaning, she might assume, that she should have no scruples about spending time with him. What she wasn't sure of was why he'd want to spend time with her—other than the obvious, and she was almost sure she didn't like the possibility of becoming sexually involved with Mike Kinnear.

She certainly couldn't believe Mike Kinnear was the kind of man likely to be smitten by love at first sight.

"You're divorced, too," he'd said. Well, he wouldn't be the first to suggest that she should want to fall into bed, "because they were both unattached and healthy."

So why did that thought make her feel so disappointed?

Shielding his eyes, Mike watched as the Tollycraft's varnished hull picked up rays from the setting sun. She handled the boat like a pro. But then she had to make this trip every day.

He'd invited her for a barbecue, for God's sake. In the years since his divorce he'd never invited a woman to his home. For some reason he'd been reluctant to introduce another female into the place Anne's mother had left.

Anne's mother, not Frances, or his wife. He understood the classification. Anne's feelings were important to him, and he didn't want her confused by a succession of females whom she might mistakenly assume to be important in his life. Anne was still grieving the loss of Frances and—how he hated the thought—daydreaming about her return.

The boat cleared the harbor and headed into the open

stretch of water leading to Brown Island. He fingered his beard. Susan might not have said she didn't like it, but her words hadn't left much doubt.

He chewed the inside of his lip. If he'd never had a woman to the house before because he didn't want his daughter seeing his casual dates, that suggested that, without conscious decision, he'd classified his interest in Susan Ackroyd as more than casual.

But that made no sense. Mike turned away, skirted an upturned rowboat and climbed the ramp. He never intended to get deeply involved again. That hadn't changed, wouldn't change. What he wanted here was simple—completely simple and uncomplicated. He wanted...what?

At the top of the ramp he paused to glance at the retreating boat once more. Trailing a narrow V of white wake, it diminished steadily into the distance. But Susan's dark hair still showed clearly. Mike drew in a slow breath of salty air. He wanted Sunday to come around—fast.

3

"**W**hat do you want?"

"Good afternoon." Susan cleared her throat and stared at the woman who had opened Mike Kinnear's front door. "I'm Susan Ackroyd. Mike's expecting me."

"Yeah." Dark eyes swept from Susan's face to her feet and back again. "He said to take you around. It's quicker through the house." She opened the door only slightly wider.

Susan made her own discreet survey. The woman's home bleach job had left brittle ends in its wake and these escaped an incongruous ponytail to stand out like a dandelion puff around a plump and shiny face.

"Are you Connie?"

"Yep." Connie stood back, a series of sagging rolls inside a pink T-shirt and gigantic blue jeans, and waited for Susan to enter. "You're early."

"I know. I'm sorry." So this was the woman Mike considered an adequate example for his twelve-year-old daughter. Hah.

On her way through a long, stone-flagged hall, Susan caught glimpses inside the rooms on either side and began to frown. She passed them too quickly to see clearly, but disorganization wasn't difficult to recognize.

"Through here," Connie instructed. Examining her

shocking pink fingernails, the housekeeper motioned Susan into the kitchen. Susan noticed that the same brain-jarring shade of pink polish ornamented Connie's toes.

Susan clamped her teeth together. She had everything to offer a child but was being treated to a sickening third degree by some social worker who had the power to deny her the chance to be a mother. Meanwhile there were children being emotionally mangled by inadequate parents who happened to be fertile.

"Where'd he pick you up, then?" Connie asked.

Shocked to her bones, Susan stood still in the middle of an incredibly messy kitchen. "I beg your pardon."

"That's all right. Doesn't bother me if he has someone over. Not that I'm used to it, since he hasn't before." Connie pushed out her lower lip to blow hair out of her eyes. It flopped and promptly fell back again. "I just wondered where—?"

"Mr. Kinnear and I have some business to discuss."

Susan regretted her pompous rejoinder even before Connie laughed. "I'm sure you have, dear. But then that's not my affair. I would have thought he'd be a bit careful with Anne around, though. Her being at a difficult age."

Tension wound Susan's skin close over her flesh. "I'm sure you aren't implying what I think you are."

Connie sniffed, her tongue moving visibly inside her cheek.

Gathering her composure, Susan rapidly took in her surroundings. This was outrageous. She figured Connie to be in her thirties and certainly fit enough to do better. Every pot, pan, dish and utensil—some clean, some dirty—appeared to be out. They were stacked on the counters, the large central cooking island, the windowsills, even the floor. Open cereal boxes, milk cartons, cookie packets—

spilling their contents—a bag of flour and one of sugar, both partially used and not closed, all sat on the table. Total chaos.

The room itself was gorgeous, though, with a wall of glass soaring along the side facing the water and a profusion of hanging plants. Mentally Susan began to remove the debris. Yes, this *could* be a very nice kitchen, indeed.

"He's out back," Connie said.

Susan gave a last sweeping look around, then without glancing at the woman, went toward the French doors. No wonder Mike's instructions had been that she should be taken around the house to reach the patio. He must know how any normal person would react to the conditions inside his home. Her temper festered. Even if Mike spent little time here, even if he'd decided to flout convention, his daughter lived in this house. The girl was at the most impressionable age. She was learning behavior patterns that would last the rest of her life. Mike Kinnear was irresponsible, unfit and... And it was none of her business.

"She's here!" Anne's voice, loud and hostile, greeted Susan as she stepped outside.

Smoke rose from a barbecue, but there was no sign of Mike.

"Hello, Anne," Susan said, giving the girl her best tame-adult smile. "It's nice to see you again."

"It's not nice to see you." A gum bubble, the same shade of green as the girl's hair, put a period on the statement.

Susan was tempted to laugh. The girl was lounging in a chaise, one leg curled beneath her, the other slung over the arm of the chair. Anne's makeup-whitened face and pouting purple lips were suggestive of a latter-day Lolita. Her black boots, presumably the ones she'd conned her father into buying, tapered to impossible points that easily added two inches to the length of her feet. Black-and-green striped socks, black stretch knee pants and a black T-shirt completed the outfit.

The girl was tiny inside her clinging clothes, a child trying to be a grown-up. Susan swallowed. She wondered if Mike ever took the time to hold his daughter, to really listen to her. If she were Susan's child...but she wasn't.

A man approached along a path that wound out of sight toward the cliffs. Susan recognized him as Mike's father, the man who had been pruning roses the last time she'd come.

Dressed as he was today, in a crisp white shirt and gray slacks, his iron-gray hair carefully combed, he resembled a retired and financially comfortable businessman far more than a gardener. Susan wrinkled her nose at the recollection of her mistake.

"Where's your dad?" he asked his granddaughter, apparently not noticing Susan.

"Dunno," Anne said, squirming to put her other leg over the arm of the chaise. "He went round there." She pointed at the path that skirted the house.

"He left a note on the cottage door," Lester said. "Said I should come and back him up. What'd he mean d'you suppose?"

"Something to do with her." Anne hooked a thumb in Susan's direction, and Lester, squinting, registered surprise. "She's that woman," Anne continued. "The pushy one who came *last* Sunday, as well."

At the girl's rudeness Susan ground her teeth but was more interested in why Mike had felt he needed "backing up" with her—if that was what he had meant.

Lester pulled himself up as tall as possible and tucked

in his chin. His mouth thinned. "That's about enough, young lady. Good afternoon, Miss, er..."

"Susan," she said hurriedly.

"Susan. I'm Lester Kinnear, Mike's dad. Now that I think about it, he did mention something about you coming. I reckon old-timer's disease must be getting me. Don't recall things as well as I used to."

He appeared ill at ease, and Susan didn't blame him. With every passing second her own discomfort increased. The enormity of the situation hit hard. That she'd been invited here at all was odd. That she'd been asked for a barbecue with Mike's family was even odder. Connie had said Mike never invited "friends" home. Susan's lips parted and she felt her mouth dry out. Could he be on the lookout for a replacement for the slovenly Connie, someone who could also fill some of his more personal needs?

She felt like fleeing.

"Mike said you live on Brown Island," Lester said politely. "Lived there long, have you?"

"About eight years," she said, watching Anne's pinched face while, at the same time, sensing Connie as a silent listener just inside the kitchen.

"What am I thinking of?" Lester fussed, pulling a chaise forward and plunking a blue-and-green flowered cushion in place. "Sit down, sit down. This is a real occasion, I must say. You *are* very pretty."

"Thank you." Susan sat down carefully, swinging up her feet while she tried to decide just what the last comment had meant. She *was* very pretty? As in, she was as pretty as Lester had been told? A blush heated her face. The only person who might have paid her that compliment was Mike.

"Did anyone offer you a drink?"

"Er, no. But that's all right. I'm not thirsty."

Lester stepped back. "I'll get you something. Iced tea? Wine? Something stronger?" He sounded flustered, anxious to please.

"No. Really. Nothing."

He clasped his hands behind his back and rocked. Susan had another thought. It was entirely possible that Lester Kinnear was anxious for his son to find a replacement for his ex-wife.

"Where did your dad say he was going?"

Anne gave a huge, bored sigh. "He didn't, Lester. He just went. You know how it is. People just go." She looked pointedly at Susan. "They do it all the time. They notice they aren't wanted and they go."

Mike and Lester might have something in mind for her, but what Anne was most interested in was seeing Susan's back, preferably retreating for the last time.

The kitchen door opened wider, and Connie wiggled through, a loaded tray in her hands. "I suppose you'll be wanting these," she said with a resigned air. "This isn't what I expect to have to do, but I'll make an exception just this once."

Silverware clattered as she plunked it in a heap in the middle of a glass-topped table. Glasses followed. "What does he want done with the corn?" she asked of no one in particular.

Lester crossed his arms and, for the first time, Susan saw a hint of exasperation in the man. "Did Mike ask you to come in today, Connie? You don't usually grace us with your presence on the weekends."

She stood up, hands on hips, and sniffed. "I'm my own boss. I come and go as I please. But I always make allowances for special occasions. I knew I'd be needed today.

Mike knows he's lucky to get someone as accommodating as I am.''

Such luck. Susan rolled in her lips to camouflage a smile. Lester met her eye, and she pitied him his obvious discomfort and frustration. Living in someone else's home and having to keep quiet about obvious disasters couldn't be easy. If she had control around here, Susan would... She coughed, suddenly self-conscious, as if these people might guess what crazy thoughts were flitting through her head.

Connie set out the silverware, slapped down napkins and fidgeted chairs into place. She smiled at Anne, the first pleasant expression Susan had seen on the woman's face. "Want to give Connie a hand, sweetie?"

"Sure." Anne got up and followed meekly into the kitchen.

Susan realized her mouth was open and closed it firmly.

"She's good with Anne," Lester said quietly, as if to justify Connie's existence. When Susan looked at him, he spread his hands. "Mike does his best, but a girl needs a woman around."

She made a noncommittal noise. Saying that Connie hardly seemed the right candidate as a role model for a twelve-year-old wouldn't be appropriate. She shouldn't have come here today. All that would have been necessary was to stand up to Mike and say Georges and Libby would contact him when they arrived.

"There you are."

At the sound of Mike's voice, she swiveled in her chair—and almost stopped breathing.

"How are you?" He was rushing, talking rapidly. "I saw your car up by the garage and I couldn't figure how you'd gotten past without me seeing you."

Susan stared, gathering her wits. "You must have gone by when Connie was bringing me through the house."

He paused in the act of depositing a bunch of roses on the table. The clippers, plunked down beside, spread clumps of dirt and leaf shreds on the glass. He didn't seem to notice. Susan could see what he was thinking. He was gauging her reaction to the neglect inside his home.

But she didn't much care what was on his mind right now. Taking her eyes from his face was an effort she didn't want to make. He'd shaved.

"Mike," Anne called, coming from the kitchen, "Connie says I don't have to stay for dinner if I don't want to. She says she'll take me to pick up Fredda so we can go to the movies."

Reluctantly Susan switched her attention from a fascinated contemplation of her host's newly revealed face to his daughter's combative stance.

"You know we're having a barbecue, pumpkin," Mike said, so levelly that Susan longed to shake him and Anne, too.

"Sunday's our day," Anne retorted with a pointed glance at Susan. "You always take me to the yard on Sunday. You didn't today. Why'd you do that to your face?"

"*Anne,*" Mike cut her off firmly, but his features were set in a patient mold. "Today's an exception, remember? I told you we were having company and—"

"*You're* having company. And it's gonna be *boring.* Lester's gonna back you up. He said you asked him. You don't need me."

Stunned, vacillating between awkwardness on her own behalf and embarrassment for Mike, Susan watched, feeling like a spectator at a tennis match. This match should be no contest, would be no contest if she had anything to do with enforcing the rules. But she had an uncomfortable sensation that she wouldn't agree with the judgment calls.

"Get me a vase, please," Mike said, and Susan recognized a new, tough note in his voice.

"But—"

"*Get* a vase, Anne."

"Ahem." Lester moved forward. He patted Mike's arm. "You said you needed me for something."

Mike colored and the effect was intriguing. "Not needed, only thought you might like to eat with us." He turned to Susan who couldn't avoid staring at his face. "My father lives in the guest cottage. Sometimes I like to make sure he gets a good meal."

Lester laughed. "I eat better than you do, son. And you know it. Frankly, if you don't mind, I'd like to get back. I've got a fair amount to do on the books yet today."

"Dad's a retired CPA. He keeps my books. Fantastic for me, since it frees me up for other things."

She couldn't help wondering exactly why she was getting all the family details. "I see. It's too bad Mike keeps you slaving on Sunday."

"He doesn't. It's what I like to do."

Lester excused himself and retraced his steps until he moved out of sight behind massive clumps of pampas grass.

"I'm glad you came," Mike said, lifting the barbecue lid and poking a fork into a foil-covered packet. "We're having salmon. One of my men caught it."

"Mmm," Susan murmured. "I love salmon."

He opened the foil and checked the delicate pink flesh inside, affording her a chance to appreciate what his razor had revealed. He was a ruggedly handsome man. The lines of his face were compelling. Deep-set eyes, broad cheek-bones, a square jaw and cleft chin—all strong and clear-cut. With a wide, firm mouth and a full lower lip, his face was impossible to ignore or forget. When he smiled, dimpled grooves formed in his cheeks.

And he'd hidden all this beneath a beard? Either he didn't care what he looked like, or he preferred to hide his assets—or some of them, anyway. The khaki shorts he wore today, with a white polo shirt, fitted like another skin and hid very little.

"What do you think?" he asked abruptly.

Susan stood up and went to look at the fish. "Not quite done, I think."

"No. About the shave."

She stayed where she was at his side, but kept her eyes on the fish. Surely he knew she was bound to think he'd shaved because he'd assumed, correctly, that she hadn't liked him with the beard.

"I think you look terrific," she said honestly, consciously letting go of her reserve. "It's a shame to hide a great face."

As soon as the words were spoken, she longed to retract them. A violent blush shot up her neck and over her cheeks.

Mike's laugh didn't help. "I think that's quite a compliment. But then, we people with great faces should back each other up, huh? We can't expect the jealous competition to toss us any bones."

She had to laugh. "How true." And she tilted her head to study him frankly. "Seriously, Mike, the beard's a masculine touch and all that, but you hardly need it..." Her voice trailed off and the heat in her face intensified. She must have been away from the company of men for too long. Mike was positively grinning with satisfaction, and she was making a fool of herself. He probably thought she was making a play for him.

"I don't like it."

Anne's voice, high and snippy, cooled everything. Mike turned around and Susan did, too, but more slowly. The girl put a stubby cut-glass bowl full of water on the table. "When'd you do that, Dad?" Her mouth turned down.

"Um." He sunk his hands into his shorts pockets and frowned.

Susan managed a closer check of his face and noted the marks of a very recent assault. His absence just before she arrived must have been longer than she'd realized, long enough to dash in and shave and grab the roses from the garden.

Mike rallied visibly. "I did it a little while ago."

"Why?"

"I like to be cooler in summer."

Why didn't he tell the kid to shape up?

"You never did it for summer before."

And with August a few days away summer was almost over. Susan favored the satisfaction of knowing he'd done it for her. She only wished he would exert some parental authority over Anne.

Mike picked up the roses, apparently grateful for something to divert his attention. He arranged them in the bowl with surprising artistry. Their fragrance rose on the warm air of early evening. Droplets clung to their velvet petals—apricot, white, palest pink. He touched them, framing them briefly with his large hands before turning a brilliant smile on Susan. "Do you like roses?"

"I love them. I've got quite a lot. Not as many as you,

of course, but enough to enjoy.'' She remembered, fleetingly, Mrs. Brock's roses. So different from Mike's.

Anne's sigh made sure she took center stage. She stood, her weight centered over one hip, the other leg bent. Her crossed arms and dismal expression showed intense ennui.

"So," she said, wrinkling her nose, "do I get to go to the movies?"

"I don't—"

"Here's the corn." Connie approached and put down a saucepan. "And the potato salad." This, too, was served in the pot that must have been used to boil the potatoes.

Susan didn't trust herself to meet Mike's eyes. He would say something now. He wouldn't let this exhibition of bad manners go on, particularly since he must know the purpose was to make her uncomfortable.

"Run along," Mike said, working his wallet from a back pocket. "Take some money. Call me when you're ready to be picked up."

If she wasn't hearing this, she wouldn't believe it. Susan considered, then quickly discarded the notion that she should offer some advice.

Anne extracted a bill and put the wallet on the table. "Fredda's dad's bringing me back."

"Right. Good." A muscle in his jaw flickered. He actually didn't care what his daughter did as long as she was out of his hair.

Susan walked to the far end of the covered patio and pretended deep interest in the hummingbird feeder—despite the fact that no birds were in evidence.

Within minutes Anne went into the house with Connie, and Mike disappeared through the kitchen door with the pots to return with their contents transferred to serving dishes. He smiled at her several times as he continued, silently, to prepare dinner.

Her exasperation dwindled. He was *trying* to hold everything together here. He just wasn't succeeding very well in some areas. No, she definitely shouldn't offer to help. Interference could be translated, correctly, as a judgment that he was inept.

"Okay," Mike said, standing back, apparently satisfied. "Let's give it a try. It's been a long time since I cooked anything."

The fish was good, the corn overcooked, the potato salad mushy. Susan ate stoically, complimenting every item, more ill at ease than she ever remembered being.

"Hell!" He pounded his forehead with a fist. "Forgot the green salad. I'll go make some."

"No." Susan clamped a hand on his forearm to stop him from leaping up. "I've had plenty. Couldn't eat another thing." She'd had more than plenty and wouldn't have eaten a bite if she hadn't been afraid of hurting his feelings.

"I forgot the wine." Now he sounded almost desperate.

"I don't drink."

"I do." He returned to the kitchen and came back, not with wine, but with what looked like a large mixed drink.

They sat on opposite sides of the table, elbows propped while they concentrated on watching the water. It stretched away forever, like a shifting blanket of foil chips, glittering and undulating.

Silence swelled to fill Susan's head. Ice cubes clinked in Mike's glass as he steadily downed his drink. The glass clipped against the tabletop, and he shifted it in circles over a ring of moisture.

"This is weird, isn't it?"

She bit her lip. Her lungs felt too full. "What do you mean?"

"This. Us sitting here having dinner. You must think I'm nuts to invite you over like this."

"Well…"

"I know you do. And I can't explain why I did. Impulse, I guess."

"It's okay." She didn't know what else to say. He was right. The whole thing was bizarre.

"No, it's not. Look—" he got up and offered her a hand "—we'll start over. You've just come to see me for the first time. Dinner didn't happen."

She pursed her lips and slowly put her hand into his. He was a strange man, but at least he wasn't dull. There had been altogether too much "dull" in her life lately.

"We'll go down to the beach and talk. Come on." He looked at her short-sleeved blue blouse and white pants. "You're dressed for it."

Not knowing what else to do, she let him lead her along the path Lester had taken. It angled steeply downward, broken at three points by short flights of steps. When they drew level with a small cottage built in the same mock-Tudor style as the house, Mike paused. "My dad lives there. Gives him some privacy and he can always go up and sleep at the house if I don't come home."

They walked on while Susan's mind reached a quick conclusion as to why Mike might not always sleep in his own bed. She shouldn't be here, shouldn't be holding his hand and shouldn't be allowing herself to feel a growing interest in Mike Kinnear.

A strong scent of brine and freshly beached kelp wafted to meet them on the shingle slipway to a broad band of tawny, driftwood-strewn sand.

* * *

Tension began to ebb from Mike. Susan's hand, warm in his, had slowly relaxed as they walked. He would do as he'd suggested and forget the disastrous encounter she'd had with his family. Later today or tomorrow Anne would hear a few of the things he'd been putting off telling her—and Connie, too.

The sun bled crimson and gilt along ridges of white cloud. Spears of gold pinned the heavens to the sea. These were the days that reminded him why he couldn't live anywhere else.

Pebbles shifted underfoot as he walked with sure, even steps. At his side Susan walked with equal ease. Her canvas tennis shoes were well worn and water-stained, probably from hopping in and out of her boat every day. They had things in common, maybe a great deal in common.

He raised his chin and breathed deeply. This…this—whatever it was he felt about her—was different from any reaction he'd had to a woman since his divorce. She was lovely and she was…nice, decent. Nothing had changed with him. Nothing would.

"Where's your boatyard?" The question was innocuous, but he felt a subtle change in her as she spoke.

"Couple of miles south."

Susan pulled her hand from his and walked to the water's edge. She bent to roll her pants up to her knees, kicked off her shoes and paddled in the sandy shallows.

Mike sat on a gray, pockmarked mast from some forgotten sailing ship. Tossed on the beach long before he'd first seen this cove, the ancient wood was warm beneath his hands. "Is the water cold?"

"Freezing," she called, but continued to range back and forth.

Libby and Georges were bound to stay in her house. His place was never private, either. Point? Where could he be alone with her, really alone?

"Are you working on a commission at the moment?"

Every question worked in the same direction. She was obsessed with this business of Georges Duclaux's boat. "Yes. And we've got months of work ahead on it yet."

This shouting at each other across a windy void irritated him. He wanted her closer, preferably right at his side. "Come and sit down." What she thought about being here was a complete mystery to him. But she had come. Despite the strangeness of his invitation, she'd come. She must at least be a little interested in him.

Slowly, her shoes dangling from one hand, dragging her heels to make trails, she approached and stood before him. "How many months?"

Damn. That was all she was interested in. But why so desperate? "Depends."

"On what?" The breeze alternately filled and flattened her shirt, hugged her high breasts.

"On how things go." He shrugged. Her small hips and beautifully shaped legs gave jeans a whole new meaning. For the first time since learning of her divorce he wondered what the hell could have possessed Bill Ackroyd to leave.

Marriage. That was the answer. It was an institution destined to destroy relationships. He'd learned that lesson well and didn't intend to forget it. Would Susan consider an affair? He had no crystal ball on that, but she was obviously no dummy. She knew she hadn't needed to come here today to fix up a meeting between him and Georges Duclaux.

That meant she was here because she wanted to be— wanted to be with him. Mike's spine stiffened, and the muscles in his gut. There was too much here that he didn't understand—about himself and about Susan.

She sat beside him, but too far away for his liking. "I know Georges won't mind how long it takes you to refurbish his boat."

"How do you know?" He got up, retrieved a stick and sat again, deliberately closer to her. "What does he intend to do with it when it's finished?"

"I don't know. I mean, I guess he'll use it, of course."

"Here? Or does he intend to take it to Europe?"

"I don't know."

"Those things are important." He drew the outline of a boat in the sand.

"So you've decided to take on the job?"

Lester had been making noises lately, suggesting that more money couldn't come too soon for the boatyard. But Mike hated feeling trapped into taking a job until he knew he could be enthusiastic. "I'm thinking about it," he told Susan.

"Why are you making such a big deal out of this?" She shot the words at him, and he saw her hands clench. "Maybe I should speak to Aaron Conrad."

Her vehemence took him aback, but not so much so that he stopped thinking clearly. "What's that supposed to mean?"

"He's your partner. From what I know of Aaron, he works hard and works for anyone who wants to use what he has to offer. I wonder how he feels about prima donnas who play games with prospective clients."

Her eyes glittered and a white line formed around her mouth. With a tinge of pink over her cheekbones, Mike decided that Susan was a very intriguing sight. She fascinated him more with every minute. And her reasons for being so…desperate? Yes, she seemed desperate for him to agree.

When he didn't respond, she turned away and stood up. "I'm sorry. I shouldn't have said that. I've had a lot on…I've been…I'm sorry."

Mike dropped the stick and got to his feet. He raised a hand, spread the fingers inches from her back and let them hover. What the hell? She could only push him away. He touched her lightly. She didn't move.

"Is there something I could help with, apart from the boat?"

"I—no." Her dark curls shimmered as she shook her head. "Thanks, though."

Carefully, very carefully, he placed his palm on her shoulder and eased her toward him. "Could we forget business? Just for a little while?" There were chances that were worth taking.

With her so near, he noticed black flecks in her navy blue eyes. Her full mouth trembled slightly. Something was affecting her deeply. Believing it was him would be satisfying, but he was a realist.

Her gaze met his, then moved to his mouth, and he smiled slightly. Her lips parted. Air became a scarce commodity.

Quickly she glanced away, up, to the side, then looked at his hair.

"What are you thinking, Susan?"

"Nothing."

That had better not be true, because he was thinking plenty.

"Fess up." He'd try for any reaction he could get. "Let me guess. The beard's out of the way, so now you've decided you can't stand the hair." She blushed so fiercely that he tipped back his head and laughed. "No words necessary, my dear."

"No, no," she blustered. "I was just wondering how...how you'd look with it, er, different...shorter, maybe."

"Aha. You think I look like a slob."

"No! I think you look wonderful and—" She gritted her teeth and closed her eyes, and they laughed together. "Open mouth, insert foot." She sighed. "I'm famous for that."

"You've got a wonderful mouth."

He felt her take in a breath and hold it. Her eyes remained closed. If she was unaffected by him, she was doing a lousy job of proving it.

"Susan, look at me." This might be too fast, but he couldn't risk missing what could be his best opportunity in the foreseeable future.

She raised her lashes slowly. The setting sun cast gold shadows over her rounded cheekbones and glistened on her mouth.

Her mouth. He felt his own lips part again. Dropping his hand from her shoulder, using all the control he had, he kept a slight space between their bodies while he lowered his head to touch his mouth to hers. A small noise came from her throat, and she rested a hand on his chest, filling her fingers with his shirt.

When she touched him, he trembled and felt an answering shiver. His body let him know he was moving into risky territory. Petting, the courting dance, would take restraint he wasn't sure he had, and he didn't understand why.

The aching heat in his body was so intense that his mind

began to slide into some dimly lit place where feeling was everything.

"Dad!"

He almost cried out. Instead he muttered, "Oh, God," as he stepped back.

Susan looked around with wide, disoriented eyes. "Oh," she murmured, clutching at the neck of her shirt.

"Anne, I thought you'd gone to the movies."

"Changed my mind." His precocious little daughter stood, legs braced apart, hands on hips, her eyes assessing slits.

"Go up to the house. Susan and I will be along shortly."

"This is awful," Susan whispered. "Wrong. I don't know what I was thinking of."

He knew, Mike thought with grim satisfaction. This was a setback, but not a defeat. "Go, Anne."

"You've got to come now," the girl said. "Mom's on the phone long-distance and she wants to talk to you. She's coming to visit."

4

A smart man knew to quit while he was ahead—or at least relatively unscathed. So apparently he wasn't very smart, Mike decided, because here he was, looking up at Susan Ackroyd's salon. Why was he trying to arrange an encounter with the wrong kind of woman? *Wrong?* Yeah, she was wrong for him. What he needed was a purely physical relationship. But unless he'd completely misjudged her, Susan would be totally turned off by that.

But then, hell, what did he have to lose by trying the direct approach? They were both single, obviously attracted to each other. Why not hand her a bald proposition: let's spend time together and let the chips fall where they may?

The air was soft, warm. He crossed his arms and rocked onto his heels, barely aware of the sound of a ship's horn or of the normal bustle around the yacht basin. The gentle day didn't have the power to tranquilize the sensations that had driven him here. Desire—raw, engrossing need—throbbed in every muscle and nerve. But there was that something else, the vague uncomfortable something that distracted the intensity. Making himself wait out yesterday, Monday, had been tough. But with the shop closed he would have had to find her house—the telephone was too easy to hang up—and he'd shied away from any risk of making her feel trapped.

On Sunday, when he walked Susan to her car, she'd insisted that they shouldn't meet again. He'd almost panicked at the thought, had found himself at a total loss for words. Their kiss had been brief, but he'd gotten the message his body had sent him: kisses weren't enough.

But he didn't want commitment. Nothing with strings. Would Susan Ackroyd slap his face when he suggested they should consider becoming "good friends"?

Mike whistled soundlessly. This was it, put-up or shut-up time. Deliberately keeping his pace leisurely, he loped to the steps and took them two at a time. A guy had to make his own opportunities. In front of her staff and customers what could she do except be polite?

Laughter, a gust of warmth, perfumed scents and the steady drone of hair dryers met him as he entered the shop. A blond woman, twentyish, sat at the reception desk. Seeing him, she held her pose, file suspended airy inches from the long, splayed fingernails of her other hand, while her pink lips slowly formed an assessing pout. Evidently she found him interesting.

He smiled warmly at her.

"Hi." Her softly rounded shoulders rose inside a white ruffled peasant blouse. "Can we help you?"

Already looking around the room for Susan, he wondered vaguely when hairdressers had stopped wearing uniforms. "Yes," he said, still searching.

One man, tall, dark-haired and thin, probably under thirty, had Mike in his sights via a mirror while he kept a smile in place and used a blow dryer on an elderly woman's hair. Two female operators were engrossed with clients.

"Sir?"

He glanced back at the girl behind the desk. "Yes?"

She frowned. "Did you want to make an appointment?"

"Ah..." Where was she? Damn, he'd been sure she'd be right here the moment he opened the door.

"Sir? Do you want an appointment?"

"Ah...no...yes." *Hell.* "Yes, I do. Right now, if possible." From the corner of his eye he saw tall, dark and thin approach. "I talked to Susan about it the other day. She thought she could do something for me." This couldn't be happening to him. These inane words couldn't be coming from his mouth.

"Everything okay, Molly?" the man said. The scissors he held in his right hand didn't appear to be grasped in hair-cutting mode.

"Well...I don't know." Molly settled adoring pale blue eyes on her scissor-wielding buddy whose name tag announced him as Jeff.

"Okay," Jeff said, putting himself between Mike and Molly. The other two hairdressers had stopped working. "Would you mind telling me what you want, sir?"

In any other situation Mike would have been amused. But this was foreign territory—Susan's territory. "Is Ms. Ackroyd around?"

"Who wants to know?"

Possessiveness? Mike squared his shoulders. He should have considered that she could be involved with someone else, only he hadn't—he just hadn't. "I'm Mike Kinnear."

"Problems?"

Susan had materialized without him seeing her approach. He tilted his head sideways to get a clear view of her beyond good old Jeff. "No problems," he said, grinning broadly. She did something to him. Even the sight of her brought partly formed visions of soft white skin, the sensation that his fingers were tangled in short silken hair.

He was losing it.

"Do you know this guy?" Jeff wasn't budging an inch.

Her lips parted, moved slightly and soundlessly.

Mike quit smiling and took a deep breath. He didn't need a map of her brain to read what she was thinking. Faint color had swept into her cheeks, and the dark and too bright glitter in her eyes said the rest. A few minutes alone on a beautiful beach were indelibly imprinted on two of the minds in this room. Unfortunately he couldn't be certain Susan wanted it that way.

"Hi," he managed. "I decided to take you up on your offer."

"Offer?" she said faintly.

The old adrenaline started to pump again, the confident rush. Give him a little time in any situation and he had his strategy down cold. "You convinced me. My image needs an overhaul. Lead me away. I'm all yours." He spread his arms and saw her take in every inch of him, all the way to his toes. The lady most certainly wasn't unaffected by him...or cold.

"It's okay, Jeff," she said as her eyes met Mike's. "Carry on." There was a hint of humor in her arresting navy blue stare—and challenge? Oh, he did hope there was challenge. Mike Kinnear thrived on that commodity. Calculated resistance sweetened the chase and ensured the absence of guilt at the finale.

The few liaisons he'd had time for since his divorce had been short and had ended by mutual agreement. He credited this satisfactory situation to his ability to choose women with no more interest in anything lasting than he had.

"Your ten o'clock lady canceled," Molly chimed from his left.

Susan's mouth tightened. "Thank you." A muscle in her jaw gave a fascinating twitch.

Mike sighed and shrugged. "Fate. You've got time on

your hands and here I am to fill it." She didn't smile and he added, "Where do you want me?"

He got the distinct impression she longed to say "Nowhere," but instead she waved him to a chair by a washbasin. When he was seated, his face turned expectantly up to hers, she snapped a dark blue nylon cape open and fastened it round his neck. Deftly she smoothed the fabric, running her fingers over his shoulders to tuck it behind his back. Her features were impassive, but her face was very close, and he felt her touch all the way to his bones.

"What exactly did you have in mind?"

And she said it without inflection, without a flicker of eye or lip! "Oh, I thought I'd leave that up to you."

A pause. And, yes, a definite flicker this time. She looked around and he followed suit—in time to catch each of her employees in sudden intense activity.

"Head back please."

Surprisingly strong hands tipped him until his neck cracked against the edge of the sink and he winced. "Easy, easy," he muttered.

She turned on the water and brought her mouth close to his ear. "You're leaving this up to me, isn't that what you said? Around here the customer always gets what he wants. Unlike some enterprises I could name."

Back to Georges's boat, not that the subject could be avoided for much longer.

"Why did you come here? What would make you do something like this to me?"

He tried to turn his head, but her fingers, firmly entwined in the hair at his nape while she directed a stinging jet onto his scalp, made sure he stayed put. "You know why I came. I had to see you."

"No you didn't." She squirted something cold, smooth

and scented like ripe pineapple into his hair and began to rub vigorously. "We have nothing to say to each other."

No one had ever suggested to Mike that having a woman wash his hair could be an erotic experience. But his toes curled inside the Gucci loafers he'd donned in honor of the occasion. This lady could wash his hair anytime.

Her hands moved more slowly, gently. When had he closed his eyes? When he opened them, Susan's attention was on his hair, then his mouth. He swallowed and resisted the temptation to reach up and touch her cheek. She wasn't like…it was there again, that feeling that didn't fit with the usual set of responses to a woman he wanted. Tenderness? No, not that, never again.

"Do you really want me to cut it?" she asked, so softly he had to strain to hear.

"Of course. I already told you that's why I came." Evidently he'd embarrassed her in front of her staff, and he regretted that. "I also thought you might like to continue what we started on Sunday."

She straightened forcefully.

He almost laughed. Did she think he'd try to kiss her here? "Our discussion about your brother-in-law's boat."

Her breasts rose beneath the bodice of her pale blue sundress. Skinny straps ran from her slender shoulders to touch the soft flesh that showed tantalizingly above the straight-edged top. Where two buttons had been left undone, the shadow of her cleavage deepened with every move of her arms.

"Susan, what's bothering you? Really bothering you?" He might be certain he already knew, but hearing it from her lips could give him an opening to push his suit.

In silence she rinsed out the soap, lathered and rinsed again, then reached to pull a towel from a shelf he couldn't see. Those little stretches did wonderful things for her supple body.

"Susan?"

"Sunday was a mistake." She was whispering again, casting surreptitious glances around.

"You regret our kiss?" He didn't think to lower his voice and rolled his head to meet a frankly curious stare from the hairdresser at the closest station.

"I don't want to discuss that," she hissed, very pink now. "It was an accident. Just one of those things that mean nothing."

"Well, I sure don't regret it. I think we should try the whole thing again—making sure there are no interruptions—and find out if there's something worth pursuing."

"Please." Desperation now. "I can't believe you're saying these things."

He wasn't being fair. Short of giving her staff an entertainment they'd probably relish and she definitely wouldn't, she had no choice but to humor him, at least in part.

"I like you, okay?" he said.

Jeff, whose client had left, sat in a chair mere feet away, supposedly reading a magazine. The pages were never turned.

"Over here." Susan rubbed his hair so vigorously his neck felt as if it might snap. She urged him unceremoniously to a spot in front of a mirror.

"Don't you like me?"

"I don't know you." She tossed the wet towel aside and replaced it with a dry one.

Their eyes met in the mirror, and a hard bolt struck low in his belly. He was a man of the world, no naive kid on the male-female block, but there was something new here and, although he had no intention of stepping away from the decisions he'd made about long-term arrangements, there was no way he would back out of a potentially satisfying interlude.

"How much shall I take off?" Her face was still pink, but she combed his hair and ran her fingers through it, bringing them to rest at the back of his neck. "Not too short, I think. Maybe I should leave it fairly long here—" her fingertips stroked the tendons behind his ears "—and take more off here." The palms of her hands swept upward over the sides of his head, and she worked with her fingers, kneading firmly as if she'd begun to forget he was there.

Mike hadn't forgotten. He closed his eyes again and wondered if his legs would still be capable of holding him should he decide to stand up.

"Does that sound okay?"

"Mmm. Wonderful."

Susan began to cut. He didn't need inside knowledge to figure out that she was good at her craft. Under her ministrations he slipped into a sensual twilight zone that he didn't want to leave. He should be plotting his next move, but he couldn't concentrate on anything except what she was doing to his equilibrium.

"What do you think?"

His eyes opened slowly. Her hands rested on his shoulders while she studied her work in the mirror.

"Are you finished already?" She couldn't be.

"I'm going to dry it. Is the length okay?"

"Fantastic." He didn't care. "Do you think it is?"

"I think it's going to be good on you."

If he covered her hands with his own, she'd only pull away. "That's all I need to hear. Will you have lunch with me?"

He immediately followed her quick glance at Jeff and caught the man's frankly fascinated stare before the apparently riveting page in the magazine reclaimed his attention.

"No, thank you," Susan said. "I've got a busy schedule today."

"Dinner?"

"No."

All the dryers had been switched off at the same time. Susan's fingers tightened on his back, and he liked the feeling much more than he was sure she intended.

"A late-night snack?"

Susan's dryer came on full blast, and hot air hit his scalp with force. The gentleness was gone, but he couldn't help smiling. She could have kicked him out the minute he'd set foot inside the shop. He wasn't fooled. Susan Ackroyd was at least a little tempted by him.

Several minutes later the dryer went off again, and she brushed and pushed, then stood back, giving an occasional pat until she appeared satisfied. "How's that?"

Dutifully he turned this way and that. A bit more *GQ* than he might have chosen, but he supposed it looked okay. Molly, passing with an armful of bottles, paused and rolled her eyes. "Susan knows how to make a man look edible," she said in a breathy voice. Jeff's magazine rustled and Molly moved hastily away. Mike deduced that the attachment here wasn't between Jeff and Susan, and the thought brought satisfaction.

"It's great," he said, giving what he hoped was a guileless smile. "How about supper?"

"No. No thanks. You can pay Molly."

He caught her hand as she whipped off the cape. "But we have business to discuss."

She twisted from his grasp and took a soft brush to his neck, automatically straightening his collar.

"I've been thinking about Georges—"

"Susan!" Molly broke in, sounding excited. She held a hand over the mouthpiece of the phone. "It's that woman. That Mrs. Brock."

Mike narrowed his eyes. Susan's face had turned several shades paler, and he'd swear sweat was breaking out on her upper lip. Without looking at what she was doing, she reached to set the brush on a table, missed and didn't even flinch at the clatter of plastic hitting the tiled floor.

He saw her swallow, then swallow again—hard.

She crossed slowly and took up the receiver. Molly stayed where she was, hands clasped tightly together as if in anticipation. A sidelong look across the salon showed that the three operators also appeared to have stopped breathing while they listened.

"Hello."

Mike raised his brows. She looked...terrified. Sounded terrified.

"Yes, Mrs. Brock. How are you? How was your vacation?" She rested an elbow on the counter and covered her eyes with her free hand. Something close to alarm clawed at Mike. Susan was definitely very affected by this conversation.

"Oh...I see." She raised her head, a stricken expression on her face. "Is that usual, group sessions, I mean?"

A pause.

"Yes, I know how many clients you have to study. I just wondered..."

Molly took hold of Susan's hand and squeezed.

"I thought you would be coming here next, to my home. Wasn't that what you told me?"

Susan tightened her grip on Molly, and Jeff went to stand beside them.

"I don't need more time to make up my mind. I told you I've considered this very carefully. No, of course not.

Yes, I realize you know what's best." She smiled at Jeff, but the corners of her mouth jerked downward. "Yes, I'll wait to hear from you. Thank you very much."

For several seconds she looked at the handset, then slowly let it drop into its cradle. "I'm not giving up, you know," she said quietly. "In the end they'll get sick of me and let me have what I want, just to get rid of me."

"This is just the way they do things," Molly said, her high voice suddenly very serious. "They aren't singling you out, just going through the normal routine."

Mike itched to ask what all this was about.

Susan shook her head. "I'm not convinced it's normal. I think that because I'm not what they deal with every day they want to see if I can be put off. I represent more work for them, and they're already too busy." She chewed a knuckle. "But Harriet Brock did tell me she'd be coming to the islands to talk to me next. What do you think her change of mind means?"

"Nothing," Jeff said. Mike noticed that the man appeared uncomfortable, as if he wasn't convinced by his own words. "Keep going along with whatever they want to do."

Susan rolled her head as if her neck hurt, and then her eyes settled on Mike. Obviously she'd entirely forgotten his presence. He shifted himself more upright and tried a smile. The hint of trembling at the corners of her mouth disturbed him. He didn't know what to say.

Every muscle in Susan's body ached. She felt tense enough to explode. The moment she'd realized Harriet Brock was on the phone she'd forgotten Mike Kinnear's very solid presence in her salon.

She needed to get out of here, to breathe some fresh air and think. Mike was a complication she could do without, regardless of the havoc the past forty minutes of his company had wreaked in her body and mind.

"Molly, make sure Mr. Kinnear has…take care of him, please. I have to go out. I'll be back in plenty of time for my next appointment."

Without giving anyone a chance to react, she hurried outside, jogged along the balcony and headed downstairs. A few hundred yards east, on a path just above the yacht basin, a shelter with a view of the water had been built. Few people stopped there and she could sit inside on a bench until she felt calm enough to go back to work.

Mike Kinnear caught up before she'd made it to the path. "Slow down." He had to do no more than lengthen his stride to keep up with her running feet, but he caught her arm and pulled her beside him.

"I can't talk to you," she told him breathlessly. Please, don't let him persist with whatever was making him badger her. Not now.

"Okay, we'll be quiet. I'll just walk with you."

"I…" What was the use? He wasn't about to go away. She walked on past an ice-cream vendor surrounded by eager customers and a woman cycling slowly with a pannier full of shrimp.

At the shelter Susan hesitated and looked at Mike. Any woman would be delighted to have him dogging her footsteps—even if he did make remarks that sounded suspiciously like invitations into his bed. Maybe with most women that would make him even more irresistible. Casual sex didn't appeal to her.

"Let's sit in here," he said as if he'd read her original intention. "You look as if you could use a little quiet time."

Ten minutes ago she'd have said that he was right, and that she needed it all on her own. Suddenly being alone was the last thing she wanted, and she couldn't think of anyone she'd rather be with than him.

She sat down first. Then he joined her.

"Want to talk about it?" He sounded...what? Concerned?

Susan averted her face. She was grasping for support from a ridiculous source. "Nothing to talk about," she lied. How could she discuss her desperate longing for children with a man who thought parenting one child was a burden?

"You're upset, Susan. I can be a good listener if it'll help. Why did you rush out of the shop after that call?"

This wasn't any of his business, not that he appeared the kind of man who ever considered whether or not he should probe into other people's lives. She shrugged and said nothing.

Mike turned toward her. "I'm sorry Anne showed up the way she did on Sunday. It embarrassed you. I'd have saved you from that if I could."

Susan's stomach did strange things. "It's her home and you're her father. She has a right to come looking for you when she needs something." As best he could, Mike seemed to be trying to comfort her, but she must try to show him that she wasn't impressed with the way he treated his daughter.

"Anne's very important to me," he said mildly. "That doesn't mean I don't deserve a life of my own. Forget that for now. You're hurting about something."

His deep voice had a gentle quality she hadn't heard in him before. "I'll be all right." Reading too much into casual concern would be a mistake.

"Somehow you don't convince me. Will you change your mind about lunch? Maybe we could both use some company." His broad hand with its calloused fingertips covered hers, and she couldn't seem to pull away. "How about it, Susan?"

"It's not possible. I've got bookings throughout the rest of the day."

"Dinner then?"

"We've already had this conversation and the answer is still no. We have nothing in common, Mike, and I don't understand why you persist in this."

"Don't you?" With his other hand he eased her face toward him, smoothed her hair, fleetingly touched the sensitive spot beneath her ear. "Well, my timing's obviously wrong because, regardless of what you say, something heavy's on your mind. I'd like to help you if you'd let me. Maybe you would if we knew each other better."

How she'd like to believe what he seemed to be offering, and how she'd like to accept it. "Thanks for being concerned, but I really am okay."

"If you say so. Susan, we do interest each other, don't we?"

She couldn't meet his eyes.

"Yes," he said softly. "We do. And it seems to me that two adults who are attracted to each other ought to do something about it." He passed his knuckles fleetingly along her jaw and dropped his hand, but not before in an incredible ache of longing made her flesh heavy. "Just as good friends."

The ache receded and she pressed her lips together. This was a first. She was almost sure she'd just received an invitation to share sex—and nothing more. "I've got to get back," she said, her throat constricted. She added with careful restraint, "Thanks for the invitation, I think. But no thanks. I must definitely have been giving off the wrong vibes."

When she got up, he joined her at once and she

thought—undoubtedly erroneously—that he appeared uncertain. Definitely an illusion.

"Susan, the last thing I want to do is insult you. I only thought—"

"I think I know what you thought. And, of course, I ought to be flattered—right?" She shouldn't have done such a good job on his hair. He looked, to quote Molly, stunning.

"Let's not part like this."

She laughed. "That sounds like an old movie line. How's Frances, by the way? Did you make arrangements for her visit?"

A blank stare gradually gave way to understanding. "She wasn't on the phone," he said in a flat voice. "My daughter's very possessive."

Anger simmered in Susan. "Children only resort to that kind of fabrication when they're afraid," she said. "Anne's a special and very bright little girl who needs to be sure she won't lose her father the way she lost her mother." She would have a child of her own and she would give that child everything she needed, not make her insecure enough to lie.

Mike's expressive brows had risen almost to his hairline. "I didn't realize you were an expert on child psychology."

She was too upset for caution. "No one's born an expert on children. Some of us are more clued in than others, that's all. Probably because we're more aware of the importance of children, and of what a gift they are. If—"
Enough. The danger signal finally sounded in her brain. "I like Anne, that's all." Even if the girl did see her as a threat, which she definitely never would be.

"Very interesting," Mike said, but he sounded markedly cooler. "My daughter and I have a very close relationship, and I think I understand her well. It's too bad you opted not to have children of your own, since you would obviously have made such a sterling mother.''

What he said, the implied sarcasm, fell like dark stones into Susan's already disturbed mind. Damn him, anyway. What did he know?

"Goodbye." She started to walk away, but he dodged around to cut her off. "Please," she said, "I really can't keep my clients waiting."

"Neither can I," he said, the winning smile back in place. His green eyes crinkled at the corners and the dimples deepened beside his mouth. "I did need the haircut, but I wanted to tell you that I'd like to offer the Duclaux an appointment on Friday. That's the day after they arrive, isn't it?"

She felt slightly disoriented. He was quicksilver, constantly adjusting, feinting, returning with a new angle when she least expected one. "They get here on Thursday. I imagine Friday would work very well."

"Wonderful." Before she could react he slid an arm around her shoulders and leaned close as he turned them toward the shop. "Why don't you bring them to the yard at, say, eleven in the morning?"

Oh, no, she wasn't being dragged into this any farther. She'd make do with Libby's comments about him. "I'm sure eleven will be fine. I'll tell Georges how to get to the yard. He can borrow my car."

They'd reached the Blue Heron Restaurant, and people streamed in for lunch. Mike guided her around the throng, his hand tightly closed on her shoulder.

"I don't think that's a good idea."

She glanced up at him, frowning. "You just said you wanted to see them."

They drew level with a gray truck parked beneath an overhanging tree, and Mike took keys from his pocket to unlock the door. Somehow, even given his new occupation, he still looked like a Mercedes man.

"Um, this is difficult to admit," he said, looking at the toes of his shoes.

Susan put a few feet between them, necessary feet to keep her mind clear. "What?"

"It really is essential that you come with your sister and brother-in-law."

"Why?"

He climbed into the truck cab, shut the door and leaned out of the window. "You will be there, won't you?"

"Why?"

The engine sprang to life. "Because I'm not good at meeting new people. I'm too shy."

Susan stood where she was, her mouth open for several minutes after he drove away. At least he'd had the grace to grin. Shy? Like a beast of prey, he was shy. And she wasn't entering his lair again.

"Over here! Over here!" Susan waved her arms above her head and jumped up and down. Georges's dark head was clearly visible above most other men in the crowd streaming from the late-afternoon ferry. Libby's straight red-gold hair blew this way and that.

"Here!" She could see Libby bobbing on tiptoe to look around, but the din and confusion separated them.

Then the striking couple turned through the gate by the ticket booth and Susan ran pell-mell for her sister. "Hi, oh, hi! The ferry's late. I thought you were never going to get here."

Libby returned Susan's bear hug and held on, her face buried in her sister's shoulder. "Oh, Sue, I'm so glad to be here. I do need you."

"You've got me," Susan said. Glancing over her taller sister's shoulder, she saw that Georges was looking anywhere but at them.

With obvious reluctance Libby released her hold and stepped back, but kept her hands on Susan's arms. The beautiful smile was there, and pale olive skin glowed over rounded features and a smooth brow that made Libby appear younger than her twenty-nine years. But the eyes—Libby's huge tawny eyes—held a heavy shadow that turned Susan's insides to lead.

At a tap on her shoulder Susan raised her face to meet

Georges's smile. There had never been any difficulty understanding why this man had swept Libby off her feet. He was gorgeous, if that was a term that could be used for someone so masculine. He exuded the confidence that came from having a fortune and incredibly good looks. His smile had an intriguing way of making dips beneath his cheekbones while it drew attention to his perfectly formed mouth and even teeth.

"Hello, Georges." She sensed a strange distance between them, which was new as was the uncertainty he seemed to feel.

"Hello?" His gallic shrug was eloquent. "Don't I get an embrace, *chérie?*"

Gently she freed herself from Libby. "Of course you do," she said, and he took her hands in his. His long fingers were strong but too cold. He studied her, his head tilted to one side. "As interesting as ever, our little Susan. And you are still alone? Such a waste." He kissed each of her cheeks.

Interesting? He was right. At best she was interesting to look at. But what had happened to the courtly flattery that he'd always been so good at?

"Georges," Libby said, sounding exasperated. "We've only just arrived. Couldn't you wait a while before telling Susan what you think is wrong with her life? She doesn't need advice on how to live."

His shrug came again. "As you say. It is none of my affair." He turned away as if totally disinterested, and Susan was left looking at his broad back. She turned to Libby, whose face was stricken.

"It's been a long journey," Libby said defensively. She glanced at Georges before leading Susan a few yards away. "Forgive us if we're snappy."

The words didn't ring true, and Susan chewed the inside

of her cheek. Georges was preoccupied now, hefting suit-cases and gesturing to a slender, dark-haired man of me-dium height. This, she deduced, must be his nephew, Jean-Claude Duclaux. Even at a distance she could tell that the conversation was in rapid French.

"So," she said brightly to Libby, "now I'm going to have you to myself for a while. How long can you stay? I have missed you."

"And I've missed you, too," Libby responded, but her smile turned a little droopy and she seemed almost on the verge of tears. "I don't know how long we'll be here." She covered her mouth, and Susan had to strain to hear what she said next. "You see how he is?"

Susan hunched her shoulders, unwilling to commit her-self if it meant making matters worse. "He's tired."

"He's more than tired. I'm hardly allowed out of his sight, and he swings from being wildly enthusiastic to…to something I don't recognize as Georges."

Susan put her arm around her sister's shoulders and squeezed. "We all go through difficult times. Maybe it's business. You must know it isn't because he doesn't care about you."

"Of course I know." Libby pulled away and stuffed her hands into the pockets of her cream-colored silk pants, which matched her short, military-style jacket. "That's never in question. Sometimes I think he loves me too much. Susan, he behaves as if he's afraid something will happen to me."

"He says that?" Susan's insides felt tacked to her spine.

"No, no. But he's constantly checking to be sure where I am. And he doesn't want me to answer the phone." Libby shook back her hair, relaxed the tension from her face. "Shh. Here they come."

Georges waved the other man, also carrying luggage,

ahead of him. "Susan, meet my nephew, Jean-Claude. Jean-Claude, this beautiful woman is my sister-in-law, Susan Ackroyd."

Susan was too accustomed to Georges to be made uncomfortable by the comment. She held out a hand that Jean-Claude ignored in favor of a very French embrace and solemn kisses planted a little too close to each corner of her mouth.

"*Madame,*" he said, stepping back and bowing slightly. "You are as lovely as Georges has said you are. But—" he waved a hand in Libby's direction "—what should we expect from Libby's sister?"

A check of Libby's reaction showed pleasure, and Susan smiled at this man whose good looks could be described, accurately, as saturnine and compelling. Upsweeping black brows, almost black eyes that followed the same line and a narrow-bridged nose complemented a wide mouth with a full lower lip. It had been a long time since little Friday Harbor had seen as handsome a pair as the hypnotic Duclaux males.

"I thought Aaron Conrad was bringing you," Susan said, suddenly remembering the arrangements. She would have gone to Seattle-Tacoma airport herself if Libby hadn't said Aaron had volunteered to meet the plane from Honolulu.

Georges flipped a hand. "He will be arriving tonight to stay with Michael Kinnear. They have a partnership," he added as if Susan didn't already know. "Aaron had business, so after meeting us at the airport he took us to the ferry in Anacortes and then returned to Seattle. But we will survive, eh?"

"Of course." But not very well if the tension around here didn't ease. "Let's get home. You'll all want a shower and a rest."

They walked to the dock, turning female heads as they passed, and climbed down the ramp to Susan's Tollycraft. Distant thunder sounded, as if to underscore the generally ominous atmosphere that lingered to mar the reunion.

"You get in, Libby," Susan said. "Sit amidships while we settle the luggage."

"Amidships," Libby repeated with a laugh. "You've become so nautical. Oh, how beautiful." She stood, her black-and-cream patent shoes planted apart on the seat, while she looked into the bottom of the boat.

Susan leaned forward and almost overbalanced. Visible through the clear plastic cover of an oversize florist's box was a heap of long-stemmed roses. Libby was already taking off the lid and removing a flower and a small envelope. She handed the envelope to Susan, who read her name there before pocketing it.

"Look at this," Libby cried. From one angle the rose appeared crystalline-white, but as she turned it, blood-red showed inside each petal. "It's like fire and ice. Who is he, Susan? You've been holding out on me."

"My sweet," Georges said from behind Susan, "could we perhaps continue your little intrigue after we arrive at Susan's? And remember, we should not interfere in the way she lives her life."

There was no malice in his voice. Susan glanced back at him and saw, gratefully, the old Georges, the one in whom laughter always shimmered just beneath the surface.

Libby made grumbling noises as she settled gingerly on the seat while Jean-Claude followed her aboard to receive the cases from Georges. By the time Georges was also in place with Susan at the helm, the old boat rode low in the water, but the engine roared predictably to life and Susan pushed off.

She gave the dock above one last glance. Her heart

missed a beat, then another. Leaning against a tree, arms crossed, was a tall, unmistakable figure—Mike Kinnear. When he raised a hand in salute, Susan turned away, determined no one should witness the incident. Just as quickly she looked back again and, unable to resist, sent a single wave. The roses had to be from him. She could hardly wait to read his card. But equally strong was her desire to wait until she was alone so she could hug the moment to herself in private.

Once more she glanced back, but he'd left.

In minutes they were threading among floatplanes and boats, heading toward Brown Island, and a fresh weight of apprehension settled over Susan. Her passengers seemed closed in their own thoughts. Libby wasn't imagining anything. There was something threatening in progress here.

Lightning shivered across the sky, a shuddering band of gold that glimmered on and on as it crackled in the distinctive way of Northwest lightning.

Georges hunched forward, rested a hand on the back of Libby's neck and resumed his oddly vigilant surveillance on all sides. He looked as if he thought they might be boarded by pirates at any moment.

The heavens darkened dramatically, turning the scene to a gray-washed canvas of dull hues. Thunder rumbled—a long, long growl that faded slowly. The scent of salt became intense. Then the first massive drops of rain fell.

Susan grimaced. The thick silence among her passengers made any attempt at conversation difficult. "We'll be there soon," she said, and was grateful when Jean-Claude, standing beside her, turned on a marvelous smile. The tilt of his eyes seemed more pronounced, and the sensual flare of his nostrils. Those eyes made a discreet but unmistakable trip from her face to her feet and back again. Evidently the fact that she was nine years his senior didn't stop him from being interested.

"I see the house," Libby said when Susan was beginning to wonder how many silent hours lay ahead. "Such a beautiful spot, Sue."

"Yes." She agreed wholeheartedly, not that she got as much pleasure out of living here since her divorce. Pleasure had to be shared, or a home built for someone else, for it to be really satisfying. As soon as there was a suitable moment, she must tell Libby about her adoption plans.

Maneuvering the boat around to approach the dock stern first, Susan stood up to grab a plank and ease them alongside. Hand over hand she moved them as close to shore as possible before dropping the fenders, leaping out and securing the lines. Immediately ahead stood her striking two-story house built in the Northwest style of dark-stained wood and weathered stone that suited the area so well.

While Susan held the boat steady, Georges and Jean-Claude unloaded the baggage. Georges immediately reached down to half lift Libby up beside him. Susan didn't miss the adoration in his eyes. Whatever was amiss, Libby was right; it didn't stem from any change in Georges and Libby's feelings for each other.

"Here." She handed the door keys to Jean-Claude. "Go ahead and get out of the rain. I'll make sure the Tolly's secure and join you. Have a drink," she added as they moved away. "Libby, you and Georges are in your usual room. Jean-Claude's in the loft." That was set up as a studio with its own sitting room and bathroom.

It might be shallow of her, but, after all, Susan was human, and getting her hands on those roses and reading the card—which probably said nothing unless it was another unacceptable suggestion—was all she could think about.

Jumping lightly back into the boat, she ignored the increasingly heavy rain and lifted the lid of the florist's box again. Feeling slightly guilty, she counted, then formed a silent whistle. She couldn't remember ever having received long-stemmed roses before, certainly not *two dozen* of them.

Using her windbreaker to keep the card dry, she slipped it from the envelope and read: "Of course I forgive you for turning me down. Your judgment was clouded. I'll make sure you have a chance to make it up to me."

Susan read and reread the note, her frown gradually dissolving as she began to laugh. The audacity of the man. Then she noticed an arrow at the bottom of the card and turned it over: "The roses reminded me of you, heat hidden inside a cool shell. That's it for the poetic stuff. I'm not giving up, Susan. Mike."

What did he want from her? She wasn't his type—even more, he wasn't hers. Not that his attention wasn't flattering.

Stuffing the card back into her pocket, she scrambled to the dock, the roses in one arm. For now she must give all her attention to Libby and Georges. Then it would be time to devote every spare minute to the problem of how to make progress with Harriet Brock.

She walked toward the house, swinging a straw shopping bag filled with fresh produce she'd bought in Friday Harbor. In Seattle Mrs. Brock had said the next step would be for her to visit Susan here and assess her home situation. Now it seemed the plan had changed. Instead there would be several group meetings with other prospective adoptive parents—married couples. Susan bit her lip, fighting down a wave of anxiety at the prospect of being the only participant without a spouse. She arrived at the back door, the one facing the water, and glanced at her flowers. If she had a man who was interested in backing her up, the whole adoption process would take on a different slant. The door stood ajar and she pushed it open. Thinking about Mike Kinnear as a prospective partner, in anything, particularly in providing a home for a baby, showed just how desperate and irrational she'd become.

"I'm not giving up," he'd written. Her skin turned first cold, then hot. She ought to wish he would give up, but she didn't.

"Hello," she called, and got no reply. They must all have gone up to get settled in their rooms.

Susan went to put the basket in the kitchen and find a vase for her roses. Distracted, she set them aside and trailed into the living room to the foot of the spiral staircase leading up to the second floor and three of the house's four bedrooms. Another short flight rose to the loft. This place was too big for one person, but it would be a great place for children to grow up. She closed her eyes. Now she was thinking children—plural. No longer of just one baby. How many other women suffered this painful longing? How many other women felt unfulfilled and yearned for a child of their own upon whom to lavish their love?

She moved closer to soaring Palladian windows overlooking the smooth lawns that swept down to the water. As always, she looked toward the green slopes of Shaw Island with its scattering of houses hugging the shore. The ocean was broken into swatches of dull steel.

Even more than Susan, her husband, Bill, had loved this spot for its isolated feeling. The view still held her captive, but in the two years since her divorce she'd discovered there could be a desolate quality to this wild place.

The living room needed dusting. With guests coming

she should have remembered that. A lover of clear expanses and no clutter, she kept the surfaces of her beautiful rough-hewn oak tables unadorned except for simple arrangements of colorful dried flowers. Heavy white twill covered the two couches that formed a bower around the used-brick fireplace. Susan loved the room as much as she had when she and Bill chose each piece, as much as when they decided to paint all the exposed crosshatched beams white and to buff the hardwood floors down to a pale shade. But it was all too much with no one to share the pleasure.

She went into the huge kitchen once more—a kitchen intended for big family meals and preparing dinners for all the guests Susan and Bill had expected to entertain.

Never meant to be. Two miscarriages led to an estrangement that had come upon them like a steadily growing malignancy, sucking away the dreams.

Tonight, at least, Susan had a reason to take some pleasure in cooking. Smiling, she began assembling salad ingredients on the butcher block island in the middle of the room. Having company did feel good. Libby would relax soon, and they'd be back to their old good-humored bantering.

Susan paused, a bunch of celery in her hand. Surely Libby was making too much of Georges's edginess. But the way he searched this way and that, watching...for what? Another thought came. Could Georges suspect that Libby had another man in the picture? Disgusted even at the notion, Susan tossed the celery into a bowl and opened a can of water chestnuts. Everyone went through stages. This was just one of Georges's. It would pass.

She went to work with more vigor. Last night she'd prepared lasagna. The salad, bread and fresh fruit would complete the meal. From the distance came the sound of water gurgling through the pipes. Soon the others would be showered and down.

The scent of roses reminded her that they needed water. After filling a Waterford vase, which had been a wedding present, she arranged the blooms carefully.

Mike Kinnear was an unexpected complication in her life. Did she dislike that complication? She smelled a rose and avoided answering her own question. She and Mike could never be anything to each other. That was certain.

He seemed self-possessed, most of the time, but occasionally she imagined she saw a hint of vulnerability. Or was she dreaming? She didn't believe she'd dreamed that he suggested they sleep together—just like that—or that he didn't particularly like being a parent.

"Can I do something to help?"

She jumped. Jean-Claude had approached noiselessly to stand at her shoulder, a hand braced on the counter beside her.

"No, thank you," she said, smiling self-consciously. The man exuded sexuality and made her distinctly uncomfortable. "Please, make yourself at home. This won't take long."

"May I keep you company?"

European charm was no myth. "Of course. Pull a stool up to the counter."

He did as she suggested and sat with his chin propped on his hand. "May I pour you a glass of wine?"

"No...yes, why not? There's a chardonnay in the refrigerator."

"What are we eating?"

"Lasagna." Listening to him, watching his elegant European mannerisms, made her wish she had planned a gourmet feast.

"Then the wine should be red, of course."

"Of course," she agreed faintly as he selected a Beaujolais from the rack above the microwave.

She found and placed a corkscrew into his outstretched hand without his having told her what he wanted.

Did she like him? Libby did. That was good enough.

Soon, with several sips of the full-bodied wine warming her veins and relaxing her muscles, Susan felt her tension ebbing.

"How do you find them?"

Susan lifted her eyes from the lettuce spinner. "I'm sorry?"

"Georges and Libby." His extremely dark eyes could undoubtedly hide most emotion, but not the troubled flatness Susan saw now. "Has Libby—er—confided in you?"

"Um..." Susan cleared her throat and used fiddling with the wineglass to buy time. "What do you mean?"

He shrugged. "Obviously she hasn't. No matter. Forget I mentioned anything, please." His thick lashes lowered as he observed the wine, which he swirled in his glass. His full mouth had come together in a firm line.

She wasn't the only one concerned about Libby and Georges. "I do know there's something wrong," she said, falling over the words. An ally in this would be such a relief. "Libby's frightened that Georges may be in some danger and—" Saying too much could be a mistake. She'd let Jean-Claude say what he knew.

"Hmm." He took a long, slow swallow. "I think perhaps she misreads the real problem."

"You know what the problem is?" Susan set down her knife and glass and leaned closer. "*Is* there danger?" Her heart began an unpleasant, irregular beat.

"Perhaps." His upper lip curled. "But not, I think, exactly in the way Libby may have decided. And I don't believe it is only the business concern that causes

Georges's change of mood. You do see that he is changed?''

"Yes, yes, of course."

"There is a certain…undertaking that brings with it some risks. Some of the people involved are—how do you say it? Shady. Criminals perhaps. But this is not what I see affecting Georges now."

Susan held her breath and remained silent.

"My uncle—who, as you must see, is more like a brother to me—is too much like someone else who was once very important in my life. That likeness has brought me much pleasure in the past, but now…'' Jean-Claude found a handkerchief and touched it to the corner of his mouth. Susan noticed his long, well-kept hands. His left small finger bore a signet ring identical to one Georges wore.

"I'd like to know what this is all about," Susan said softly. "They both mean so much to me."

"I can rely upon your absolute discretion?" The black eyes pinned her.

"Yes." Her hands scrunched into fists. Before she had felt apprehensive. Now she was deeply afraid.

"Your sister is a beautiful woman, a sensual woman who has every right to expect her man to meet every need." Now the eyes didn't connect with Susan's.

She opened and closed her mouth, trying to unscramble what he might really be saying. "Georges *is* everything my sister needs."

"He's not sure of that anymore."

Nausea turned her clammy. "Are you suggesting that Georges thinks Libby has been unfaithful? If you are, I assure—"

"What I am suggesting is that Georges appears to have

some doubts. These doubts may be leading him in a very dangerous direction.''

"I don't understand.'' Indignant, Susan walked around the island to stand at Jean-Claude's elbow. "That makes absolutely no sense.''

"Ah, but I think it does. This madness over the boat is all part of his desperation to keep wooing her. It will be a gift to his love. Has he told you what it will be called?''

"No.'' Taking a breath had become a feat.

"*Ma Libby*. My Libby.''

Susan swallowed. "That's beautiful.''

"Yes, I suppose so. It also suggests obsession, which is never healthy.''

"I don't know what point you're trying to make.''

"It's simple, Susan.'' He ran a finger back and forth along the tendons in her hand. "Georges thinks, perhaps correctly, that a passionate woman, even one as good as Libby, can become distracted by, er, exciting diversions.''

Susan bridled. "Whatever you're implying, I know I don't like it. Libby has left me with no doubt that she and Georges are happy—in every way.''

"Ah, yes,'' Jean-Claude said too softly. "Libby knows this. And she assumes Georges is also certain of her. But there are things she doesn't know because he had never told her, and I do not feel it my place to do so.''

Susan's heart beat faster and faster. "Make your point.''

"Did you know that Georges's brother, my father, took his own life?''

She looked away. "No. I'm sorry.''

"So am I. Like Georges, my father loved his wife—my mother—obsessively. And she loved him, but he was never certain of her. He imagined that she tired of him. I assure you that he was wrong. To this day, my mother is still alone. She has never cared for another man.''

Susan didn't know what to say.

"My father's jealousy made him unbalanced. When he...when he drowned himself, he left a note. It said he could not live without my mother."

"How sad," Susan whispered. "How terrible for you and your mother."

Jean-Claude raised his chin, and she saw his chest expand as he sighed deeply. "Yes. I don't think I can face another such tragedy."

She touched his arm and he smiled sadly.

"What does this have to do with Georges and Libby?" Susan wished she could ease this man's evident pain.

"Forget I said anything."

Susan moved closer. "Please tell me."

"If you insist." His face became remote. "I see in Georges the signs I saw in my father, even though I was young at the time. I am concerned for Georges's stability."

"No. I'm sure he wouldn't—"

"Are you?" His dark eyes passed over her face. "I am not. I believe it is possible that Georges suspects his wife is slipping away from him. And I am afraid he could choose to take the same course as his brother—suicide."

A restless night had left Susan with gritty eyes and a heavy sensation in her limbs. Coffee would put her right. As soon as she ferried Georges and Libby to Friday Harbor, it would be time to get to the salon. Jeff, with Pearl and Lynne—and with Molly on the desk—managed very well, but Susan never felt quite secure if she didn't put in a good day's work.

When she entered the kitchen, she was less than pleased to find Jean-Claude, looking fresh and too handsome in a white polo shirt and white cotton pants, lounging at the table. The smell of freshly brewed coffee assailed her, and when he leapt up to pour her a cup, her hostility quickly faded.

"*Bonjour*, Susan," he said, smiling engagingly. "A beautiful day. I wanted a chance to—as I think you say—mend fences. I believe I upset you last night. That was not my intention."

She wanted to forget the whole incident. "You were worried and trying to be honest. Let's leave it at that." Sliding into a chair in front of the cup of coffee he'd set on the table, she worked on her socks and tennis shoes. She'd had no opportunity for a private talk with Libby. That must be remedied.

"I was too dramatic," Jean-Claude said. "You may have got the impression that I thought Libby might be, er, looking elsewhere. That is not what I meant. Simply that I sometimes think Georges is afraid she is."

"Please don't worry anymore. I'm not going to." Last night at dinner Georges and Libby had appeared relaxed and happy, and Susan had tried to put Jean-Claude's frightening suggestions out of her mind.

"I have let my imagination go too far, I fear. It is simply this foolish deal of Georges's that is the real trouble." Jean-Claude turned down the corners of his mouth. "But he will not listen to me. I only hope it won't be too late when he finally realizes—shh." He held up a hand. "They are coming. Please do not mention what I have said."

Completely frustrated, Susan screwed up her face but held her tongue as Georges and Libby came in with their arms around each other. Libby gazed adoringly up at Georges and fingered a necklace Susan didn't remember seeing before.

"Georges is spoiling me again," Libby said, breaking away to lean close to Susan. "Cartier. He ordered it specially and had it sent. It was under my pillow. Can you imagine that? I need many necks and wrists and ears to wear all the lovely things he buys me. Honestly, Georges—'' she shook a finger at him ''—you have to stop spoiling me.''

''Never,'' he said, laughing as he handed Susan a small box. ''I didn't forget you.''

She looked away from the band of gold and diamonds at Libby's throat to examine her own gift—earrings of sapphires and diamonds that must have cost a fortune. Of course they would complement her eyes wonderfully, and she loved them, but still the generosity made her uncomfortable. ''Thank you, Georges,'' she said, bobbing up to kiss him. As she sat, she caught Jean-Claude's speculative glance that clearly said, ''I told you so.'' Georges did appear to feel he needed to keep buying his wife.

The phone rang and Libby snatched it up as if this were her home. ''Hello!''

Susan couldn't help smiling.

''No, this is Libby, her sister. I bet you're the man with the roses.''

Susan covered her face and groaned.

''Of course she liked them—at least I think she did. She didn't say.'' A laugh. ''Who knows what she really thinks?''

''Libby,'' Susan growled in a low voice.

''Yes, she did tell us about the appointment. At your boatyard. She made what you do sound fascinating.''

Susan glared at the ceiling and muttered, ''I don't *know* what he does.''

''Shh. Be calm.'' Jean-Claude patted her arm on the table.

''Is there any change in our arrangements? Libby, let me speak to him.'' The tightness in Georges's voice immediately caught Susan's attention.

"Eleven is still all right? Good. No, I...no." Libby covered the mouthpiece. "You don't need to speak to him, Georges. Susan, Mike says you're coming, too. He called to make sure you knew."

"I have to get to work," she said honestly. "You don't need me."

"She says we don't need her," Libby repeated into the phone. "She says she has to go to work." Silence. "Yes, certainly. Susan, Mike wants a word with you."

Unwilling to make a scene, Susan painted on a smile, got up and took the receiver. "Hello."

"Hello yourself. You've decided to avoid me, haven't you?"

"I don't think this is the... Of course we'll talk about this again."

"Oh, no, you don't." He tutted. "And I thought you were above deceit. Shows how little I know about human nature. Susan, my love, I've just realized that I, too, have to work this morning. Perhaps you'd let Georges and Libby know I'll get in touch with them later."

She turned her back to the others. "No."

"Oh, good. So you'll be here at eleven?"

"Yes." She hung up. *Blackmailed.* Why, when she'd always avoided manipulative men, did she turn to heated jelly at the very sound of Mike Kinnear's voice? He was, without a doubt, the most unscrupulously conniving male she'd ever met. The biggest puzzle was why he'd zeroed in on her as a target for his attention—unless her reluctance was a challenge he couldn't resist.

This ploy to get at her had worked this time. There wouldn't be a next time.

Kinnear was the only word on the sign, as if no other explanation of what went on in this boatyard was necessary.

Susan drove between the gates and downhill past piles of lumber, drums of who-knew-what, great wooden spools of metal hawser as thick as a man's wrist and dozens of other supplies that must be necessary to "Kinnear."

"This is so exciting," Libby said. She sat beside Susan who felt more lighthearted than she had since her sister's first call from Hawaii. Libby seemed completely at ease again and, since last night, had made no mention of her previous concerns.

Jean-Claude had stayed on Brown Island to work, but Georges's long body was folded into the tiny back seat of the Volkswagen Beetle and from time to time, whenever they drove over a bump, he groaned.

"Did Mike say where we should go?" he asked.

Before Susan could respond, a tall athletically built man with curly brown hair stepped into their path, one hand held up.

"Thank God," Georges said, sounding very sincere. "There's Aaron. Let me out of this traveling tomb."

Laughing, Susan applied the brakes. The man she recognized as Georges and Libby's old friend, Aaron Conrad, opened her door and stood back until she got out beside him. An overpowering scent of varnish wrinkled her nose, and the sound of high-powered saws and hammering fractured a bright blue day. Libby, a finger in each ear, was already on her way around the hood of the car.

Aaron, even more serious-faced than Susan recalled, extended his hand to shake. "It's good to see you again," he said in a distant tone that suggested he'd memorized suitable words for the occasion.

"Aaron!" Libby launched herself at him, wrapped her

arms around his neck and kissed him enthusiastically. "You're here."

He raised his finely arched brows and smiled, crinkling the corners of his very dark brown eyes. "We did this yesterday, Libby. But I'm always glad to be hugged by you. You can hug me again tomorrow if you like. I've promised Mike I'll spend a few days with him."

Aaron's tan suggested long hours in the outdoors. Since he owned a ski lodge and sold sports equipment, Susan supposed that was to be expected. His looks were certainly arresting. In fact, she'd been exposed to more knock-'em-dead males in the past few weeks than she remembered seeing in years. Not such a terrible ordeal, even if they were all around on a temporary basis.

"Hello, Aaron," Georges said.

"Hi, there, Georges," Aaron said, smiling. "I got in last night. Mike's in his office. He sent me down to lead the way."

"Come on," Libby said to Georges, taking his hand. "This is what you've been waiting for for weeks."

There was no more time to consider the dilemma now. A short distance ahead, placed with a clear view of the water, stood what appeared to be a workshop with rooms above it. Mike Kinnear had emerged through an open door.

He wore almost-new blue jeans and a pristine short-sleeved shirt of fine black-and-gray checked cotton. She noted that the haircut she'd given him had definitely added to his already overwhelming appeal.

"Good morning," he called, one thumb hooked into a pocket.

Susan's breathing sped up. This would be the last time she had to see him, she reminded herself—if that was what she wanted.

Georges and Libby moved forward rapidly. Aaron hung back and Susan stayed with him.

"You and Mike are old friends," she said conversationally.

"Yes." Aaron dropped to his haunches and looked toward the sea. He was at once contemplative, a handsome reserved man who seemed to possess the ability to withdraw quickly and easily from a situation.

Susan shifted from foot to foot. "Is that where the boats are worked on?" An oversize, open-ended building stood below them.

"Yes."

She had never, she realized, had any reason to talk to Aaron before. Just as well, since he seemed to prefer silence.

"How many people does Mike have working for him?" she asked. Anything was preferable to standing around feeling like a fool.

"Five."

"I see." She glanced up at Georges, Libby and Mike. The latter looked directly back at her. He wasn't smiling…simply looking.

"They're working on an incredible boat," Aaron said, startling her. "Fifty-one feet. A full-keel gaff schooner. Mahogany and ash. Her hull is single-unit construction, sandblasted to…" He raised his face, frowning, as if coming out of a dream. "Good boat."

Susan had a sudden glimmer that there were mysterious depths to Aaron Conrad. Indeed, he was a *most* intriguing man…almost as intriguing as Mike Kinnear.

"Susan!" Libby called. "Come on."

"I don't want to," Susan muttered before she could stop herself.

Aaron hopped to his feet and ran a hand through his tousled hair. "Why don't you want to?"

She hunched her shoulders. "Oh, no reason, really. It's nicer outside."

"How do you know? You haven't been inside. Mike's a good man. He likes you."

Susan stared at him. He whistled, turned on his heel and walked away.

Reluctant, but jumpily excited, Susan leaned into the slope and hurried to join the others.

"We're going to talk about the boat," Libby said. "Mike would like you to be there, too." A mischievous grin turned up the corners of her mouth.

Asking why wouldn't accomplish a thing. Resigned, Susan gave her sibling a warning glare and trailed along into a workshop where a man on a stool was bent low over an intricately carved piece of wood. Paper-thin curls of wood littered the workbench and spilled onto the floor.

"This is Rudy," Mike said. Dutifully Rudy waved a chisel in acknowledgment. "He's refurbishing panels from the salon aboard the *Sultan*. That's the schooner we're working on."

Georges took a closer look and made admiring sounds. Seeing how animated he looked, Susan experienced a pang of anxiety. For some reason her brother-in-law had turned his boat into a passion and had convinced himself that Mike Kinnear was the man to transform his purchase into a dream ship. What if Mike turned him down, after all?

"Up there," Mike said, indicating open-tread wooden stairs leading to a loft.

Georges held Libby's hand and led her up. Susan followed and quickly found Mike at her shoulder...and felt his hand resting lightly at her waist. His fingers slipped to her side and she drew in a breath. He was determined to pursue her and, damn her own weakness, she liked it. Right now her skin burned beneath his touch and her legs felt heavy.

His office was a surprise. Having had a brief glimpse inside his home, she expected similar disorganization here. She couldn't have been more wrong. In one corner a low, tan leather couch and two matching love seats were arranged around a square rosewood table. Nautical sketches, black-and-white line drawings of sailing vessels, adorned walls paneled in light oak. Windows covered two walls, meeting at a corner that overlooked the entire yard. Under one window was a desk piled with orderly stacks of papers. The other window spread light over a huge drafting table covered with blueprints.

One other item in the room caught and held Susan's attention. A bed, covered with an old and faded afghan, occupied a space along a wall beneath a skylight. She gave the bed a long look. It could just be that on at least some of those occasions when he didn't make it home at night, he was guilty of no more than working late and becoming too tired to do anything other than sleep right here.

"Sit down," Mike invited. "Coffee?"

"Thank you," Libby said at the same time as Susan shook her head. Georges added, "Black please." Susan walked to the windows while husband and wife settled on the couch. Mike went directly to a coffee maker on a small table by the bed and filled four mugs.

Susan waited until he'd set the mugs in front of his guests and seated himself on a love seat. This way she could make sure she didn't end up with his thigh pressed to hers again.

Once she'd sunk into the buttery leather, Mike jumped up again. "Anyone for cream or sugar?"

"Cream, please," Libby said.

He found a carton in a portable refrigerator and brought it to her. Then he sat beside Susan on the love seat. "I'm glad you were able to come, too," he said guilelessly. "Anne was asking about you. I told her you'd be sure to visit us again soon."

Susan blinked.

"Susan has really worked hard on your behalf," he said to Georges. "She was good enough to accommodate my schedule by coming all the way out to the house. I have a twelve-year-old daughter from my former marriage. Anne's at what they so diplomatically call 'an interesting age,' and Susan made quite an impact on her."

Good old Susan was suddenly an old and willing friend. Well, enough was enough. She wasn't going along with the charade. "Anne's a lovely little girl. Unfortunately, with me I think it was hate at first sight—on her part of course."

"Not at all," Mike said, looking into his coffee. "You don't understand the thinking of the preadolescent mind. It isn't in to get along with adults. But she told me she thought you were cool—for someone so old."

It sounded like something Anne might say, but she didn't believe him. Nor did she understand why he was taking the conversation in this direction, unless…unless he was still trying to make points with her. And she didn't understand the preadolescent mind, huh? He, of course, did. What a laugh. He was totally inept with his daughter, and Susan was sick of being reminded that she hadn't had children.

She glanced around to find Georges and Libby watching her curiously. Libby's pursed grin suggested she "saw all"—namely, that there was something significant in progress between Mike Kinnear and her sister.

"Susan tells me you will need a lot of persuading to

take on *Ma Libby*,'' Georges said. He glanced at Libby, smiled so gently that Susan's heart turned, and placed his wife's hand on his knee.

Libby's determinedly cheerful countenance slipped and the deep love she felt for Georges shone in her marvelous eyes.

Susan saw Mike watching them and saw the way his mouth tightened. What, she wondered, was that all about? Surely this confirmed single didn't secretly envy marital bliss? Immediately she felt mean and unfeeling. He'd loved once and lost. Those things, as she knew only too well, never entirely stopped hurting.

"So," Georges said as the silence began to stretch, "it will be up to me to convince you our boat is so special that you would not want her to be touched by other hands."

"I don't think that will be necessary," Mike said evenly. His long, broad hand rested on his knee. Sun-bleached hairs glinted on the backs of splayed fingers. For a crazy instant Susan longed for those fingers to be entwined with hers.

"Her hull is magnificent," Georges said. "Three-inch-thick diagonal double-planked Alaskan cedar over four-inch cedar-and-oak frames. So beautiful. I'm told she was built in the Seattle area in the forties and used very little until this, er, prince bought her. He made her into the—how do you say it—party boat? Red velvet and much fussiness that will all have to be removed. But—"

"Susan told me all about it," Mike said.

She didn't have to look to feel his eyes on her. Could ego be strong enough to make a man who was obviously very successful, very good at what he did, play these games? Surely he was playing games. She hadn't been allowed to tell him very much about the boat.

"Ah," Georges said, "so you must already have had some time to decide whether or not you will be interested in my proposition."

"Mmm."

Now she had to turn her face to his. He seemed oblivious of the fact that his prospective customers would observe the single-minded attention he lavished on her. But then he probably had no intention of taking the commission. He'd brought Georges and Libby all the way down here for nothing. The rat.

"Did Susan tell you the topsides are white?" George went on, his voice dreamy.

He wasn't noticing Mike's behavior, Susan thought, feeling vaguely sick.

"White," Mike repeated. "I like that. I understand she's pretty run-down, though."

"Outrageously so," Georges agreed. "But she will emerge a beauty, I assure you. We do have the engineer's assurance that the engines are sound."

"Tell him about the brass, Georges," Libby said, hanging on to his arm.

Georges shrugged. "Libby was very taken with the brass. What could be seen of it."

"Hmm."

After all this he was going to turn them down.

"You will, of course, want to see the plans and discuss my expectations," Georges said. "But I want you to know that, should you decide to consider my proposition, yours would be the final say—in everything."

Susan began to feel really angry. Mike Kinnear had no right to give Georges hope when he had no intention of doing the work.

"I'm sure we'll be able to come to a mutual agreement." Mike picked up Susan's coffee and handed it to her. He held her eyes for longer than was comfortable. "There would seem to be a challenge here, and I've never been a man to run from a challenge."

She could have sworn a cool breeze slicked over her skin. Why else would she have goose bumps on a warm day?

"So—" Georges leaned forward "—you are telling us you accept the job?"

"I'm telling you it sounds like something I'd like to do and I'll be more than happy to enter into further discussion on the project. Where's the boat now?"

"In Kauai. Nawiliwili Harbor."

"Oh, Susan," Libby said, her eyes gleaming, "I knew things would start turning out all right once we were here." Smiling, she bowed her head and didn't see her husband's frown.

"You will want to see her, of course," Georges said. His fingers were laced tightly together in his lap. There *were* problems here. But surely they didn't stem from the grisly roots Jean-Claude had suggested.

"That would be necessary," Mike said, and Susan was even more aware of his almost unwavering scrutiny of her. Georges and Libby must see it, too. What would they think?

"We'd better get back," she said, anxious to put breathing space between herself and this unsettling man— and to try to figure out a way to help Georges and Libby. The prospect made her shudder.

"Are you cold?" Mike asked softly.

She had to glance up. His concentration on her might be unsettling, but it was also having other effects on her. "I'm not cold, thank you. You'll need time to decide how to answer Georges's proposal."

"Quite." Georges said, and he and Libby rose. "Susan

has said you prefer only to deal with boats you buy yourself. Of course, we shall be very disappointed if you decide—''

''But I've already decided.'' Mike interrupted. ''At least I've decided what to do for the immediate future. I'm surprised Susan would think otherwise.''

''Otherwise than what?'' she asked, unable to stop herself.

''Well, you should know that I never walk away from something without being certain I won't regret the decision later.''

The phone rang twice. When Susan picked it up and said, ''Hello,'' the line was dead. ''I hate that,'' she told Libby, who sat visibly agitated at the other end of a couch near the living room fireplace.

''No one there?'' Libby said absently. ''That happens all the time to me.''

Since they'd returned to Brown Island Libby had had little to say, and Susan still hadn't found the courage to try to draw her sister out.

The phone rang once more. When Susan picked it up, she again heard the empty pinging of a disconnected line. ''Silliness,'' she said. ''I should check in with the salon. They aren't used to me being out on Saturday.'' Yet she didn't feel she could leave Libby until they'd talked.

Again the phone rang and Susan watched it, counting. Four, five. She picked up the receiver and frowned.

''What is it?''

She shook her head at Libby, a hand over the mouthpiece. ''I don't know. I can't understand what— Oh, French. Georges has it.'' She started to hang up, but Libby took the receiver from her and held it to her ear.

She covered her mouth and her eyes filled with tears.

When Susan tried to come closer, Libby waved her away. Only seconds passed before she hung up.

"What is it? Libby, tell me!"

Tears coursed down Libby's cheeks and she shook uncontrollably. "I should have known it wouldn't stop."

Susan took her in her arms and rocked. "Nothing can be this bad."

"It was the man. I heard him once before…by mistake." There was the merest flash of guilt in Libby's amber eyes.

"What did he say? This time, I mean?"

"That Georges had better rethink his decision if he knows what's good for him."

The questions couldn't wait any longer. "Libby, please tell me what's worrying you."

"It's complicated." Libby rested her head against the back of the couch. "Everything and nothing…nothing I can really pin down."

"Try to explain," Susan said encouragingly.

"Georges is involved in a large project that may involve some risk—personal risk, I think."

Susan made an encouraging noise and decided against mentioning that Jean-Claude had already alluded to all this.

"That call more or less confirms my suspicions. Someone doesn't want Georges to go ahead with the project, and they're prepared to do whatever it takes to stop him." Libby turned her face toward Susan. "They may have used a threat against me to try to persuade him. That could explain why he watches me so closely. And… Oh, Susan, I'm almost sure they've already tried to do something awful to Georges."

"You can't be sure of that if he hasn't told you so."

"I think I can. Susan, the man on the phone said that 'next time' Georges won't be so lucky."

6

The plastic coffee cup had become Susan's anchor. Its contents had long since grown cold, but she continued to curl her fingers around the flexible shell. Voices became a distant blur. When she looked up, the faces around the long scarred table seemed to shift. Only Harriet Brock's remained clear. She was smiling at Susan.

Silence.

Mrs. Brock had asked her something. Susan shifted in her seat and returned the serene smile. "I beg your pardon?"

"I asked if you had any picture in your mind of a child—a child you think could become yours."

Susan took her hands from the cup, afraid she might crush it and spill the coffee. "Well..." She turned her palms up. In the hour since they'd started this group meeting, she hadn't been capable of forming a coherent sentence. The others—the three couples who sat holding hands—were so sure of themselves, so secure.

"Perhaps not." Mrs. Brock laughed. A sympathetic laugh? An impatient why-is-she-wasting-my-time laugh?

"Yes...yes, I do. Sometimes I do." Susan's eyes hurt from holding back tears. "But maybe I feel her more. I don't know. Perhaps that's silly." Everything she said sounded silly.

"I don't think so," the woman to her left said softly.

"I think about holding my own baby. Is that what you mean?"

Susan nodded gratefully and, regardless of how hard she tried to stop them, tears welled. "I...um...I was pregnant twice. Both times I miscarried at twelve weeks. Afterward I would try to imagine what the baby would have been like if she'd lived—they were both girls—and I sort of saw impressions. Blond hair." She giggled nervously. "Stupid when she would probably have been dark. But I could feel—" Oh, God, she was going to cry and blow it all. This wasn't what it was all about here.

"Go on," Harriet Brock said.

"I haven't held many babies." Everything she said was wrong. "I...you can feel how your own baby would be in your arms. A small weight—light and soft and warm. You look at other people's babies and it hurts so much. You can't reconcile why they have theirs and you don't have yours. And no one wants to listen to you, not as often as you want to talk about it. My husband..."

Someone sniffed, and she focused on a man across the table. His name was David something, and the anguish in his eyes amazed her.

"What about your husband?" Mrs. Brock prompted.

"Well, he was upset, too, but he probably got tired of hearing me go on about how much I wanted a baby." All she could do was be herself. She puffed out her cheeks and tilted her head up to stop the tears. "They shouldn't put you in a maternity unit when you've had a miscarriage. You hear other women in labor. And you hear babies cry."

In the quiet that followed she felt numb and very, very still. The woman next to her rested a hand on her arm, but she couldn't seem to respond.

"I was put there after my hysterectomy, too." There was no mistaking the break in David's wife voice. Her name was Natalie. "I guess they just don't have enough room elsewhere sometimes."

"Yes, well," Harriet Brock said after a while, "it's important to put some of the emotion behind us, isn't it?"

Us? Susan stared at the caseworker, at her impeccable suit and her hair that was never out of place. "Do you have children?" she asked. There appeared to be an unwritten rule that Harriet Brock had immunity from the personal questions she asked everyone else. To Susan that seemed wrong.

"Two," Mrs. Brock answered. "I don't think we should go much farther today. It usually works well for an established group to continue to work together. Does that seem agreeable to everyone?"

There was a chorused "Yes."

"Very well. We'll meet here again in four weeks. Ms. Ackroyd, perhaps you'd stay a little longer since your situation is different."

Sickness swept into Susan. "Of course." Would this be it, the time she'd be told to forget the whole thing? Certainly she hadn't contributed much to the meeting, although the three couples had made every effort to include her in the discussion.

Mrs. Brock stood as the others filed out. "Oh, and there's something I'd like you all to think about by the next time we meet. Children need to believe they're worthwhile. I think we all agree there."

Six heads nodded.

"That means they have to be convinced they aren't the product of worthless biological parents. I'd like you to come up with some ideas about how you could instill a child with the conviction that their real parents were special, and that they made a brave choice in giving them up."

After the door closed, Mrs. Brock returned to her seat, separated from Susan by the length of the table. In the center stood a vase of huge, overblown pink roses. Mrs. Brock's trademark. Susan fastened her eyes on the roses while she waited for the woman to speak.

"So?"

Susan inclined her head. "Yes?"

"Do you understand why I particularly wanted you to come into a group of the kind of people we usually deal with?"

She did, but she wouldn't make Mrs. Brock's job too easy. "Why don't you explain it to me?"

"You should understand what you're up against. It's obvious how much each of these couples has to offer a child."

And because she didn't have a husband she didn't have anything to offer? "Many children grow up in single-parent homes. More and more today."

"That doesn't make it the most desirable situation."

"A home with one parent and a lot of love is preferable to one with two parents and constant dissension."

Mrs. Brock sighed and leaned back in her chair. "True. But that isn't the issue here. With the children I deal with I have some control over the type of people who will become their parents."

Control. Yes, that was obviously very important to this woman. "I will be a good parent," Susan said firmly.

"So you still want to be considered?"

"Yes!" She must not lose her composure. "Of course I do, Mrs. Brock. I should have thought that was obvious by now."

"Most single people who want to adopt find it easier to be selected if they agree to take an older child. Or one with handicaps."

Susan looked up slowly, becoming appalled. "You mean a single person is suddenly considered a highly eligible parent if he or she can take...slightly shopworn merchandise?"

"I didn't say that." Mrs. Brock sounded flustered, a new development.

"The one thing I don't think I could handle would be a child who needed exceptional attention, either emotional or physical. Not because I don't want to, but because I also have to earn a living." Susan sighed. "I wish I could adopt a handicapped child. But as you keep pointing out, I'm single. It wouldn't be fair to the child."

Mrs. Brock stood up and Susan noticed a surprising spot of bright color on each of the woman's cheeks. "All right, Ms. Ackroyd, that will be all for now. Four weeks from today, then."

"Thank you." Mrs. Brock had said nothing to make her believe she was as much as an inch closer to her goal. "Is there anything I could to do speed up the process?"

"No."

"But I will get a child eventually?"

"In the four weeks between now and your next appointment here I'd like you to consider something."

Susan walked toward the door. "Anything."

"Would you feel comfortable keeping a picture of a child's real mother in a prominent place in your home? This would be a child you had been selected to adopt."

"Why?"

"Don't answer questions with questions, Ms. Ackroyd. Could you do that?"

"If I don't know why—"

"I think you've already given me an answer." Mrs. Brock picked up her briefcase.

"No, I haven't. And you didn't ask the others that."

"I didn't feel the anger in them that I feel in you." The door opened wide under Mrs. Brock's hand. "You've made it clear you resent women who've had children. As I told you, it's important for a child to believe his or her parents had value. I don't believe you could do that."

"But I think I could." Susan's scalp felt so tight that it hurt. She should never have asked this woman a personal question.

"I'm not convinced. And until I am we won't make much progress, will we?" Fine brows arched over Mrs. Brock's gray eyes. They'd turned steely hard. "Which means you have a very long way to go to reach your goal—if you ever do."

What he'd decided to do was dangerous at best. On the other hand, he'd made very little progress with conventional approaches. Even a large bouquet of roses hadn't made a chip in Susan's glacial attitude toward him. In fact, she hadn't even thanked him.

Aaron had egged him on today. If this turned out badly, he'd blame Aaron's bad judgment and call it quits.

Before long someone who knew him would start to notice the amount of time he spent hanging around the waterfront in Friday Harbor and start asking questions.

The ferry from Anacortes approached steadily, and he positioned himself where every foot passenger would have to pass him to disembark. He knew Susan had had some sort of appointment in Seattle this morning. Libby and Georges had traveled into the city with her and would be there for the night to have dinner and see a show.

They wouldn't be back until tomorrow.

He paced back and forth. Sometimes a man's plans worked. With Jean-Claude Duclaux off in the mountains with Aaron, who'd taken him to see Aaron's skiing operation and spend the night at the lodge he owned, there might never be a better opportunity for Mike to be alone with Susan.

She might not be on this ferry. She hadn't been on the last one.

He liked her. But he didn't want anything more than a satisfying liaison. Yes, that was true, absolutely true. Well, sure, he *liked* her, but there was no reason he couldn't desire a woman and like her, too.

Only he'd already established that she wasn't the type to be interested in a no-strings affair. So why was he continuing with this?

Because he *liked* her, damn it. And she made him feel what he hadn't felt for a long time—warm inside, as if he didn't just want to say, "Hi, goodbye, it was great." He wanted her to like him, too.

She made him feel protective. He screwed up his eyes. *Protective?* The only other human being who ever made him feel protective was Anne.

Frances had raised entirely different emotions. Possessiveness because she was beautiful? Yep, and…sure, love, for as long as it had taken him to find out that a man couldn't keep on loving a woman with no love to give back.

The ferry docked, shaking the ground beneath his feet. The smart thing to do was hotfoot it out of here before he made even more of an ass of himself than he already had.

Passengers straggled off. He watched until the last people had come through and outbound passengers began to board. This was it, a sign: *Give it up, Kinnear. She only interested you because she didn't fall into your arms.*

There she was.

His jaw slackened. What was it he felt when he saw her? His heart beat faster, for crying out loud! Second childhood, that had to be it—or worse—second adolescence.

He didn't need this.

"Watch where you're going, lady!"

Mike had half turned away. Looking back, he was just in time to see a burly man scowling at Susan. In a dirty white T-shirt and jeans that rode below a bulging belly, the guy wasn't a pleasant sight. Mike could have cared less if he hadn't seen the distress in Susan's blue eyes. He shouldered his way through the milling people to reach her.

"That's enough," he said to the man while he slipped his fingers beneath Susan's elbow. "The lady hasn't done anything to you."

"Oh, yeah? Only knocked my newspaper all over the place."

Sections of paper were spread on the ground. Mumbling apologies, Susan pulled free and crouched to gather up the sections. Mike gave the man a glare and bent to help. "Here." When he had all the parts he handed them over.

"Dippy broad."

Mike didn't bother to pursue that. His attention was on Susan, who didn't appear totally aware of her surroundings. He frowned. "That guy really upset you, didn't he?"

"What?" She raised her face. Her almost waxen pallor added to the impression of preoccupation.

"Are you okay?"

"Yes. Yes, of course I am."

"I suppose you have to go to work now. I was hoping to have a few words with you first." Now she'd ask how he knew she'd be on the ferry, and unless he talked fast, she'd figure out he'd had his spies—Aaron Conrad for one—watching her movements. And if she figured that out, she'd likely tell him to get lost.

She squinted in the general direction of her salon. "No, I don't think I'll go to work yet." Her eyes looked as if they hurt her.

"Do you have a headache?"

For the first time since he'd approached her, she actually looked directly at him. "What are you doing here?"

Honesty, he reminded himself without too much conviction, was the best approach. "Aaron said Georges had told him you'd be going into Seattle and then coming back on one of the early-afternoon ferries. I just happened to, er, be around when this one came in and there you were." He smiled and his mouth felt stretched.

"Yes. Well, that's nice. I've got to get home."

There was something he was missing here. Susan seemed upset, and that bothered him a lot. "Have you had lunch?"

"No."

"You haven't? That's great. Why don't we—"

"I've got to get home and think."

Mike crossed his arms. If he didn't watch himself, he'd be gathering her to him like a child in need of comfort. With Susan Ackroyd that approach was unlikely to go over well. "Susan, this is none of my business. You can tell me to get lost if you like. But I think you're upset at the moment. Am I right?"

Prepare yourself, he thought, this is where she tells you to butt out—again.

"I'm very upset."

He swallowed. "Can I do something to help?"

"No. No one can."

She walked past him toward the small boat moorings, and he took a few seconds to decide to run after her.

Without a backward glance Susan walked down the

ramp and along the dock to her Tollycraft. Mike reached her as she finished tossing in the lines and climbed aboard.

"May I come with you?"

"Why?" The empty eyes she turned up to him touched something he'd forgotten he had—his soul.

"Because I don't think you should be alone."

She appeared puzzled. "I won't be. Georges's nephew will be there and—"

"No. Jean-Claude went to Alpine Ridge with Aaron. They'll be there overnight." And Mike was very glad the too-smooth Jean-Claude wouldn't be around to hold Susan's hand. He stepped down beside her in the boat and hauled in the fenders.

"I want to be alone," she said.

"I don't think so," he countered. If badgering a troubled woman was a sin, then he was prepared to be a sinner. "Sit down. I'll be your chauffeur."

"You don't have to do this. How will you get back?"

"One of my men will come over and get me."

"Oh." She settled into a corner while he turned on the ignition, revved the engine and steered out into the channel.

"Where to?" he asked when they'd cleared the dock area.

"My house faces Shaw Island. Head straight for the eastern shore. Beyond the farthest headland there's an inlet. I'm on the other side of that."

They traveled without speaking. The sun brought out beads of sweat on Mike's brow, and he wiped them away with the back of his forearm. In her blue cotton wraparound blouse and matching full skirt, Susan appeared impervious to the heat. He noted that she wore hose and navy blue pumps. What had taken her into Seattle on an eighty-five-degree day, dressed as she was, and why had she returned with "depression" written in every slumped line of her face and body?

Could he come right out and ask where she'd been? No. But he didn't need special insight to figure out that whatever she'd been doing, the outcome had been one very upset lady.

"It's hot."

She didn't answer, and he looked at her over his shoulder. Her arms were crossed and she held a fist to her mouth.

A cigarette boat loaded with bleached, bronzed and screaming teenagers shot into his field of vision to starboard. "Hold on," he called to Susan, smiling as he braced his feet wider apart.

Rap music, blasted at a glass-fracturing level, reached him at the same time as he turned the little Tollycraft's nose sharply into the first ridge of a wide fan of wake. Then they were nose down with a following thud as the stern landed in the trough.

Mike ducked, instinctively protecting his neck from the shock. Again he glanced back at Susan, and this time their eyes met. He smiled. "Kids!" he said over the dissipating roar of the other boat.

She nodded and smiled absently. "They used to annoy me."

Whatever that meant. Maybe she was telling him she'd mellowed out with age. Well, he hadn't. Children let loose with big, dangerous toys still made him feel like leading a campaign to legalize the arrest of negligent parents. But he kept his opinion to himself. Since Susan had never been a parent, she was unlikely to relate to his feelings on the subject.

After twenty more minutes or so she said, "There it is," and came to stand beside him. The wind blew her short hair away from her face and whipped color into her cheeks. Her blouse flattened to her breasts, and her skirt billowed behind her. She was small-boned, but not skinny. No, anything but skinny.

Her house surprised him. It was much bigger than he'd expected and probably worth a bundle. Certainly it was too big for one woman, and he wondered why she'd continued to live there when one of the condos close to her salon would have been so much more convenient.

It wasn't until they'd tied up and stood on a path leading to the house that she hesitated.

"What is it?" he asked when he realized she'd hung back.

"I don't know."

Mike stuffed his hands into his pockets. Coming with her probably hadn't been such a good idea. As quickly as the thought formed, he classified himself as spineless. If he was so sure he wanted to know this woman better, he should be prepared to help out when she was in trouble. And he had no doubt that she was in some sort of trouble.

"Come on in the house and—" He laughed. "This is a bit mixed up, huh? I'm inviting you into your own house and I'm going to suggest you have a drink there. Am I presumptuous or what?"

"You're nice," she said in a small voice, and continued up the path and into the house.

After digesting the compliment, Mike followed her. He was nice. He liked that. It made him glow.

Inside, Mike found himself in the middle of a large living room that gave a pale and airy impression. He appreciated the effect. But after seeing how much she'd accomplished in a small space at the salon, he shouldn't have expected anything less from her here.

"You wanted a drink," she said. She ran her fingers

through her hair and straightened her skirt, giving Mike hope that she was coming out of her funk.

"Actually, it was you who wanted the drink."

"I said that?" She frowned. "I never say that."

"Well, you didn't exactly. I just thought it was a good idea, I guess. What do you like?"

She looked dubious. "Sometimes I drink wine. There's a bottle in the refrigerator."

"The kitchen's over there?" He pointed to an archway through which he could see champagne-colored tile and white appliances.

"Yes."

Without waiting for further discussion, Mike located the refrigerator, took out an already-open bottle of chardonnay and slipped two glasses from a rack. White wine wasn't his favorite drink, but he only needed to show himself willing to keep her company.

Susan grimaced at her first, very large swallow of the wine and her eyes teared. He'd barely sat beside her on one of two matching white couches when she downed the rest of her drink. Giving him a watery smile, she kicked off her shoes and tucked her feet beneath her.

"Good wine?" He doubted she'd tasted it.

Susan nodded, holding out her glass. He filled it again and poured an inch into the bottom of his own.

Fascinated, he watched the second glass go the way of the first. Her eyes took on a feverish sheen. Taking advantage of a drunk wasn't what he'd had in mind. With what he hoped was nonchalance, he slid the bottle onto the table and took up his own wine.

"When a woman gets pregnant, no one comes along and asks if she's qualified for the job."

Mike's teeth came together so hard that he winced.

"Do they?" Susan extended her hand, wiggling the stem of her glass. "You tell me that."

"No." He glanced at her very flat tummy. She couldn't be saying she was pregnant, could she?

"Forget it. Can I have some more of this?"

"I don't think…" He wasn't her father. "Sure."

When he poured again, she looked down into the wine but made no attempt to drink. "It's discrimination."

Susan Ackroyd definitely was no drinker. There could be no other explanation for her heightened color or her nonsensical comments.

"I told her I'm going to make a very good parent, and she said she didn't think I would."

Whoa. He was out of his depth. "Who's she?"

"She—" Susan took a sip "—is Harriet Brock. Controller. She decides who's an *eligible* parent."

"When is the…when will the baby be born?" Anything—she could have hit him with anything but this—and he'd have taken it in stride.

"Don't know."

Boy, she sounded tipsy. He couldn't abandon her in this condition. "They can't just take a baby away from its mother, so I wouldn't worry." Another thought. "And the father has something to say, too."

"You don't understand. The mother decides on her own to let the baby go."

"With coercion, or what?"

"After being counseled that it's for the best. The father isn't in the picture by then, so it doesn't matter what he says."

Mike bridled. "Does he even know about the baby? It's his, too, y'know."

"I don't know if he knows. It can happen that the

mother doesn't know who the father is. You're a man of the world. That shouldn't shock you.''

It did in this case. "Let's take this slowly. I'd like to help you if I can. You went in for a doctor's appointment this morning and they tried to persuade you to give up on the idea of keeping your baby.''

She turned her head slightly as if having difficulty keeping him in focus. "I don't have a baby yet. That's the problem. And you don't go to a doctor for these things. Not unless it's a private adoption and that's real expensive and you have to know someone.''

"I'm not sure I follow.''

Without warning Susan burst into tears. He caught her glass the instant she would have dropped it to wrap her arms around her knees and sob.

"That…that woman deliberately put me in a group with married couples to make me feel bad.''

His heart turned. She needed comfort, and the least he could do was offer her that. Gently he slipped his arms around her and cradled her against him. "It's okay. You're upset and the wine went to your head. And you didn't have lunch.''

"N-no.''

And pregnant women shouldn't drink. "Tell me what I can do to help you. Does Libby know about all this?''

"No. But I'm going to tell her and she'll back me up. She'll understand.''

"Of course she will. Maybe they're worried about how you'll care for a baby and work. Or are you going to quit for a while?''

"No! That's not the problem." She burrowed her head beneath his chin—and his body began to react to the feel of her, damn it.

"But it could be their concern.''

"Every one of the other women, the ones at the meeting, works outside the home. They don't intend to stay home after they adopt. I'm being discriminated against, I tell you."

Adopt. His fingers were in her hair, stroking, tangling in the curls. His other hand rested at her side, the thumb pressed into the firm curve of her breast. She wasn't pregnant, merely interested in adoption.

Susan nestled closer, then turned up her face until he felt her lips against his throat. "You understand how it is, don't you, Mike? Needing a child to love?"

"Yes, I understand." She felt…wonderful, pliant.

"Children need to be loved."

"Everyone needs to be loved." He paused, his hand inches from her hair. Getting more involved than he wanted would be too easy with this woman. She made him say things he didn't want to admit.

"They want me to give up trying to get a baby, but I'm not going to."

The mixed-up sensations invading his body and brain were too much. An urge to flee hit him, followed rapidly by an urge to stay.

"Kiss me, Mike."

A bolt of white heat speared him. Her face was raised, her full lips parted, her eyes closed. Where her wraparound blouse had worked awry, much of one pale breast was exposed.

Was this taking advantage? He was only human. Slowly he lowered his mouth over hers and moved it very gently back and forth. The faint taste of salt tears mingled with wine to incite him with its headiness. He heard his own muffled groan, and then her tongue slipped past his teeth to meet his and he twisted, gripped her arms and deepened the kiss.

Breathless, he lifted his head.

"Again," she murmured, arching her back to reach him. Her breast totally escaped the lacy thing she wore beneath her blouse, and Mike drew in a breath. His erection pressed painfully against his zipper. With a shaking hand he stroked that white flesh. She was beautiful, and she wanted him as much as he wanted her.

"Mike." Her voice was an urgent whisper.

Leaving his hand where it was, he nipped a trail along her neck. "Yes, sweetheart?"

"Bill couldn't understand why I cared so much about having a baby."

He rested his mouth just below her ear and opened his eyes. His chest rose and fell rapidly, and the heat continued to mount in his groin.

"He sort of cared, too," Susan continued in a dreamy faraway tone. "But he didn't think about it when we were making love."

Mike swallowed. "He didn't?" No woman had ever spoken to him of her previous sex life while he'd been making love to her.

"No, I'm sure he didn't think about anything but sex and gratification."

"He didn't think about anything else?" This couldn't be happening to him.

"No. And every time got to be the same for me."

"How was that?"

"The only thing that made sex worthwhile was the hope I'd get pregnant." Her voice had become very, very drowsy. Her eyes closed. Her head drooped. She was asleep. Mike moved carefully off the couch. If Susan wanted a baby, she'd definitely come to the wrong man.

7

Humiliated didn't come close to the way Susan felt.

She blessed the afternoon air that blew on her hot face as she drove across the island in the direction of Mike's house. She owed him an apology. She'd owed it to him yesterday, as soon as she'd awakened to find herself curled up beneath a blanket on her own couch with a note from him on the table. He'd written that he was sorry he hadn't stopped her from drinking too much, but he'd had no idea so little would affect her. Then he'd told her to call him if she needed anything.

She gritted her teeth. If she hadn't felt so sick and had such a headache, she would have called him last night. This morning she'd had another thunderous headache. Already late for work and reluctant to contact him at the boatyard, anyway, she'd put off her apology to the afternoon.

Georges and Libby had arrived back in the middle of the morning. Susan had taken them to Brown Island and decided from the strained atmosphere that it was best to leave them alone as soon as possible.

A bug flew into the car and she flapped at it. It took very little to irritate her today.

After Friday when she overheard the telephone call to Georges, Libby had stopped sharing her concerns. Then she'd become determinedly cheerful, as if she were trying to prove to herself that everything was fine. Susan hadn't had the heart to bring up the subject again. All she could do was pray for easier times ahead.

The garage at the top of Mike's driveway came into view, and the dense fuchsia bushes loaded with red blossoms that formed a hedge along the top of his property.

She parked, got out and started down the pathway. To hesitate even for a moment might mean she'd lose her nerve and turn back. When she woke up on the couch, she'd been fully dressed, her skirt pulled demurely over her legs, her head propped on a cushion, and she couldn't remember what she'd said to him before she…passed out. Not exactly. But there had been some talk about children; she recalled that. She had told him about the adoption meeting, that was pretty clear. And they'd kissed. Her idea, not his. Blood sang in her ears. She'd thrown herself at him, and now she had to apologize. This had been a truly rotten week.

Scents from Mike's rose garden assailed her, warm and sweet. Not like Harriet Brock's sickly blooms.

A noise came from Susan's left, and she paused, scanning the bushes. Probably a raccoon or a squirrel. She took several more steps and stopped completely. This time there was no mistaking the giggles she heard—multiple giggles coming from behind a high wall of privet that backed the rose garden.

Making no attempt to move quietly, she veered from the path and approached the source of the noise…and the smell. A lifelong nonsmoker, Susan was very sensitive to cigarette smoke.

She walked to the end of the hedge and went around to the back.

"Anne!" The name was out in a censorious tone before Susan could stop herself.

The girl sat cross-legged on the ground. Two other girls and a boy sat with her to form a circle. They each held a cigarette.

"Who's she?" a dark-haired girl asked. She had the same hairstyle as Anne—long on one side, shaved on the other. The girl's ear sported six or seven dangling earrings.

"She's no one," Anne said, but she quickly stubbed out the cigarette and threw the butt away. "Are you?" she challenged.

"What are you doing?" Susan asked lamely.

"We're cleaning our teeth." The third girl, taller, also dark-haired and wearing leather everything, smirked and took a long drag. Smoke issued through her nose and she coughed violently. "Right, Eric? We're cleaning our teeth," she said through spasms.

The boy, his baby face showing the signs of early acne, had turned an ugly shade of red. He put out his cigarette and muttered something unintelligible. Boys at this age, Susan recalled, were said to be unbearably uncomfortable with almost every element in their lives.

"Where's your father?" Susan was too angry to be amused at the silliness.

"Is she your old lady or something?" the girl in leather said.

"Don't be dumb," the other girl said. "Anne's old lady sings in Vegas. She wouldn't let a little thing like a few weeds get to her. She's cool, right, Anne?"

"Shut up, Fredda," Anne said. "My dad's not here," she told Susan. "He's gonna stay at the yard and work—probably all night."

Susan resisted the temptation to tell the girl she was a compulsive liar. "Is that a fact? Thanks for the information." She swung away, walked out of sight of the kids and headed for the house. If Mike wasn't there, she'd be very surprised. There and totally oblivious to his daughter's antics and to the very real possibility that she was heading for trouble.

Marching downhill, Susan gained confidence. Now she had ammunition. She'd be failing in her duty as a concerned adult if she didn't let Mike know the risks he was running by neglecting his child.

Several rings and a rap or two on the front door brought no response. She refused to believe Mike wasn't in. By the time she reached the patio at the back of the house, she was sure. Smiling grimly, she approached the open French doors from which issued the voice of a male crooner, wailing his incoherent message. The choice of music surprised her, but then what did she really know about the man?

In the kitchen the sight that confronted Susan momentarily swept away her anger. Connie, this time with her jeans topped by a red sweatshirt trimmed with white fringe, swayed around the room, her eyelids lowered in a parody of seduction.

Embarrassment overtook Susan. She stepped back and called out, "Hello! Hello! Anyone at home?"

Within seconds the volume was lowered and Connie appeared in the doorway, her arms crossed.

Susan attempted a smile, but her anger had begun to simmer again. "Is Mike here?"

"He never said you were coming."

"He didn't know." She approached and Connie had to choose between a collision or letting her pass. Connie stood aside. Susan walked as far as the cluttered table and turned to face the woman. "Is he here?"

"No. Polite people call first."

Susan tried to count silently to ten and failed. "You, of course, would know about polite people."

Connie sniffed.

So did Susan. More cigarette smoke. She glanced around. A butt smoldered among a heap of others in an ashtray on the counter beside a bowl of raw batter.

"I don't believe it." Susan shook her head. "Does Mike know you smoke around food?"

Connie's bosom rose impressively. "What does and doesn't happen in this house, and who knows about it, is nothing to do with you. There's the door."

"Are you supposed to be looking after Anne?"

"Supposed to be? What does that mean? I am looking after her, and anyone will tell you I do a good job. Why, when that little scrap's mother walked—"

"I'm not interested in that. Where is Anne now?"

"I'll tell Mike about—"

"You do that. Someone should tell him something, and the first thing is that you're not fit to have responsibility for a child."

"Well!" Connie buried her fists in her billowing hips. "I've never in all my days been spoken to like that. I'm respected for what I do and—"

"What's going on around here?"

Susan jumped so hard that she jarred her spine. Mike, unheard by Connie or herself, had come into the kitchen from the hall.

"I just got here and—"

"She goes or I do," Connie broke in. "I'm going, anyway. My nerves won't take this. I'll be back in the morning and you can let me know if I'm to continue around here. If I do, it'll be without this...this woman's interference."

"Connie—!"

She cut Mike off with a flap of the hand, gathered a white straw bag decorated with multicolored plastic flowers and sailed from the room. The slam of the front door shook the house.

"Okay." He dragged out a chair and flopped down. "Welcome to my happy home. Now, would you—or someone—tell me what's going on?"

"Look at this place."

He frowned at her first but looked, anyway. "It's a mess."

"Just like that. *It's a mess.*" She spread her slender arms. "How can you live like this?"

This was something. After yesterday he couldn't believe she was here at all, let alone that she was acting as if she owned the place. Could be bravado to cover embarrassment, he decided.

"I asked you something, Mike. How can you continue to employ a hopelessly slovenly woman like Connie and how can you live in this sty?"

"Hey." He wasn't amused. "Things get a bit messy, but I made the decision a long time ago that I was sick of a house that was a showplace. I had years of that. Now I want a home—for Anne. A place where she can let her hair down."

Susan turned her back. "I can't take this in. Homey is one thing. Dirty is another. Can't you see that?" She swung to face him.

She had a point. But he didn't have the time—or the inclination—to look for another housekeeper. Besides, Anne liked Connie. "Connie gets along with Anne," he said, feeling defensive. "When a girl's had a difficult time it's more important for her to feel some continuity and security in her primary caretakers than it is to be able to eat off the bathroom floors."

Susan wrinkled her pert nose. "I'm not sure I'd even want to walk on the bathroom floors."

"It's not that bad." He shouldn't be the one to retreat. She was out of line.

"Maybe. But that's not all—not even what bothers me most. It's Anne."

His stomach clenched. "Anne's fine. A bit wild but only in a small way. She's a real individual."

"Right. Letting her hair down, huh? What there is of it."

He shrugged. The hairstyle didn't please him, either, but he wasn't going to admit it to Susan.

"How often can you say you know what your own daughter's doing?"

Damn, where was this all coming from? Yesterday he'd left a sexy, tipsy and helpless bundle on her couch to sleep. He'd been a gentleman. Today she was strutting around his kitchen, telling him how to be a parent, although she'd never been one herself.

She'd stopped pacing and leaned against the sink to stare at him.

Gorgeous, and a waste. Sex was only good for making babies. He raised his chin and studied the ceiling. Not with this guy, no matter how much he might enjoy the process.

"I'm sorry."

"What?" Surely he'd misheard her.

"I said I'm sorry. That's what I came here to say. My behavior yesterday was unforgivable. I was so embarrassed when I woke up. I want you to know that I don't go around throwing myself at men and making them kiss me. I don't get drunk, either."

Making men kiss her? The way he remembered it, he'd definitely *enjoyed* kissing her.

"And I know I bored you sick with all that maudlin stuff about adoption. Well, I want you to forget every word I said. I'm not upset. Really I'm not. I'm really a very capable and sensible woman—'' she drew in a quick breath

''—and I don't know what came over me. The heat probably, and a long day. You know how that can be sometimes. The last time I kissed—well, honestly, I probably haven't kissed a man since Bill, which proves I'm not the type to do that kind of thing.''

''Of course not.'' He tried not to smile. Telling her she could kiss him anytime certainly wouldn't be the thing to do.

''Right then. I'd better get back.''

''Right.'' He racked his brain for a way to keep her here. She went to the door.

Mike stood up and escorted her outside. ''Goodbye. Um—are you working tomorrow?''

''Of course.'' She crossed her arms tightly.

''I've got to go into Friday Harbor.'' He had to do something about this new streak of dishonesty. ''Do you suppose we could have coffee?''

''I've got a busy day.''

''Me, too. But we could both spare half an hour. There's that little coffee place below your salon. The one that sells ice cream and chocolate and things.'' He shouldn't feel so desperate for her to agree.

''Okay.''

Nerves twitched all over his body. She made him feel like a kid, and when she showed signs of coming over to his side, she made him feel like a kid on Christmas morning.

''I'll come for you at eleven,'' he said. ''We'll beat the lunch rush.''

''I'll meet you there.'' She definitely wasn't in the mood for conversation. All worn out from her apology, he supposed.

"It was wrong of me to criticize the way you deal with your home and with Anne. I'm sorry about that, too."

Unfortunately she could just have a point. "Forget it."

They walked slowly uphill, in silence now.

A screech came from somewhere to his right. He stopped and peered across the rose garden. "Did you hear that?"

"Yes—no, I don't think so."

He stared at her, bemused. "You don't think...listen, over there." On the other side of the roses. Jogging, he set off in the direction of the noise and went around the hedge that backed the plantings.

"Mike!" Susan's voice accompanied her thudding footsteps. "Wait!"

Anne and her three buddies were still smoking.

"You little idiot." A pulse thundered in Mike's temples. "Get up!"

"Mike—"

"*Don't* interfere," he ordered Susan, who was a blur of red at the edge of his vision.

"Dad—"

"Get out of here. All of you."

"Dad—"

"Shut up!"

He clenched his fists at his sides while Fredda and the others got up. Eric and the girl he didn't know scrambled. Fredda rose with insolent nonchalance. He'd known this wasn't a good friend for Anne. Why hadn't he done something about it before now?

"Okay. Out!" He pointed to the road. All the children had to live within walking distance. "Go on. Out. And I never want to see you again. From now on you and my daughter don't know each other. Got that?"

"Dad." Anne was crying now, wailing. About time he

took a stand. Look what being an understanding father, a friend, had accomplished.

"Mike, maybe—"

"Please don't interfere," he told Susan. He never remembered being this angry with Anne. "Why did you do this? What's wrong with you? If I'd done such a thing when I was your age, my father would have grounded me forever."

"We were only smoking."

"*Only!*" He was yelling and it felt good. "*Only?* You little idiot. That's it. I'm grounding you. You don't go anywhere or do anything until winter break. Have you got that?"

Anne only cried.

"And you're right about Connie." He glowered at Susan. "She's a bad influence on my daughter and she doesn't do her job. I'll fire her in the morning. I suppose that makes you happy."

"It doesn't."

"Well, it's easy to look at someone else's life and figure out what ought to be done with it. Try having more than yourself to think about— What did you say?"

"I think you're overreacting."

The pounding in his head diminished. "You were the one who said I wasn't a good parent because I was oblivious. I just said you were right, and even that doesn't satisfy you?"

"I had no right to interfere. But I do think this is going too far." She looked at Anne, who had moved nearer to her. They were aligning themselves against him. Mike couldn't believe it.

"Regardless, I'm not changing my mind."

"Of course not." Susan's voice was very soft with that compelling quality he'd noticed before. It made him feel like leaning closer. "Would you consider giving all this twenty-four hours, though? Just so you can make your decisions when you're calm. I'm not saying Anne shouldn't be punished at all, am I, Anne?"

His daughter now stood side by side with Susan and shook her head emphatically at her.

"But you might want to…adjust the sentence a little."

Was that a smothered smile he saw? "Sentence? She isn't on trial."

"No. Exactly. So you'll think about it?"

"If you think that's best?" She was lovely, and…sweet. A bright, reasonable woman with the courage to admit when she thought she'd made a mistake. Susan Ackroyd was special, too special for a man adamantly opposed to total commitment—a man like himself.

She was smiling at Anne. "I think that would be best. And it could be that Connie would, er, it could be that Connie just needs some, er, guidance?"

"Don't get rid of Connie, Dad."

Well, he probably shouldn't do anything in a rush of anger. "I'll think about it," he told Anne. "Now go to your room and I'll talk to you later."

"Yes, Dad." With a last baleful glance at Susan, a glance that said, "You're my only friend in the world," she slunk away.

Mike straightened his shoulders. Suddenly he'd become "Dad" instead of "Mike," and he thought he liked it enough to try to make sure it stayed that way.

"Well?" Susan said.

"Yes. Sorry about all that. I'll walk you to your car."

They made their way back to the path and continued up. He regretted his outburst in front of her, and as happened every time he was with her, he dreaded the parting. "So I'll see you at the café tomorrow?"

She studied her feet as she walked. "Maybe that isn't such a good idea."

"Yes, it is," he said quickly. "We need to talk."

"What do we need to talk about?"

"How I should deal with Anne and Connie." A stroke of genius on his part. "I value your level head."

"You don't need my advice."

"But you will come?"

They reached the road, and she opened the door of her old yellow VW. "I shouldn't."

"Why?"

"Because I'm not sure what it is I feel about you. Or what it is you're feeling about me. I'm not a fool, Mike. I know when I'm being chased, and I'm not your type."

His mouth opened, but he couldn't come up with a thing to say.

"Think about that, too, Mike." She closed herself into the car with a mighty slam that rattled his ears. "It's pointless to play games with people who aren't into sports."

"But—"

The engine roared, drowning him out, then settled down to a cranky chug.

"If you decide you don't want to have coffee, I'd appreciate a call," she said. "You can leave a message if I'm not around."

Never—he had never dealt with a woman like her. "Susan, are you suggesting I'm some sort of wolf?"

She turned the wheel and the little car putted away from the curb. "By the way—" she looked back at him and her hair blew across her face "—the roses are lovely. Thank you."

8

"I know it's ten past eleven," Susan told Molly. "There's a big clock right up there."

"Then go," the girl said, wiggling with excitement while she held a manicure customer's nails beneath a heat lamp to dry a layer of polish. "If he thinks you've stood him up and leaves before you get there, I'll die."

Susan pursed her lips grimly. She wouldn't tell Molly, or anyone else, that she knew Mike would still be there, but that she was afraid of him and of her reaction to the man. Every instinct warned her that he could be dangerous to her emotional health.

"Will you *please* go?" Jeff, sneaking up behind, put an arm around her shoulders and whispered in her ear, "Before we all have heart attacks."

She shouldn't have told them who she was meeting. "Yes, I'll go. But don't get any ideas. This is purely a business appointment. I'll be back in plenty of time for my noon customer. And I just want you to know that I've noticed I don't get no respect around here." Waving a finger, she opened the door. "Think about that. You're altogether too familiar."

"Go," Jeff repeated, and Susan shook her head as she closed the door behind her.

Clouds had rolled in overnight, but the breeze was warm. She walked down from the balcony and turned along the boardwalk toward the café Mike had mentioned. The overcast day hadn't kept tourists away, and she had to dodge to avoid preoccupied wanderers.

"Susan! There you are."

Mike, pushing back his chair, stood up by a table outside the café. Aaron Conrad stood with him and smiled his reticent, solemn-eyed smile.

"Hello." She shook Aaron's outstretched hand and sat in the chair he pulled out for her.

"Coffee?" Mike asked.

"That would be nice."

Aaron waved Mike aside. "I'll get it. Anything in it?"

"Cream, please."

As soon as they were alone, Susan was sure she shouldn't have agreed to come. The sexual electricity between them wasn't a product of her imagination.

"Great day, huh?" Mike said, expanding his chest inside his denim shirt.

"It's muggy."

He smiled broadly at her. Unforgettable face. Unforgettable man. She could no longer pretend she didn't want to be with him.

"Everything's perfect as far as I'm concerned," he said, leaning forward suddenly. "You don't know Aaron very well, do you?"

"Not personally. But Georges and Libby talk about him so much I often feel as if I do."

"He's a great guy. A lifesaver to me."

Before Mike could say more, Aaron returned with a mug of coffee. "Are we all set then?" he said to Mike. "I need to call the bank."

Mike stood again and pumped his friend's hand. "You won't regret this."

"I know that. Goodbye, Susan. Say hi to Libby for me."

"He's set me free again," Mike said when Aaron had left. "I honestly thought I was headed for an assembly line operation."

Asking questions might not be polite, but he was inviting curiosity. "Assembly line?"

He hesitated, running a hand through his hair. "I don't know why I feel I can tell you anything, but I do. Susan, my boatyard is an expensive operation and we've had a cash-flow problem."

She made a sympathetic noise but couldn't help feeling surprised. "You seem very successful."

"I thought I was. And I am." He nodded as if reassuring himself. "But the figures just haven't been there lately. Dad thinks we haven't been charging enough, and he's obviously right. I think the first thing we tell a prospective customer should be that if he or she can't afford the best, we aren't their boys."

"Really?" She wasn't sure how he expected her to react.

"Really. Anything's better than having to take on just any project that's thrown our way. That kind of mass production was never my intention."

He really was a prima donna about his work. "Most of us have to do a few things we'd rather not do to make a living."

"I went that route for years. I don't want to again. Thanks to Aaron it won't be necessary."

"What did Aaron do?"

Mike's expression became serious. "He showed how much he believes in me—in us. Money, big bucks until things even out, is what I need and Aaron's giving me that."

His attitude rankled. Rather than step up production and become less picky in the commissions he accepted, he would allow Aaron to sink even more money into the business. "It must be nice to be coddled."

A speculative gleam entered his eyes. "I'm not sure I follow you."

What he did wasn't her problem. "Did you think things through—about Connie and Anne?"

"Everything's under control. And you're evading my question."

Okay, since he insisted. "You sound spoiled. Everything has to be your way, on your terms."

He crossed his arms and studied her, his mouth compressed. "How can you make a judgment like that? You haven't given us a chance to really get to know each other."

"It isn't going to happen. We're too different." Her heart hammered. Even as she told him, she hoped he'd disagree.

"We're different because I'm spoiled and want to take, and you only want to give, is that right?"

Susan picked up her coffee, wishing she'd kept her mouth shut.

"And with you the giving extends to your personal life. Is that right, Susan?"

She looked at him squarely. "Yes, that's right."

"You want to adopt a child because there's one who deserves what you have to give."

She felt her face turn scarlet. "I don't want to talk about that." Or remember the episode at her house.

"Of course not. You're good at dishing out the advice and the criticisms, but not so good at taking it. I've known a lot of people like you."

She moved to stand up, but he clamped a hand on top of hers. "What's the matter? Can't face the truth?"

"You don't know the truth—not about me."

"Sounds as if we don't know much about each other, period."

"Absolutely. And there's no point in continuing this." She felt sick.

"I'm sorry you feel that way. I think we might have been very good for each other." He looked at their hands on the table. "You expect people to take notice of your opinions, so here's mine. I think you need a man in your life, someone to take your mind off loneliness."

"I'm not lonely." But she was and it hurt to hear it said aloud.

Mike shrugged. "If you say so. But think about this. If you were involved with a man, would you be making excuses for wanting a child?"

"No...I'm not making—"

"So you say. I think you're the selfish one. And you're frightened. You want a child to fill *your* needs and you're terrified of being deeply involved with a man again."

"How dare you—?"

"I dare most things. I've made some decisions in my life that most men would never have made because they would have been afraid of the risk. And I don't intend to tolerate criticism from a mixed-up woman."

"Mixed up?"

"I'd say that blaming your husband for the breakup of your marriage because he didn't think about pregnancy every time you had sex was pretty mixed up."

She closed her eyes and slumped. God, had she said that?

His grip on her hand tightened, but she couldn't look at him.

"Susan." He spoke her name urgently. "Susan, look at me."

"Leave me alone."

"Look, I'm sorry. I shouldn't have said that, but you made me so angry."

"Don't worry about it." Numb, she wrenched away and stood up.

"I'm really sorry..."

"Don't be. I'm not part of your life in any way. I never will be."

Susan tossed her bag onto the living room floor and sank, sighing gratefully, onto a couch. Saturday was always a busy day at the salon. Since noon she'd been longing for home and this moment.

"You haven't forgotten our date, have you?" Libby came from the kitchen with two glasses of iced tea.

"No. Of course not." But she had forgotten her promise to take Libby to the salon and do her hair. "We'll go after dinner."

"Change of plans," Libby said, perching on the edge of the coffee table. "Georges and Jean-Claude have been hidden away all day. I pouted, so Georges insists he take the two of us to dinner when we're finished at the salon."

Susan squelched the impulse to say she'd rather get to bed early. "Sounds like fun." Since the fiasco with Mike on Thursday, she'd felt depressed and embarrassed...and disappointed, damn it. She'd never had him, but she missed him.

"You don't look as if you think it'll be fun."

She met her sister's all-seeing eyes. "Sorry, I've been in a funk. I don't mean to put a damper on things."

"It's Mike, isn't it?"

Susan wondered briefly if Libby was getting information from other sources. "No."

"If you say so." Libby held her glass aloft as if interested in its contents. "I think you like him—a lot. And I think he likes you."

"Past tense," Susan said, forgetting caution.

"Oh. Something did happen between you two." Libby moved to sit beside Susan. "Tell me about it."

"There's nothing to tell." She kicked off her shoes and wiggled her sore toes.

Footsteps thudded on the stairs as Georges and Jean-Claude descended from the sitting room in the loft they'd been using as an office. Georges came into sight first, his handsome face tightly drawn. "No," he said over his shoulder. "Absolutely not." He automatically spoke English whenever he entered Susan's presence—only one of the many considerations he showed her.

"I think you are wrong, Georges." Jean-Claude followed him into the living room. "These people are unscrupulous. We already know they're capable—"

"Enough." Georges held up a hand, but not before casting a quick glance at Libby. "We are here for a break, *chérie*. I am becoming a dull man in that little room. And you are lonely."

Libby smiled as Georges sat on the couch opposite Susan and Libby. Jean-Claude paced back and forth before the fireplace.

"Oh, I forgot." Libby sprang up, hurried to the kitchen and returned with an envelope. "This came in the mail, and it's so fat I thought it might be important."

Susan accepted the package gingerly and read the return address. Her heart and stomach collided. H. Brock at the adoption agency had sent her a missive.

Unable to wait, she ripped open the envelope and read the letter accompanying some forms. More forms. Minutes later, so upset that she could scarcely keep from leaping off the couch, she looked up to find three pairs of eyes on her. She met the mysteriously dark ones that belonged to Jean-Claude and stuffed the envelope and its contents into her pocket. He made every effort to be friendly and she liked him well enough, but this was something she couldn't bring herself to discuss in his presence.

"What is it?" Libby asked, her eyes wide and troubled.

Susan turned up the corners of her mouth. "Just some business stuff I was expecting. It can wait."

The phone rang and Libby picked it up. *"Oui,"* she said after a few seconds. *"Un moment, s'il vous plaît."* She held the receiver against her chest. "It's Geneva, Georges. An angry man asking for you."

Georges moved to sit beside her and took the phone. The French immediately became too rapid for Susan to catch even a word. Her brother-in-law's increasing agitation, however, needed no translation. He alternated between waving his free hand and jamming it into his hair. At one point he slumped back to rest his head and close his eyes.

Susan looked from Libby to Jean-Claude. The latter continued to pace, pausing from time to time to gesture wildly. Libby subsided into a tight ball on the couch and hugged her arms around her middle.

"Merde!" Georges hung up. "They will not get the message. They will not believe that once committed I will not withdraw."

"I think you are wrong." Jean-Claude went to stand beside his uncle. "There is danger here."

"Shh." Georges shook his head sharply. "Enough."

"You know how I feel about this," Jean-Claude continued, evidently undaunted. "That was Sportes, correct?"

"Correct."

"And he wants out of the spa project."

Georges got up and walked to the window. "What he

wants now is not what he wanted a year ago. Now we have progressed too far and there is too much at stake for too many. I will not be intimidated and he must deal with his own—" He swung around. "I cannot soothe his nerves."

"If we got out now, it would be with minimal loss to ourselves. In fact, we would lose nothing since we still have the property."

Georges scowled and advanced to stand toe-to-toe with Jean-Claude. "I have more scruples than that, and so should you. We would not be hurt, but others, who started with so much less, would lose everything."

"We cannot be responsible for the troubles of the world."

"No. But what we can affect, we must. This spa will be built, regardless of how much certain other factions would like to be assured that we will not give them competition."

Susan looked from one man to the other, absorbing what she heard. This was definitely the root of Georges's ill humor of late. It had to be. He was caught in the middle of a high-stakes investment feud and didn't even have the total support of his nephew.

After a charged silence, Jean-Claude bowed faintly and stepped back. "You are right, Georges. As usual. I'm afraid you have the courage I lack. I apologize."

Immediately Georges's frown was transformed into a fond smile. "You are an exceptional businessman for one so young. That is why you are so important to me. I wish my brother had lived to... I miss him."

Jean-Claude turned away. "So do I. I think I will go up and make some calls."

"Won't you join us for dinner in Friday Harbor?" Libby asked, sounding anxious. "I'm going over with Susan to get my hair done. Then I'll return for you and Georges while Susan does her busywork at the salon.''

He looked at her, smiling. "I think not. But thank you. I feel in need of a talk with a certain friend." The smile became a grin.

"Ah," Georges said, inclining his head, "the beautiful Simone. Give her our love."

Jean-Claude murmured assent and walked upstairs.

"He has a significant friend?" Susan asked. It seemed everyone did, except her.

"Oh, yes. Very much so. They are to be engaged shortly."

"Is she…" Susan paused, listening. "Was that someone at the door?"

The next knock was louder, and Georges strode to open the back door. Aaron Conrad, as serious-faced as ever and with an anxious look about his eyes, stood on the threshold.

Susan only hesitated briefly before saying, "Come in, Aaron." He entered hesitantly, as if expecting to have to flee at any second. "I thought I'd drop by and see how everyone is." His smile was a dismal effort.

"We're glad you did," Libby said, patting the place beside her. "We're not seeing enough of you."

He advanced, rubbing his hands together and glancing around. "You have a lovely home, Susan."

"Thank you, Aaron." It was obvious he wasn't here just for this chitchat. "How did you get here, by the way? I didn't know you had a boat."

He stopped in the act of sitting down and stood erect again. "It's Mike's."

Oh, why did everything have to be related to Mike Kinnear? Remembering their argument, Susan began to get angry all over again. But she had to remember her manners. "Would you like a drink?" she asked Aaron.

"No thanks. I can only stay a few minutes."

"Well," Susan said, deciding she was probably the cause of his discomfort, "I expect the three of you would like to visit. I'll be ready to go when you are, Libby."

"I'm keeping you from something?" Aaron looked stricken.

"Not at all," Libby said, smiling. "Susan and I are going to the salon for a while, but there's no hurry. Maybe you'd like to join us for dinner later. I'm coming back for Georges. Around eight, I hope. So—"

"Oh, no," Aaron said. "Thank you, anyway, but I've got to get over to Seattle for a while tonight."

Yet he'd taken time to come here first. Puzzling. "If you'll excuse me," Susan said. "Call me when you want to leave, Libby."

"No!" Aaron said, making Susan jump. "No. I wouldn't hear of chasing you out of your own living room. I mean, I'd like you to stay. Wouldn't you?" He turned to Libby. "Like Susan to stay, I mean?"

Susan had a fleeting desire to laugh. Fortunately very fleeting. She couldn't remember ever seeing a man who was usually so self-contained appear this uncomfortable.

"Stay, Susan," Georges said. His expression showed frank bafflement. He sat down and Aaron followed suit. "So, Aaron, are you beginning to think snow?"

"Yes." Aaron nodded. "Definitely I'm thinking snow."

"You hope to open for skiing by your Thanksgiving, *n'est-ce pas?*"

"Absolutely so. Thanksgiving."

"Do you ever miss our racing days? I do." Georges gazed into the distance, smiling slightly as if remembering when he and Aaron had been giant slalom contenders in world competition.

"Often," Aaron said. "And I still do ski a lot—all winter. You must come back next season, Georges. We'd have a good time together."

"Perhaps I will," Georges said. "And you must come to our chalet in Madonna di Lago. Libby and I wish we could always be there. Correct, *chérie?*"

"Yes," Libby agreed. "Do come to Italy with us again, Aaron. It's been so long since you did."

"Maybe I will." He looked at Susan. "Have you been?"

"No." Making sense of her life after the divorce hadn't left time for travel.

"You should." He ran his palms up and down his muscular jean-clad thighs. "Maybe you could talk Mike into going with you. He needs a vacation and, um—"

Susan felt her lips part in astonishment at what Aaron had just suggested.

"Does Mike ski?" Georges asked blithely.

Susan met Libby's eyes and quickly looked away.

"He has. He could be good given more time," Aaron said, turning pink again. "He's a neat guy. One of the best."

"He seems interesting," Georges said, beginning to frown. Susan saw him raise his brows fractionally at Libby, who shrugged almost imperceptibly.

"Mike isn't always a diplomat," Aaron said. "His, er, mouth gets him into a lot of trouble sometimes. But he doesn't mean anything by it. When you get to know him, you realize a lot of it comes from being unsure of the impression he gives." Aaron paused and wiped his hand across his brow. "He's had some rough times in his personal life, and they've made him a bit prickly. But when you get beneath that, it's like…sort of like peeling an onion. No, more like…he's worth getting to know for the man he is inside all that toughness."

Moving to the edge of the seat, Aaron looked directly at Susan and extended a hand. "Do you know what I mean when I say how rough it is to see someone you care about feeling bad and not knowing what to do to help out?"

She nodded. Everything within her yearned to go and hold this special man's hands. Mike must have talked about the disaster his last meeting with her had been, and for some reason Aaron had gotten the impression his friend was disturbed by the event. Now, despite being naturally reticent, Aaron was trying to smooth the troubled waters. Unfortunately he didn't know his pigheaded buddy as well as he thought he did.

Aaron's expression had cleared. "I knew you'd understand." He got to his feet. Near the door he paused. "Everything will be all right."

When he left, Georges turned to Susan. "I think he did not come to see me and Libby his old friends. He came to see you. Can you explain what he was saying?"

She thought she could, but she wouldn't. "He wasn't saying anything to me. He's not comfortable in social situations, I should think. That must explain it."

The noise Libby made sounded suspiciously like a muffled giggle, and Susan shot her a warning glare.

Georges was too preoccupied to notice. "What you say explains nothing. Aaron has been my friend for fifteen years. He is quiet, yes, but also very poised. I have never seen him so awkward. Most strange."

"Yes, well, you and I should get to the salon if we're not going to be eating at midnight," Susan said to Libby, anxious to terminate this conversation. She wondered if Mike could have suggested that Aaron come to her. No, not Mr. Kinnear's style. Aaron had taken it on himself to deliver his message.

Libby had gathered her purse, slipped a lightweight white poplin jacket over her fuchsia silk shirt and black pants and now she picked up Susan's purse. "Ready when you are."

"I wish you would let me buy you a new boat," Georges said, walking them to the door. "Your old Tollycraft may be a classic, but it worries me."

"Why?" Susan laughed. "I've been using it for years. And the man who owned it before me never had a bit of trouble. I intend to keep it forever."

"If you say so," Georges said. He waved to them from the door. "Please be very careful. Call me before you leave to come back, Libby."

Susan hurried down the steps from the salon. It was already after nine. She was tired, but Libby was obviously looking forward to a relaxed time at the restaurant and Susan was loath to disappoint her by backing out. At least Libby hadn't given her an argument when Susan suggested she needed a change of pace and would be the one to return to Brown Island for Georges. Since Libby didn't have much experience handling a boat, Susan would rather be the one to go while Libby cleaned up at the salon.

With darkness the air had grown cool. Ribbons of mist slithered along the pier, following Susan to where she docked her Tollycraft. Once aboard, she took a final look at the lighted salon before starting the engine and steering carefully among the moored boats toward open water. She preferred not to make the crossing between Brown Island and Friday Harbor at night, but this was one occasion when she was glad of the chance to be completely alone. The letter from Mrs. Brock, with its fresh list of intimidating

MIRA ®

AN IMPORTANT MESSAGE
FROM
THE EDITORS

Dear Reader,

Because you've chosen to read one of our
fine novels, we'd like to say "thank you"!
And, as a **special** way to thank you, we've
selected <u>two more</u> of the books you love so
well, **and** a mystery gift to send you
absolutely **_FREE!_**

Please enjoy them with our compliments...

Editor,
The Best of the Best

P.S. And <u>because</u> we value our
customers, we've attached something
extra inside...

Peel off seal and
place inside...

EDITOR'S
**FREE
GIFTS
SEAL**
THANK YOU

HOW TO VALIDATE
YOUR
EDITOR'S FREE GIFT
"THANK YOU"

1. Peel off the FREE GIFTS SEAL from front cover. Place it in the space provided at right. This automatically entitles you to receive two free books and an exciting gift.

2. Send back this card and you'll get 2 "The Best of the Best™" novels. These books have a combined cover price of $11.00 or more, but they are yours to keep absolutely free.

3. There's no catch. You're under no obligation to buy anything. We charge nothing—ZERO—for your first shipment. And you don't have to make any minimum number of purchases—not even one!

4. We call this line "The Best of the Best" because each month you'll receive the best books by the world's hottest authors. These authors show up time and time again on all the major bestseller lists and their books sell out as soon as they hit the stores. You'll love getting them conveniently delivered to your home...and you'll love our discount prices.

5. We hope that after receiving your free books you'll want to remain a subscriber. But the choice is yours—to continue or cancel, anytime at all! So why not take us up on our invitation, with no risk of any kind. You'll be glad you did!

6. Don't forget to detach your FREE BOOKMARK. And remember... just for validating your Editor's Free Gift Offer, we'll send you THREE gifts, *ABSOLUTELY FREE!*

YOURS FREE!

We'll send you a fabulous mystery gift absolutely FREE, simply for accepting our no-risk offer!

® and TM are trademarks of Harlequin Enterprises Limited.

DETACH AND MAIL CARD TODAY!

The Best of the Best™ — Here's How it Works:

Accepting your 2 free books and gift places you under no obligation to buy anything. You may keep the books and gift and return the shipping statement marked "cancel." If you do not cancel, about a month later we will send you 3 additional novels and bill you just $4.24 each in the U.S., or $4.74 each in Canada, plus 25¢ delivery per book and applicable sales tax, if any.* That's the complete price, and — compared to cover prices of $5.50 each in the U.S. and $6.50 each in Canada — it's quite a bargain! You may cancel at any time, but if you choose to continue, every month we'll send you 3 more books, which you may either purchase at the discount price…or return to us and cancel your subscription.

*Terms and prices subject to change without notice. Sales tax applicable in N.Y. Canadian residents will be charged applicable provincial taxes and GST.

obstacles had been on her mind all evening. She'd been unwilling to burden Libby with her own problems, but the strain of appearing cheerful had worn her temper thin.

There was a special beauty to night on the silken black deep. The mist's white wraiths played around pilings as the Tollycraft chugged from the harbor. Susan stood at the wheel, her apprehension waning as peace overtook her. The world was a softly swishing velvet place scented with pine and salt.

Susan opened the throttle wider. If she didn't hurry, dinner would be breakfast.

True to form, the Tolly roared gamely, her bow lifting higher to cut a clean path toward the shadowy hulk of Brown...then the engine sputtered.

"Come on," Susan said aloud to the little boat. "Don't give me trouble tonight."

The engine died.

Susan peered at the gas gauge and her throat closed. Empty. When had she filled the tank? Not today, but certainly not long ago. Darn her carelessness. She must have been too preoccupied with everything that was going on. This was one mistake she'd never made before.

Scrabbling in a locker, she located the can of spare gas. Before she lifted it clear she knew she was in bad trouble. It was too light. Unscrewing the cap, she shook the can. Nothing inside.

Her heart beat hard and erratically. Closer to Friday Harbor there would have been a good chance of someone hearing her shout. Unfortunately she'd traveled too far out to a point opposite an almost unpopulated part off the shore of Brown Island. She had to try. "Help!" No answer. Susan's scalp tingled.

She shouted again and again...to no avail.

Wrapping her jacket more tightly around her, she sat

amidships and searched in all directions. *Keep calm,* she told herself. *Someone will pass close by, and then you'll shout.*

More time elapsed and the sound of lapping water seemed to grow louder. She swam well but was increasingly aware of the opaque blackness shifting beneath her. In that cold water, in the dark, how long would she last? How far was it to shore? How long would it be before she was missed? She'd already been stranded out here for a long time.

The boat was fine, strong. All she had to do was wait.

An engine sounded to port. Susan stood up and strained to see, but the noise quickly died.

Her feet were wet. Looking down, she clutched her stomach. Water sloshed back and forth, seeping from beneath the central bench.

Slowly she turned, braced her hands on the bench and stared into the well of the boat. There were inches of water and more seeping in steadily. The stern was already perceptibly lower than the bow.

The boat was sinking.

9

Mike braced his hips against the Boston whaler's wheel and swept the waters with his powerful flashlight. Only swelling darkness and mist lay ahead as far as he could see. He was afraid. More afraid than he'd ever been before.

Chance had put him in the right area at the right time— or he hoped he was in the right place. If he hadn't let Aaron talk him into going to the salon tonight, he wouldn't have been there when Georges called.

"Susan!" The darkness took his voice, and there was no reply.

"Oh, God." He cut back the engine to minimize noise. Desperation made him want to travel fast, but he had to hear and try to see.

Other engines rumbled. Other voices called. Gratitude raised a spark of hope. Aaron was out there somewhere with Libby. And Rudy and Neil had promised to raise as much help as possible before setting out in their respective boats. The Coast Guard had been alerted, too, but altogether they'd only been searching for thirty minutes.

Thirty minutes since Georges had become worried enough to call Libby at the salon to ask if Susan had left when they'd said she would. Mike tried not to let himself imagine what might have happened to that antiquated little boat of Susan's...or to her.

Scanning the surface constantly, he zigzagged. Something stung his eyes. Sweat. It was cold, but he was sweating.

A searchlight came on. Coast Guard, he figured. They were heading along the passage between Brown Island and San Juan.

"Help!"

He drew in a giant breath and blinked against the sweat. "Susan. Where are you?"

Silent seconds passed. He must have imagined her voice. "Susan?"

"Here. Quick. Please."

When he saw her, he had to pull sharply to port to avoid a collision. Dark hair plastered to her head made her almost invisible, like a slick seal with a pale face. Inching closer, he reached for her. "Give me your hand."

As her arm came up, she sank.

Mike stood up and kicked off his shoes, ready to dive in.

"Mike!"

She'd surfaced again, and this time he grabbed her windbreaker. Slowly, afraid the fabric would give way, he towed her against the boat and hauled her in.

"Thank God." Clasping her against him, he was aware of the icy wetness that drenched the front of his clothes. He didn't care. "I thought...I thought you were dead."

"No way." Her clattering teeth garbled her voice.

"Ahoy!"

Another small boat had approached. "Hi. Who is it?" The whaler rocked wildly, and Mike leaned against the instrument panel, still holding Susan tightly.

"It's Rudy. Any luck?"

"Yes." He felt shaky, shaky enough to collapse. "I've got her. Could you get back to Friday Harbor and call off the Coast Guard?"

"Will do. Is she okay?"

"Yes," Susan answered, wobbly but determined as ever. "Thank you for coming."

"My pleasure," the master carpenter called back. "I'll spread the good news."

"I ran out of gas," Susan said, shuddering ever more violently. "Can't understand what I was thinking of."

"You're all right now, love." In a sharp, clear instant he identified what he felt. Not just the casual relief of one human being for another, but overwhelming gratitude for the safety of someone who meant a great deal to him. Maybe no one but Anne had meant this much to him before.

"I don't know why my boat sank."

He stroked back her hair and maneuvered them to a locker. From inside he retrieved a blanket. Then he wrapped it around Susan and settled her on a seat. She needed warmth and quickly.

Her Tollycraft had sunk? "Of course, you were in the water. I wasn't thinking there for a minute. Did you turn her over?" The boat still shouldn't have gone down.

"No. I must have hit a deadhead without knowing it and holed her. She went down so fast, Mike. I tried to bail, but it was useless. I thought…I was only in there a little while, but I didn't know how long I could last. I'm so cold."

"We need to get you back now. Hypothermia isn't something you want." Or that he wanted her to have. With gentle firmness he pulled her to her feet again and wrapped the blanket around both of them, trying to close her in with his warmth while he opened the throttle and headed for Brown Island.

At Susan's dock Mike made them secure as quickly as

he could, then helped Susan ashore. He swept her into his arms. She weighed so little.

"I c-can walk." She struggled, but weakly.

He hoisted her higher, cradling her face into his neck. "I'm sure you can, but you're not going to."

"P-pushing me around."

Her jerky laugh pleased him. The lady had guts. "I'm like that. Always picking on the helpless little people." The lights in her house blazed and two shapes, Georges and Jean-Claude, were visible at the windows.

"Thank you, Mike."

He checked his stride and allowed himself a moment's pause. "I went to the salon looking for you, Susan. There's so much I want to say to you."

"Mike." She sounded drowsy, and he recognized the danger sign immediately. "I want to talk to you, too."

"Later." He rushed on, but fresh hopes poured warmth into his veins. Maybe he hadn't entirely blown his chances with her.

The door was thrown open. "Who is it?" Georges stepped outside, bending his head to peer into the darkness.

"Susan's okay," Mike said. "I've got her."

Running footsteps behind them made him pause and turn around.

"Susan!" Libby caught up, with Aaron a step behind. "Oh, Susan. Take her upstairs, Mike. She needs to get warm."

Mike passed Georges, who looked like a wild man, and Jean-Claude, whose countenance was more ruffled than Mike would have thought possible. "Tea," he told them. "Hot and sweet—and fast. Get a doctor out here."

"No," Susan said faintly. She stirred against him as Mike reached the stairs, and he looked into her pale face before resting his chin atop her head. "Don't get a doctor, please. I wasn't in the water long. A couple of minutes. A hot bath and the tea and I'll be fine.''

"We'll see," he told her. "Which room, Libby?"

At the top of the stairs Libby pushed past and ran ahead to open the door onto a big bedroom decorated with bold geometric shapes and designs in gray, black and white. Mike had little time to take in his surroundings before Libby, one hand in the middle of his back, urged him into an all-white bathroom relieved only by a black glazed ceramic statue of a mother and child.

"Sit her on the toilet," Libby said, all business. "Thanks, Mike. We'll take it from here."

He backed away, but his eyes were held by Susan's dark blue stare. She didn't want him to leave her, but this wasn't the time to explore the deeper meaning of that revelation.

Georges met him at the foot of the stairs. "Should we call the doctor?"

Mike shook his head. "No. I don't think it's going to be necessary. We were lucky. I must have come upon her minutes after the boat went."

"Jean-Claude went to use the phone in his sitting room. He will make sure the search has been called off."

"I already did that, but it doesn't matter." There was a distance between him and these Swiss, almost imperceptible, but there nevertheless.

Georges insisted on fixing him a drink, and they sat in silence until Georges drew in an audible breath and stood up. "I would like to talk to you. Now is an awkward moment, but we must find a convenient one. There have been, er, developments that make it necessary for me to put a limit on our time here." He glanced upward. "Libby does not know this, and I would prefer that she not find out—not yet."

Mike rested his forearms on his knees. Despite the cultural differences, he liked this man. "Is there something I can do to help you? I'm sure Aaron would do anything he could, too."

"No, no." He waved his hands. "I realize tomorrow is Sunday, but could I come to your office? Say at nine?"

"Tomorrow at nine," Mike agreed, deeply curious.

"Ah, thank goodness everything's okay," Libby said, coming down the stairs and going to sit by her husband. "Susan's tougher than she looks. Why don't you go up and see her, Mike? Take some brandy. I think that would be better than tea—in a lot of ways."

He stood up but hovered, uncertain.

"Do it," Georges said, smiling. He reached to pour a glass of brandy from a decanter on the table. "Here."

Mike took the glass and went up to Susan's room. He knocked and heard her muffled "Come in." This time he took a longer look at the huge platform bed in which she was propped against a heap of pillows. A bed intended for more than one, surely. He shied quickly away from thinking of it as her marital bed. Black-and-white striped drapes were caught back each side of three narrow floor-to-ceiling windows. The same stripe had been used for the quilt. There was a chair and ottoman in gray, black and white check, a white carpet and black lacquered chests. He could have claimed this room as his own with no problem. Not that he was likely to be invited as more than a onetime visitor.

"You do like to analyze your surroundings, don't you?" Susan's voice roused him. "Habit. I think you can judge a person by her decor." He moved close and sat, without being invited, on the edge of the bed. When he offered the brandy, she shook her head and he put the glass on her bedside table.

"And what does my decor tell you about me?" Her hair

had dried to a curly cap, and devoid of makeup, her face had a healthy sheen. Apart from a light tan on her arms, every inch revealed by a low-cut ivory satin nightgown was pale and smooth.

Mike concentrated on the chair. "You're dramatic, a maverick. But you aren't comfortable letting the rest of the world know the true you, so you hide it in places not usually seen by too many people."

"I rather like that. You're very perceptive." She extended her hand, palm up, and he didn't hesitate to sandwich it between his own.

"You're still cold." He raised her fingers to his mouth and kissed each one, watching the changing shadows in her eyes. "But only your skin, dear Susan, nothing else."

She colored, that wonderful pink blush he'd come to love. "I'll never be able to thank you enough for coming after me this evening."

"If I hadn't found you, someone else would have." He wanted to lighten the horror for her.

"I didn't want anyone else." She spoke very softly and finished with her lips slightly parted and glistening.

"Oh, Susan, what am I going to do with you?" Releasing her hand, he slipped his hands over her silken shoulders and down her back to the gentle roundness of her hips. "I know what I'd like to do, but not with your family on guard."

She gave a shaky sigh. "Just hold me for a little while."

Susan pushed back the covers to expose her provocative satin-clad length. The fabric was as arousing in its effect as bare skin. His breath caught in his throat. She crawled to sit on his lap and drape her arms around his neck. Lifting her face, she kissed his jaw again and again. When he bent toward her, she captured his head, and her tongue darted to outline his mouth with hot little strokes.

Mike groaned and tried to remind himself that they could be interrupted at any moment.

"Hold me," she whispered, pressing her breasts against him. "Touch me."

Not cold. Not cold at all. Controlling the temptation to rip away what was probably an expensive piece of satin, he held her waist and claimed her mouth in a hard kiss. One hard kiss, another, and another more gentle one, before he firmly lifted her back against the pillows and pulled up the covers.

She pouted, and the effect was both surprising and charming. "I wanted to do that," she said. "I'm sorry you didn't."

He laughed. "You aren't going to draw me into an argument that way, my sweet. What I want is very evident to both of us. We'll just have to make sure our timing gets better."

A thoughtful expression stole her smile. "Perhaps."

"What do you mean, 'perhaps'?"

"Nothing. You should get home. They'll be wondering where you are."

As usual, the damn coolness was seeping in again. Was she remembering his reaction to her notion about sex and pregnancy? Was she assessing whether or not to waste passion on a man who didn't share her views? He stood up. There had to be a way to make her forget her screwy ideas.

"You'll want to rest tomorrow," he said, picking up the brandy and holding it to her lips until she took a sip and wrinkled her nose. "But by Monday you should be fine, and it's your day off."

"Yes." She coughed and pushed the glass away.

"So we'll have dinner."

"Just like that? We'll have dinner?"

"Sorry. Will you please have dinner with me?"

She wriggled against the pillows, exposing more of the tantalizing flesh that he already knew was firm...and ready.

"Will you, Susan?"

"We'll only end up getting mad at each other about something."

Desire was making him unbearably uncomfortable. "True. But that's better than the alternative."

"What's that?" Again her lips parted just enough to show very white teeth.

"Not being together at all."

He left before she could reply, closing the door and standing there long enough to be sure no one would guess he was aroused. Libby and Georges met him in the living room.

"Will you have something to eat?" Libby asked.

"No. Thank you, but I'd like to get home to my daughter." And he couldn't be this close to Susan and not be with her, not tonight.

"We understand," Georges said, sounding formal once more. "Again we cannot thank you enough."

The Duclaux escorted him outside and to the dock. "I'm glad this evening ended like this," he called up from his boat, aware that he could think of a far better ending.

"Indeed," Georges said, tossing him the bowline.

"Me, too," Libby added, her face invisible in the darkness. "And for selfish reasons I'm glad Susan persuaded me to let her be the one to come back for Georges."

"You should explain that, *chérie*," Georges said as Mike began to wonder how she could be so overtly selfish.

"I was supposed to come. If I had, there'd be one less person present, because unlike Susan, I can't swim."

* * *

Libby and Susan sat side by side on a swing beneath an old madrona tree in Susan's yard. From here they could see a constant parade of Sunday boaters moving in and out of Friday Harbor.

"With the sun and all this blue water it's hard to imagine how awful last night was," Susan said.

"Let's not talk about it. I'll never forget how scared I was for you."

They rocked back and forth, each with a toe on the ground. Bees buzzed loudly along a hedge of heavily scented honeysuckle blossoms.

"I saw the address on that envelope that you got yesterday," Libby said suddenly. "All the time you were doing my hair last night I was trying to think of a way to talk about it."

In unison they stopped swaying. "I was going to talk to you about it," Susan said. "There doesn't seem to have been a right time."

"Is now okay?"

"Uh-huh. I guess. I'm going to adopt a little girl, Libby."

"Oh, Sue—" Libby twisted to face her "—I just knew that's what it was. You always wanted children. This is the right thing for you to do."

Tell Harriet Brock, Susan thought. "Thanks. It isn't so easy, though."

Briefly she outlined the nonprogress she felt she'd made so far.

"That doesn't sound so bad to me," Libby said, her voice bubbly. "You're impatient, that's all. Why did you look so funny yesterday when you opened the letter?"

Susan exhaled gustily. "The latest curve is that Mrs. Brock wants me to consider a cosponsor. I ask you, Libby—" she clasped her sister's forearm "—a *cospon-*

sor? I don't have anyone just dying to sign up for that kind of responsibility, but what Mrs. Brock is suggesting is that without one I may never get a child.''

"Shh. Calm down. Are you sure that isn't something you're reading into this?''

Susan thought about that. "No, I'm not sure. But I don't have anyone to cosponsor with me, and I don't want anyone.''

"Do me a favor, Sue, and take this a step at a time. That's what we'll have to do.''

Susan stared. "You? What do you mean?''

"Georges and I.'' Libby laced her fingers and propped her chin. "When we get back to Geneva, we're going to start adoption proceedings. We can't have children of our own. Something to do with me—hormones. The egg fertilizes, but it doesn't survive. That's the best explanation I can give.''

"I see,'' Susan said when she could speak.

"We were disappointed at first, of course, but not anymore. So, you see, we'll have something else in common, you and I.'' Libby smiled, but her eyes were sad, and a lump formed in Susan's throat. "We'll both adopt our children.''

"Yes.'' Susan couldn't think of anything comforting to say, nor did she know if she should try.

Libby checked her watch. "Oh, no. Noon already. When Georges called, I promised I'd be ready for him to pick me up at one. We're going to Seattle. Will you come and poke around with us?''

She was tired. They both knew as much. "No, thank you. Enjoy yourselves. Where did Georges go so early this morning?''

"Oh—'' Libby made an airy gesture "—he said he had something to do in Friday Harbor. Don't ask me what.''

Susan had been impressed by the ease with which Georges had been able to summon up a new twenty-two-foot motorboat by eight-thirty in the morning. He seemed daunted by nothing. He'd calmly informed her that this beautiful new boat was hers. She'd known argument would be pointless.

"Okay, then." Libby hovered. "See you later. By the way, something else I almost forgot. We leave for Hawaii again on Saturday."

Susan gripped the chain beside her. "Will you come back here before you go home?" She couldn't bear to give Libby up so soon.

"Probably. Georges has to go back to Geneva on business for a few days. Then he'll join me in Kauai. But you'll be with us, anyway."

"I'm...in Hawaii?"

"Of course in Hawaii. Kauai to be precise. Georges is making the arrangements, and he won't hear of you staying behind. We have to go and look at the boat with Mike."

Jumping to the ground, Susan pushed her hands into her pant pockets and studied her feet, deciding how to deal with this and not hurt Libby's feelings. "Nice try, but it won't work. For one thing, I can't leave the salon. For another, Mike Kinnear and I can't be together for more than five minutes without trying to kill each other."

Libby smirked. "Didn't look that way last night."

"Exceptional circumstances."

"Your ticket's been ordered and you're coming. You have a perfectly good staff to look after things for you at the salon, and Jean-Claude will be here to keep an eye on the house. He doesn't like Hawaii. Says the humidity gets to him, and he's got a pile of work to do."

"I'm not going, I tell you," Susan said breathlessly. "And I'm surprised Mike can. He has a twelve-year-old daughter, you know." Not that Susan was surprised that he was willing to walk away from Anne at a moment's notice.

"Mike's father and housekeeper are going to look after Anne."

"His *housekeeper?* Good grief."

Libby sniffed. "You are so difficult sometimes, Sue. He said to tell you that Connie Bangs has cleaned up her act, whatever that means. He said he wouldn't leave Anne if he wasn't sure she'd be fine, and he knew you'd want to hear that."

"You discussed me with Mike Kinnear?" She was incredulous and angry.

"No!" Libby started walking away. "He sent that message via Georges, that's all."

"I'm not going."

"Fine." Libby stopped on the path and faced Susan, her fists on her slender hips. "Then I can't go, either. Georges won't hear of the two of us being separated when we have so little time together—and neither will I. So I guess I'll have to give up my trip to Kauai to look at my boat."

"Oh, wonderful." Susan tipped her head back and scowled at scudding clouds. "My sister resorts to blackmail."

"It works, though, doesn't it?" Libby said very softly. "And you'll have a wonderful time, I promise."

"I didn't say I'd come."

"But you will." A smile crinkled the corners of Libby's eyes, a mischievous smile.

"Yes...yes, you little manipulator. Some things never change. You always did get your own way."

As Libby ran toward the house, humming, Susan felt her own smile slip. Her sister seemed so happy. *Please don't let anything take that away.* The foreboding she hadn't felt in days now flowed over Susan again. Why couldn't she believe the future held the things she and Libby wanted?

Susan ran into the foyer of the bank, shaking rain from her umbrella. She'd awakened to the downpour this morning, and it showed no sign of easing.

She checked for the shortest teller line, then stood quite still, her hand halfway into her purse.

Mike stood leaning over the teller's counter, with no one lined up behind him. Susan finished pulling out her deposit and walked slowly toward his broad back. He'd called yesterday to ask how she was. Their conversation had been short but had left her feeling cared about and longing to be with him again. She would never forget what he'd done for her on Saturday night, or how right it had seemed that he be the one to find her.

"Hi." She tapped his shoulder and he turned. There could be no missing what happened to his expression. His delight at seeing her shone in his smile. The faint narrowing of his eyes, the glint there, sent a clear message.

"Hello," he said. "Would you believe me if I said I was thinking about you?"

Suddenly breathless, Susan glanced away.

"You're turning pink, my love. I like it when you do that."

She laughed self-consciously. "Not exactly the cool woman of the world, am I?"

"I like you the way you are, Susan," he said, bringing his mouth close to her ear, making her feel they were sealed off from the world.

"And I like you the way you are," she whispered, and felt what he called "pink" turn to scarlet.

"Good." He straightened. "I'll make a forward woman of you yet."

"Mike," the man behind the counter said, "what name do you want on the cashier's check?"

"Frances Kinnear," Mike replied.

Susan swallowed with difficulty and fumbled with the papers she held. He was sending money to his ex-wife. Surely any support he gave her would be dealt with through other means than this.

Mike stood aside while Susan dealt with her transaction. Then he shepherded her out to stand in the vestibule. Rain fell from the gutters in a solid curtain.

"So we have a date tonight." He smiled again and touched her cheek with a knuckle. The spot felt singed, and her shortness of breath increased. "I thought we might keep it simple. What we need most is to talk. Agreed?"

"Agreed." She could see the check, which he still held. Although it was folded, a row of zeros suggested it wasn't for a small sum.

"Good. Then how about pizza and conversation at the yard? My office digs are comfortable—but you know that. Would you feel okay there?"

Achy heaviness invaded her body. If she went there with him, the end result would be inevitable. They would almost certainly make love. "I'd feel comfortable. It's a good idea."

His eyes lingered on hers, then flickered to her mouth. "Too bad we can't just go now."

Susan laughed. "One in the afternoon's a little early for dinner, don't you think? And won't you have people working all over the place? We wouldn't want to have to share our pizza."

"No," he said, abruptly sober. "No, we wouldn't want

to share anything. I'm looking forward to being with you in Hawaii, Susan.''

''Yes, Hawaii.'' This hadn't been mentioned on the phone yesterday. Susan was still uncertain about the trip but saw no way out.

A small figure dashed through the rain and collided with Mike. He held her off. ''There you are, pumpkin. Say hello to Susan.''

Anne's polite, almost shy ''Hello'' caught Susan off guard. So did the subtle change in the girl's appearance. Soft hair had started to grow on the shaved side of her head, while the longer side had been washed free of green and shone pale blond as Susan had suspected it would. Very little makeup was in evidence.

''Hi, Anne. You look great.'' She could have kissed her—and Mike, who must have worked miracles in the past week or so.

''Thank you.'' She turned her face up to her father. ''Mike, I put all the packages in the truck. Seattle was cool. We bought all kinds of stuff for school.''

Susan frowned, wondering who had taken Anne to Seattle to shop and who had given her advice on what to buy.

''Here are your cards.'' Anne fished several credit cards from her pocket and handed them over. ''I got stuff for when Mom comes to visit, too.''

''That's great, pumpkin.'' The rigidity of his face belied his casual comment. ''We'd better get you home.''

''No, no.'' She jiggled up and down. ''I've been invited to a party with some kids I met at the movies on Saturday. It's at one of their houses.''

''Where?'' Mike asked.

''I don't know. But one of the girl's moms is driving, so it's okay. I'll call if I need a ride home.''

Mike was putting away his credit cards. "Okay. But behave yourself, huh?"

Susan's hands opened and closed convulsively. This was incredible, this lack of responsibility.

"Mike," Anne said in the act of walking back into the rain, "you did get the money for Mom, didn't you?"

"Yes, honey."

"Good, 'cause she's really gonna be able to use it to come and see me this time." With that, she ran out of sight.

"Well," Mike sighed, "she really seems happier these days."

Susan couldn't keep quiet an instant longer. Even as she coped with the sick feeling caused by the mention of a visit by Mike's ex-wife, she continued to seethe over his casual attitude toward his daughter. "I thought you were going to be firmer with Anne."

He frowned at her. "I am being firmer. What makes you think I'm not?"

"Letting her loose with your credit cards. Allowing her to go who knows where to a party without any idea of who she'll be with and when she's coming home."

"Wait a minute." His big hand settled, slightly too roughly, on her forearm. "Weren't you the one who told me not to overreact to a little bad behavior?"

"Yes. I told you to rethink a decision about punishment for a silly piece of naughtiness. I didn't tell you to go mad in the other direction."

"Go mad?" His voice was dangerously low. "I'm not going mad. I know my daughter and I trust her. She won't do anything foolish."

Susan's pulse roared. "Nothing foolish? Like smoking in the garden wasn't foolish?"

His grip became iron. "Didn't you just say that was a silly piece of naughtiness, nothing more?"

"You twist everything." Her voice was too loud, but she didn't care. "You don't understand that you have to be consistent in dealing with a child."

"I can't believe…" He rubbed a hand over his face. "You're really something. I've never met anyone with as much nerve as you've got."

"What you mean is that you've never met anyone who had the guts to tell you what they really think." She'd passed beyond caution.

His deeply indrawn breath was visible. He smoothed back his hair and zipped up his windbreaker. "Let's forget this, Susan. Anne isn't your problem. She's mine. And I'll do what's best for her."

"Sure."

"Please, let it go. Tonight we'll be calmer, and then I'll be happy to discuss the differences in our philosophies on child-rearing."

"I don't think so."

Mike grimaced. "You don't think what, for God's sake? You are the most infuriating woman sometimes."

"Obviously. All the more reason for us not to get together. Tonight or any night. We don't agree—on anything. Why prolong the aggravation of being together."

"Because I *want* to be with you. I'm not always sure why, but—"

"I'm not sure, either. So I'll make it easy on both of us. I'm too tired to go anywhere tonight." Disappointment was almost a pain in her leaden stomach.

"Look—" he swung her to face him "—Anne's my daughter. Got it? I'll bring her up any way I damn well please. I've said this before, but I'll say it again. What do you know about bringing up children? You've never had any. Wishing you had doesn't change that.''

She throbbed with chagrin and hurt. ''No, it doesn't. Thanks for reminding me. Don't call. I won't talk to you.''

''I won't call.''

Without a backward glance she stalked out into the sodden day.

10

Below the lanai, raindrops from a recent squall still glistened on the flat, round leaves of a giant pua tree. Mike rested his forearms on the white railing. From the vantage point afforded by the house's high stilts, he could scan the perfect curve of Ke'e Beach, empty now that the scattering of tourists had fled the shower. This was part of a daily ritual he'd discovered. Stay in the lush magic of the north shore only until the predictable series of warm showers blew in, then head for the more arid southern beaches.

The ocean that foamed against the shore stretched before him endlessly. Turquoise, jade-green and purple; color and mood constantly shifting over banks of coral. Here and there an intrepid snorkeler still plied back and forth between the shadows of submerged shelves, unable to leave the shoals of brilliant fish Mike had already found himself helpless to resist.

This was another world. In Hawaii time seemed to stop, and he wished he could stop with it. But in the rambling house behind him Libby and Susan were talking to Georges, who had arrived in Kauai an hour earlier. Talking to him or trying to appease him? Mike felt awkward, superfluous. Although he'd kept a smile on his face, Georges's mood was almost tangibly foul. He'd deftly avoided any real explanation of why he'd arrived on Monday morning, a day sooner than planned. To Mike the

change in Georges's plans was a relief in at least one respect. The diversion would make the awkwardness between him and Susan less obvious. In the week since their
disastrous encounter at the bank they'd both maintained
silence. But he'd thought about Susan. He'd thought about
her until his fingers itched to snatch up the phone.

He turned his back on the sea and leaned on his elbows.
Sheer white drapes billowed from doors that opened onto
the lanai from a living room reminiscent of missionary
days—koa wood floors polished to a reddish gleam, white
rattan furniture, coarse, cream-colored hala rugs and tapa
hangings. Yes, Mike could like it here for a very long time.

He looked at his bare feet beneath the bottoms of his
beige cotton drawstring pants. Bare-chested and already
more deeply tanned than ever, his body felt good—except
when he looked at Susan or thought about her. And he'd
done one or the other constantly since yesterday's tense
journey to the islands.

"Codeine, then." Libby's voice drifted from the house,
followed by a muffled masculine rumble.

Georges had admitted to a migraine. Mike, never subject
to headaches, sympathized without having any idea how
bad the pain might be. But there was far more wrong with
Georges Duclaux than a headache. Mike would stake a lot
on that. In their discussion the previous Sunday Georges
had made Mike more of a confidant than he really cared
to be and Georges had revealed enough of his business
deals to give any man one hell of a headache.

With the sweeping away of the tropical ministorm, a
pungent scent rose from the warm, wet red earth. Gnarled
plumeria trees with creamy white and yellow blossoms, or
pale pink and red, seemed to breathe out their sweet fragrance in great wafts.

Mike sank his hands into his pockets and paced. If only

he and Susan could have time alone, really alone, he knew they could overcome their differences. The old question rattled around his brain yet again: why was Susan so important to him? The possible answer alternately thrilled and terrified him. How could he, a confirmed single, be even considering that he might be able to love a nut like Susan Ackroyd? Not that she was even speaking to him.

He stood still. The breeze whipped at his hair, his face, but he felt so still. Overhead, coconut palms bent, rustled, their fronds clicking gently. The inner stillness. Did he already love her?

He felt Susan coming before she pulled the drapes aside and stepped onto the lanai. That happened frequently—the awareness of her presence even when he couldn't see her. Scary.

She walked to stand almost shoulder to shoulder with him, facing the sea. "Did you see the cut on his neck?"

The silence was broken. He looked sideways at her. "No."

"He tried to cover it up with a scarf, but Libby pulled it off before he could stop her. It's deep. It should be sutured, but he says that's garbage." Her eyes were the color of the navy blue water over the deepest bands of coral. "Probably too late now, anyway."

"Some people don't like to make a fuss about those things." Like himself, and Susan, too. "I remember a woman I dragged out of freezing water who wouldn't see a doctor." And, as far as he was concerned, that incident was far from closed.

She hunched her shoulders. "I suppose. Georges says he was leaning out of one of those sash windows and it slipped down on him."

"But you don't believe that." Moving between Susan

and the railing, he leaned back and studied her, arms crossed. "Why not? Sounds reasonable to me."

"I'm not sure why. Maybe it's because he looked funny when he said it, as if he was making it up as he went along." She chewed her lip, a crease between her brows. "Do you know what I mean? That feeling?"

"Yes," he said slowly. And he didn't think of Susan as a woman into fantasies. "Any theories about what might have really happened?"

She surprised him by settling her hands on his forearms. "You don't know about this, but Georges has been involved in a business venture that's become messy. Someone else with a big stake in it wants out because there's been some pretty nasty opposition. They're building a spa. I think there's another outfit planning a similar project, and they want to stop the one Georges is financing."

He didn't tell her Georges had already discussed some of this with him. "What would that have to do with Georges cutting his neck?"

"If he did cut his neck."

"Meaning?"

"Oh, I don't know. Jean-Claude made some comment about the other people being unscrupulous, and then the man who's in with Georges called as if he was frightened. I wonder, that's all."

He laughed but didn't feel remotely amused. "So you're active imagination has hoods sneaking around beating up on Georges to persuade him to back out?" Actually, he'd had much the same thought himself. "Georges is a big boy and he's been playing big-stake games for a lot of years. Trust him. He knows what he's doing."

She breathed deeply, her breasts rising beneath her white gauze halter top. Her matching ankle-length skirt blew around her bare legs. A light tan made the white fabric whiter, her hair appear blue-black. Preoccupied as she was now, her face mirrored her deep concern for her sister and her husband. Mike liked her all the more for that, for her unselfish concern for others. In the past day or two he'd also begun to think she'd been right about the way he handled Anne. And he had no doubt Susan's forthrightness in that area was motivated by fearless conviction that children deserved the best. He needed to apologize to her—again.

"I feel like a fifth wheel here today," she said abruptly. "I'm going to take one of the cars and go for a drive. Tell them where I've gone—if they ever come out of their room."

"May I come, too?"

She folded her arms under her breasts and raised her brows at him. "Are you sure you want to?"

"I feel like a fifth wheel, too. We might as well keep each other company. We could decide not to talk at all. That should be safe."

Her laugh, the slow way the corners of her mouth turned up, unleashed a delicious warmth in him.

"Won't Georges want to get you right over to Nawili-wili to see the boat?"

"While he's got a migraine?" Mike had mentioned the boat as soon as Georges had arrived and gained the surprising impression that the man's enthusiasm might have dwindled. Susan didn't need that insight added to her other concerns. "Anyway, he already said he wants to wait until late this afternoon because he's got to have a long talk with Jean-Claude."

"More business," she muttered tightly.

"Probably. Let it go, Susan. You can't do anything to help." Mike wished he could do something, mostly because he hated seeing Susan upset. And he also wished the question of the Duclaux boat could be settled quickly. This trip had come at a bad time. He was needed at the yard and couldn't afford not to be there, but he also needed more work. Georges's boat had begun to interest him, and he hoped it would be the answer to taking Kinnear more strongly into the black. Aaron's added investment was a help, but still not enough.

"You're right," Susan said. "I can't do anything here and neither can you. We might as well get out of the way and give them some privacy. It's probably hot at Poipu Beach. You're a sun lover. Shall we drive there?"

He glanced from her sandals to his bare feet, then looked at the woolly green mountains that rose to sheer, saw-toothed heights behind the house. "How about a hike instead? Would you like that?"

"The NaPali Trail," she said, reading his mind. "The guidebooks say it's for hikers who enjoy a challenge. Which means you, of course. Tennis shoes are the best I can do."

"We won't go too far in." He studied the mysterious shadowed slopes again. Here and there silvery white streaks slashed downward, some of the hundreds of waterfalls that fed the lush valleys of the Garden Island. An odd excitement caught at him. "This place is something. We don't have long to make the best of it."

"No." She turned toward the door. "I'm already worried about being away from the salon."

"I know what you mean," he murmured. Then he added, "The skirt had better go. You'll never be able to climb in that."

"Thanks for the tip."

After one hour and several miles of plodding, Susan plopped down on a rock and fished a handkerchief from the pocket of her shorts. Mike strode steadily upward, unaware she'd fallen behind. Let him go. She hated to slow him down and she'd catch up when her heart rate was back to normal.

Mike's sneakers thudded on the rust-colored earth, as he stepped nimbly around large boulders in the trail. He'd told her they'd been put there to mark the path by native Hawaiians long before missionaries and whalers had arrived to "enlighten" the island's people. Since leaving Washington, she and Mike had been repeatedly together but always with Libby present. Susan knew they needed to talk. More apologies would probably be coming—from both of them.

She looked at him, moving higher and higher above her between the glistening leaves of philodendron vines. He'd also changed into shorts, and his legs were even more tanned than she remembered from their first few meetings. Tanned, with long, lean muscles and sun-bronzed hair. No perspiration showed on the back of the pale blue polo shirt he'd put on. He was a strong, well-conditioned man. He mesmerized her…and in the weeks she'd known him she'd been furious more often than at any other time in her life.

Resting her elbows on her knees, she propped her chin on her hands. She couldn't stand him, but she couldn't stand to be without him. She couldn't bear even to *think* about being without him.

But it would happen, and probably soon.

"Hey!"

She jumped. Grinning, Mike loped downhill toward her.

"What's so funny?" Standing up wasn't out of the question, just undesirable while she was comfortable on her rock.

"This is what happens when you take a walk with a wimp. You end up making care trips."

Shading her eyes, she squinted up at him. "Care trips?"

"Yeah." He came to a stop beside her, and she noticed he wasn't even breathing hard. "Every mile or so you look back and find out you're alone. Then you have to go back to make sure the wimp doesn't need CPR."

"I'm not... You're grinning again."

"Am I? Are you sure you don't need CPR?"

Lascivious would describe his smirk nicely. "It's hot up here. And it's steep. You didn't say it would be this steep."

Slipping off the day pack he'd brought to carry drinks, he dropped beside her on the rock, edging her along with his rump to make enough room for both of them—barely. "You need more exercise."

"Not this kind." Susan didn't trust herself to look at him. Everything he said seemed loaded, and her responses played right into his hands. This time he didn't come back with a quip. His arm rested on her shoulder, and their sides touched all the way to where his hair-rough thigh relaxed against her knee. Warm, male skin...companionable closeness laced with harnessed sexuality...nice.

"If you can make it around the next bend, there's a place where we could get down to the water." Mike bent so that she had to look at him. He raised his brows. "Of course, if you'd rather, I'll just carry you back to the trailhead...."

"I'm perfectly capable of making it as far as I want to go."

His eyes seemed even greener in the vivid light here. "So we'll go paddle?"

He was definitely too close for comfort. "I didn't think you could get to the north shore beaches." She stood up and peered downward through the dense vegetation to where the ocean ceaselessly shifted. "It's a long way down there."

"You can't get to the beaches by car. That doesn't mean they aren't there—for the pregeriatric folks."

Ignoring the barb, she started uphill. Every few steps her tennis shoes slipped on the mud and she leaned farther into the incline.

Mike's footsteps fell in behind her. Within minutes the humid air shortened her breath. Slowing, she pointed at a tree. "Look at the pineapples."

"Pineapples?" He drew level as she stopped. "Pineapples don't grow on trees."

As she well knew, but her comment bought breathing time. The lauhala tree, balanced on its campfire style tent of air roots, sported pods that resembled the fruit.

"Those are pods," Mike was expounding. "They're used for applying the die for tapa. You know, like the bark hangings back at the house?"

She knew. "Really? They do look like pineapples, though, don't they?"

"And the fronds are what they make into hala rugs. That's from lauhala—the name of the tree."

"Really?" And she was wicked, but this was a case of employing whatever came to hand for simple survival. "Where did you say it was that we could start downhill?"

"Here."

Veering to the right, he dropped from the trail onto a barely visible track that appeared to lead nowhere. Susan stayed where she was.

"Come on," Mike called over his shoulder.

Susan took a few tentative, slithering steps.

"You're proving my point." He plodded back, pulled her hand from her hip and set off at a slow but determined pace. "It's all downhill. It'll give you a chance to catch your breath."

"And it'll be all uphill going back."

"We'll wait until it's cooler."

And how late would that be? Susan didn't ask, but kept a firm grip on his hand and her eyes on the treacherous terrain.

Forty minutes brought them to a band of black lava rock overhanging a long, narrow strip of white sand. Mike smiled at her triumphantly. "A little piece of paradise?"

"Oh, yes." She breathed the tangy, warm pine scent of casuarina trees. Stunted by the elements, their trunks overhung the drop to the beach. "How did you know it was here?" He'd seemed to know exactly where he was going.

"Aaron told me about it."

"I didn't realize he'd been here."

"You probably don't realize a lot of things about Aaron. He's a complex man."

She wouldn't argue with that analysis. "My turn to lead." Picking her way, Susan climbed, using feet, her fingers and her bottom to clamber over the rocks. Prickly cones from the casuarinas scratched her arms and legs and she winced.

"Ha!" Landing on the sand beside her, Mike whipped his shirt over his head and threw wide his arms. "Our own beach. How about that?"

Susan glanced away. Tall, straight, his muscular chest the color of warm gold, his strong legs braced apart—Mike Kinnear probably knew he was overwhelmingly sexy. She certainly did.

"I'm getting out of the sun," she said, hoping she didn't sound as affected as she felt. "Over there under the ledge."

By the time she'd crawled beneath the mossy overhang

and sat down cross-legged, Mike was in front of her, arms braced on the rock above. "You really feel the heat, don't you?"

"Uh-huh. That's why I like living where I do. This is a great place to visit, but I'd shrivel up if I had to stay here. At least you can take your shirt off."

"So can you." His eyes didn't move from hers, but he did give one of his delightfully evil grins. "Okay if I sit with you?"

"Why shouldn't it be?"

"We haven't had our mandatory 'sorry' session yet."

"You're right. I'm sorry I seem to make a habit of telling you how to run your life." Folding her arms on her knees, she rested her forehead. That way she didn't have to look at him. "Sit," she added.

His body, settling next to hers, was warm and smelled clean and salty. "I shouldn't have made the crack...you know, *the* crack. I'm sorry."

"There," she said. "That's done. We're getting pretty good at it."

He settled an arm over her shoulders, but she didn't raise her head. When he pulled her to rest against him, her heart made a huge leap.

"I think you've made some good points about the way I deal with Anne."

Susan slipped a hand hesitantly around his waist and shifted her cheek to his shoulder. As she listened to him, the gentle, thoughtful quality of his deep voice calmed her.

"I don't want to bore you with my life history," he said.

Didn't he know, couldn't he sense there was nothing about him that would bore her? "I'm a good listener."

"Yes, I think you are." The hand on her shoulder chafed rhythmically to her elbow and back. "I've got a brother, Ed. He's a couple of years older than me. We've always been close, but since he went into the service—navy—we haven't been able to spend as much time together as we'd like. When we were growing up, we were more like twins than most twins. We thought alike. Looking back, I think it was probably because most of the time we were a survival team.''

He paused and she tilted her face up to his. Mike stared straight ahead as if seeing his past.

''Our parents seemed very involved with each other. They were one of those couples who did everything together. There was never any doubt that we were loved, but we came in a distant second to their relationship.''

Susan bit her lip. ''My folks are a bit like that.''

His short laugh caught at her. ''Unfortunately when Ed and I were in our middle teens, Mother decided she wanted a change. One night she packed her bags and left. Never came back, never wrote to us or called.''

''Oh, Mike. But there must have been more to it than you realized. People don't take that kind of step for no reason.''

Mike put his chin on top of her head. ''You're probably right. Dad would never talk about it. Still hasn't, and I don't think I'll ever be able to raise the subject. I think she got bored and probably found someone else.''

''Oh.''

''Yeah. Oh. Oh, nothing. The end. Dad reacted by turning into the heavy father. Back then I could feel sorry for him and try to please him, which I did by becoming a success in the business world. Ed's version was the navy. Dad approved of that, too. Ed's happy. I really believe that. But I wasn't cut out for the nine-to-five, chalk-stripe suit number. Trying to please my dad wasted a lot of good years and got me into a... I went off in the wrong direction for me. I don't want that for Anne.''

The jerky way he stroked her arm, the tightness of his hold, spelled preoccupation and a need for human comfort.

''Anyway, I'm going to have to review what's the best approach with my daughter. Thanks for making me stop to think.''

''You're a good father,'' she told him, not only because it was what he needed to hear, but because he loved his daughter and that was the greatest gift he could give her. ''Single parenting isn't easy.''

He leaned away to look at her. ''Remember you said that.''

''Let's go down by the water.'' She couldn't believe she had said the one thing she avoided thinking about.

When she moved to get up, he stopped her. ''Not yet. I like sitting here...holding you.''

And ensnaring her tighter and tighter in the web of sensuality he could spin about her with no apparent effort. ''What about Frances?'' This was the acid test of trust and openness.

''Frances got bored, too,'' he said without hesitation. ''She didn't marry a tradesman who worked with his hands on expensive boats he could no longer afford to own.''

''I think what you do is wonderful.''

''Thanks. But I don't completely blame her. I changed the rules. Welshed on the contract, I guess you could say. She agreed to...she agreed to stay with a guy who said he'd be one thing and then became something else. Not really fair, huh? Kind of gave her the right to say, 'Okay, I'm changing a few things, too.' She's trying to be a singer. Her road hasn't been all roses.''

Somehow Susan couldn't summon up a whole lot of

sympathy for Frances. "You sound as if you still care for her."

He looked thoughtful. "I care what happens to her. She was my wife and she is my daughter's mother. But I don't love her anymore, if that's what you mean. Sometimes it's hard to be sure I ever did." He stirred and smiled absently. "My record with the women in my life hasn't been brilliant. They seem to end up finding me expendable."

The revelation, his interpretation of what had happened with him and his mother and then, between him and his wife told far more than he could have realized. This was a man determined not to be wounded again.

Susan said, "I know what you mean."

When he didn't pursue the comment, she was grateful. Enough had already been said about her marriage—at least for now.

"Let's take that walk." Mike ducked his head and scrambled from the shade, pulling Susan with him. He kicked off his shoes and pushed them into a pile with his shirt and pack.

"Georges and Libby seem like a perfect match," he said as they strolled slowly through the shallows. "Very much in love."

"They are. But no one has everything. They very much want children and can't have them. They intend to adopt, too."

He kicked up a spray of water, and Susan felt a slight drawing away. She'd reminded him that there were differences between them that were unlikely ever to be resolved. "I imagine it's very important to a man like Georges to have an heir," he said. "Someone to carry on what he's built."

That angle had never occurred to her. "Yes, I suppose so. But most of all, I think he'd make a wonderful father.

And Libby needs to be a mother. Most women do,'' she added with a note of defiance.

"Maybe."

"Not maybe. Definitely."

"So you say." Swinging her toward him, he lowered his face until she felt his breath on her lips. "I think what most women need even more is to be wanted by a man."

Her swift sidestepping motion caught him off guard. She ran several yards before he caught her around the waist and clamped her against him. "Why don't you like it when I say that? When I do, I'm also saying that a man needs a woman."

"And it's just a physical thing, isn't it, Mike? Physical need."

"I didn't say that. But it certainly comes into it." His fingertips, spread wide on her bare back, were calloused. A tradesman's hands. The sensation inflamed her.

"This isn't a great idea," she murmured.

Mike smiled. "Sunshine does beautiful things for you. But so does rain and fog…and anything else I can think of. White gauzy fabric is particularly effective." A knuckle, slowly rubbed from her collarbone, along the edge of her halter, brought a shudder she couldn't hide.

She cleared her throat. "I thought you'd worn out your poetic bent."

"Does that have a deeper meaning?" His smile was playful.

"The card with the roses."

"Oh, that." He bowed his head, then looked directly at her. "Could we be serious? I'd like that."

"The roses were wonderful." Her heart flipflopped. He couldn't know how limited her experience with men was. There had been no other deserted tropical beaches and wild sexual longings while she stood in the arms of a man she wanted as she'd never wanted...anything?

He watched her closely. "We're feeling the same things. Could we do something about that?"

"What are you saying?" Blood pounded in her ears.

"I don't know what we can have together. Long-range. But I think it could be that we're meant to find out."

Sex. The now. Could she take that, enjoy that, and not crumble when there was nothing more?

"It's become important for me to be with you," he said. "When I'm not, I think about you. Do you suppose that's a symptom of something?"

"Not unless—" No, she couldn't do this. Twisting away, she stumbled, then began to run.

"Susan!"

The water hampered her. She ran on regardless, barely aware of the sound of splashing behind her.

"Susan, stop!" He grabbed for her arm, but with a strength she hadn't known she possessed, Susan pulled free—and tripped.

"You...damn." Mike tried to catch her, and they fell together, landing on wet sand amid a shimmering spray. "You little idiot. Susan, you're driving me mad."

Droplets clung to his face and body. Lying beside her, braced on one forearm, he wiped his face. They were soaked. Water slipped beneath them, barely an inch deep, then softly receded only to ripple in again.

Supporting herself on her elbows, Susan rested her chin on her chest and closed her eyes.

"Why do you do that?" His voice was softly insistent. "Whenever you feel me getting too close, you shut your eyes or run or pull me into an argument. You're avoiding the inevitable, Susan."

She looked up at him. "How did you get to be so sure of yourself?"

"I'm not—except where you're concerned. We want the same things. I've already told you that. You think so, too, only you try to deny it."

"We should start back."

"No." His hand on her shoulder stopped her from moving. "We should be right here—together."

"What if I say I don't want this?"

"I'll listen. Then I'll ask you to prove it."

"How would I do that?" Surely he could hear her hammering heart.

Without warning, his mouth descended upon hers, not roughly, but with unmistakable assurance. His firm lips brushed back and forth before he carefully sucked her lower lip between his teeth. When his tongue sought and found hers, and circled, she let her head fall back and sank to the tide-soaked sand.

"This is how you'd prove you don't want to be with me," he whispered against her cheek. His hands spanned her ribs and his thumbs rested on the sensitive undersides of her breasts. He blew gently against her ear. "Right now you tell me to get lost."

Telling him he was unfair would be pointless. Turning her head, she sought his mouth again and showed him that instinct could teach all a woman needed to know about kissing a man thoroughly. When he was breathless, she rested her head on the sand again and watched the changing shadows in his eyes.

"You didn't tell me," he said. In one fluid motion he knelt and anchored her hands, leaned over, then settled swift, hard kisses on her face and neck. Another move brought him astride her hips, and he tipped his head to one side to study her.

"Mike—"

"Shh. I just want to look at you. You might as well be naked in this." The backs of his fingers passed from her shoulders and over wet gauze to her nipples.

Susan arched her back. "Mike—"

"Uh-uh." With those wonderful calloused fingertips he incited quivering ecstasy that burned rods from the turgid flesh beneath his hands to the waiting places in her body. "See what I mean?"

He kissed her lips again, still leisurely and controlled, then rolled her face from side to side. Supporting her, he slipped his mouth to her breast and kissed her through the sodden fabric.

Her belly contracted sharply and she bent her knees.

"See?" He raised his face and she saw her breasts, the nipples dark and hard, straining inside the now-transparent fabric.

Susan lay down again and ran a hand over the glistening hair on his chest. She stroked his sides and turned her fingers to reach his belly. Mike's lips parted, then drew back from his teeth. Muscles in his jaw jerked.

"I see a lot," Susan whispered. The playing water rushed around them again. Pressing downward, she found the proof of their shared desire and smiled at his indrawn breath and tightly shut eyes. "Whose eyes are closed now?" She explored more daringly, finding room for her fingers beneath the leg of his shorts, touching his groin with her nails, probing until his next breath was a hiss and he snatched her wrist away.

He made the mistake of releasing his grip to fumble with the tie behind her neck, and she promptly returned to her exploration.

"Stop, or I'm going to lose it." His kiss opened her mouth wide while he stripped the halter to her waist. She wrapped her arms around him. The hair on his chest, the firm muscle, worked a softly stimulating magic on her skin. The kiss went on and on, and the insistent massage of his flesh on hers. Her breasts were afire and her womb and her achy, trembling thighs.

Mike sat back on his heels, his nostrils flared, the veins in his neck distended. With one finger on each hand he drew circles over every sensitive, exposed piece of skin until she wriggled and reached for him. Capturing her hands, he held them to his tensed middle and this time moved them himself to cover the heaviness between his legs.

They played on, touching, kissing, tracing with lips and tongues until Mike let his head hang back and a cry escaped him. Susan laughed and squirmed to sit up. She worked at the fastenings on his shorts until he stopped her and finished the job himself. Susan was naked before he'd tossed the shorts aside.

"Do you have any doubts about this anymore?"

Susan shook her head, knowing what restraint was costing him. He sat, cross-legged, and she caught her breath as she looked at him. Then he was pulling her down, spreading her legs—and sinking into her. Linking her feet behind his waist felt so good, so natural.

"Relax," he ordered, but gently. Bracing the weight of both of them on his locked arms, he thrust his hips, and Susan's body flamed. His chest rose and fell, and he seemed to force himself to be still and quiet. With his thumbs he found the small hot place that jolted every nerve in her body.

"You don't have...don't."

He only smiled, and reached forward to take a nipple between his teeth. And his thumbs kept moving. Susan opened her mouth but couldn't make a sound. She felt his spasm, the swelling within her.

"Mike!" Liquid heat traveled from his probing touch to tighten her around him, and reason burned up. Susan heard herself pant, and Mike—and their mingled cries.

She moved to her knees, his hips between her thighs, his hands around her waist. Then it was all Mike. He carried her with him, and she wanted to go as far as he wanted to go, rising higher and higher until their moans were part of the sea and the wind.

A mighty, searing surge. Susan panted, reached for and found his neck, holding on as they fell together side by side on the blessedly cool sand. Replete.

Mike pulled her face against his chest and cradled her, their bodies facing, still joined. "You managed to surprise me—again," he murmured.

"Hmm." She couldn't manage words.

"All that fire, my girl. Intoxicating stuff. Don't think you're going to get rid of me now."

Oh, she hoped not. "We're going to have to stay here until we drown."

"Why?" He looked into her half-open eyes. "Don't answer that. I know. Neither of us will ever be able to move again. Your fault, my sexy friend."

Friend. She wasn't just a friend anymore. Something brushed her side and she strained to see. Her halter floated by.

"Mike!" Struggling, ignoring his protests, she made a grab for the wispy garment and caught it. "Where are our shorts?"

His eyes cleared slowly. "Shorts? Who cares?" But he slowly withdrew from her, leaving her throbbing and longing to draw him back.

Struggling to his legs, which were obviously rubbery,

he rounded up the rest of their clothes and offered her a hand. She held on and he hauled her up beside him.

Immediately they kissed, and it didn't matter that salt-water streamed from their hair into their eyes. Laughing, they ran hand in hand to the hollow beneath the ledge.

Hopping, Mike worked his shorts on over his damp skin and Susan did the same. When she held up the halter, Mike stole it.

"Gimme," Susan demanded.

"Nope." He put it behind his back. "Take it from me."

Susan grabbed, dodging from side to side until she landed breast to chest, pulsing all over again, their mouths fused. When the kiss ended, she was gasping, and Mike fell flat on his back, spread-eagle, eyes rolled up.

"I've killed you, huh? Great. Now I'll be safe."

"Don't bet on it. I'm not finished with you yet."

Susan scrambled, still half-naked, beneath the ledge and Mike joined her. He put the halter out of her reach and pulled her against him. "We can't stay here forever," he said, and regret hung heavy in his voice. "But I'm not going yet."

They fell silent, kissing from time to time, stroking each other. Their skin felt like fields of exposed nerves. Mike played with her breasts, using his lips and teeth, his tongue and his hands until Susan reached for the waistband of his shorts.

Mike held her wrist. "We really don't have time for that."

"No." She couldn't hide her regret. "Mike."

"Yes."

"Nothing."

"Yes, there is." He tilted up her chin and kissed the spot between her brows. "Tell me."

"Why aren't you worried about birth control?"

He didn't, as she'd expected, look as if she'd thrown cold water on him.

"Why do you think?"

"Maybe you wouldn't mind that much if I became pregnant?"

He smiled and she thought he seemed wistful. "Sorry, sweet. I'd mind very much."

For the first time Susan was conscious of her nakedness. She crossed her arms over her breasts. "Then, why?"

"You're taking birth control pills."

Her mouth opened. Goose bumps shot out all over her body.

Mike wrapped his arms around her and held her gently. "I saw them in your bathroom, Susan. Susan Ackroyd was on the label and the days of the cycle when you're supposed to take them. I've been around long enough to know about those things. And you're up-to-date with the dose."

"Yes," she whispered. "They're to regulate my cycle."

"I thought about that as a reason, too. You wouldn't mind at all being pregnant. I know that."

He was so gentle, so honest. "No, I wouldn't. I wish I could be."

"And I wish you'd forget the whole thing. Susan, I'm not interested in being a father again. And if you had my child, I wouldn't be able to do anything but take responsibility. I'm not the type who could turn away, even if you insisted the baby was all you wanted from me. Do you understand?"

How could she not understand? She'd met a man, been made love to by a man who was completely honorable and true to himself. What he was telling her was that he wanted an affair with her, but nothing more.

"Can you accept what I'm telling you, Susan?"

"I understand it."

"Okay. But I've wanted you from the day we met. Today only made sure I found out how much. I'm not giving up. We're going to have to reach a compromise."

"Sex without strings."

She heard him swallow. "I'd rather you didn't put it like that. Couldn't we say we'll take this a day at a time and not try to make decisions for the rest of our lives?"

"I could try, but I don't know. I'm new to this."

"Yes, I know. But you were intended to be a woman with a man and I intend to be that man."

She picked up her halter and reached back to tie the straps at her back. Mike finished the job for her, fastening the knot behind her neck before holding her face between his hands. "We're going on from here, my love, because we can't go back and we sure can't stop."

"I'm not sure—"

"What did you think about when we were making love? Having a baby?"

She tried unsuccessfully to turn away. "No, I didn't."

"Then I'm very sure what's going to happen. There'll be many more days like today for us. I'm going to make sure you'll need the loving more than you need air."

11

Georges preceded Mike on the long path to the house. They'd driven in silence from Nawiliwili Harbor where *Ma Libby* was anchored, and Mike sensed tightly harnessed tension in the other man. Whatever was said now had to be thought through very carefully, for everyone's sake.

The moon cast a silver gleam over the scene. From a nearby pond, bullfrogs set up their nightly symphony, the bass sound muted by the whine of a strong wind through the sighing palms and the crash of the ocean below.

For the first time since he'd arrived, Mike felt a pall in paradise, a premonition of darkness to come. He shuddered slightly. But at any moment he would see Susan... This afternoon was clear in his mind, so clear that it played like a movie in full color with stereo sound and relived feelings. He gritted his teeth against his body's response.

"Hello!" Libby called from the door as Georges approached ahead of Mike. "How did it go? What do you think, Mike?"

It was coming. No more putting off reality, and he didn't know what the outcome would be.

"Give the man time, *chérie*," Georges said, waiting for Mike to pass before closing the door. "I think he has a great deal to think about. Am I correct?"

"Yes and no," Mike said, going into the living room

where all he saw was Susan, dressed in a yellow tank top that didn't hit the waist of her white Bermuda shorts.

"What does that mean?" Libby rushed around him, a frown creasing her smooth brow.

"It means that I've already done a lot of thinking. Now I have to discuss those thoughts with you and Georges and decide what, if anything, should be done."

"We should sit." Georges tossed his keys onto the glass top of a bentwood table and sat in a white wing chair.

Susan lay on a rattan couch, her head propped on a mauve cushion at one end. Her bare midriff was tanned and the tank top hugged her breasts. Mike walked to the couch and looked down at her. She moved her feet to make room for him to sit, and their eyes met. Could they be together tonight?

"So," Georges said, his smile not reaching his eyes. "Perhaps you should trust us with your conclusions, Mike."

"She's a wonderful boat…potentially." Beneath his apprehension excitement trembled. He mustn't allow his judgment to be clouded by his desire to turn *Ma Libby* into the masterpiece she was meant to be.

Georges let out a great sigh. Libby dropped to sit at his feet and they held hands. She smiled delightedly.

"You don't believe I bought a…a load of junk."

Mike chuckled at the odd sound of the words on Georges's lips. "No, anything but. What I do believe is that I may not be the man for the job that needs to be done." He held up a hand to cut off Georges's protest. "Please let me finish. It isn't that I don't *want* to do it, or that I don't think I'd do it better than anyone else. But there are other considerations, and for your sake as well as mine, I've got to be objective."

The Duclaux watched him, patently confused, and Susan

scooted to sit cross-legged, where she could see him clearly. He wished he could hold her hand without worrying about embarrassing her.

"If there were a known crime called boat abuse, I'd know where to take people to show an excellent example. Only morons would do what was done there."

"She does look awful," Georges agreed. "Ridiculous."

"She's ruined—at least to the naked eye. Everything has to be stripped—absolutely everything. Gutted would be a better word." He turned to Susan. "There are beams in the salon. They're covered with discolored pegboard tiles. When I pried one off, I found beautiful, intricate stenciling and mahogany molding. It's all damaged but could be restored."

"Exactly." Georges leaned forward. "I can see that you appreciate what can be achieved."

"Oh, I appreciate it, okay. Then take that playroom, or whatever you'd call the main stateroom. Mirror tile on the overhead and pink velvet drapes on a four-poster bed. We have to pull everything out and see if we can find clues to what the area looked like before." He paused. His anxiousness, his too-childlike longing to be the one to resurrect the old beauty, was in danger of showing through. "Of course, you may not want to recreate her exactly. That was only my thought."

"And you read Georges's mind, didn't he darling?" Libby turned her face up to her husband whose expression softened. He laid a finger on her lips.

"Yes, Mike. You've read my mind. *Ma Libby* is a piece of history that should be made as beautiful as she once was."

Mike got up and poured a Scotch. "The points I've mentioned are nothing. Only two in a list of hundreds.

Have you given any thought to the cost of a project like this?''

"It will be enormous," Georges said calmly.

"And you're prepared to pay." He made the question a statement. "But I'm the one with problems. I might as well lay them out for you now."

"Please." Georges went to fix himself a drink and poured wine for Libby and Susan. She promptly set her glass on the table and, recalling her low tolerance for alcohol, Mike had to smile.

He sobered quickly. "Money," he said shortly. "I'm the one who is worried about money. To put this commission into production, my outlay would be fantastic. For one thing, since we already have work in progress, I'd need more staff. The kind of people I'm talking about are hard to find, and they don't work for peanuts. To be honest, I'm already having cash-flow problems, and I don't think I can swing this until the present job is completed and paid for."

Taking a deep breath, he plowed on, praying his compromise would keep him in the running. "Could you consider waiting that long? Possibly another six months?"

"No." Georges returned to his seat. "Absolutely out of the question."

Mike nodded slowly. He should have known this would be the response. "I'm sorry. In that case I'll try to help you find another—"

"If you recall, finance is my business. I'll deal with the initial capital you'll need to get started with the project."

For a moment, Mike couldn't believe what he'd heard. He smiled and wished he could feel elated. "That's incredibly generous." He slowly returned to his spot beside Susan. "Unfortunately it wouldn't be enough. I'd need the entire cost of the renovation up front."

"I had expected you to say as much," Georges said, smiling slightly. "I have taken certain steps in anticipation that you will agree with what I propose. Of course, it would not be possible for me to loan that kind of capital without some guarantee of return. However, if you would consider my assuming an interest in your business..."

Mike let out a long breath. "You consider Kinnear that good a risk?" This was an option he'd considered and decided not to suggest. He hadn't been able to visualize Georges getting deeply involved with an undertaking over which he'd have so little control.

Georges was smiling. "Aaron and I have been friends for many years. He is already your partner. What is good enough for Aaron is good enough for me. My friend is a shrewd man."

Mike felt Susan move and glanced at her. She'd gripped her ankles and was staring at him. He couldn't read her expression.

"What do you say?" Georges asked.

"We could be looking at two years of work on your boat alone. And, if something were to go wrong and the project were never completed..." How badly he wanted to say yes and grab the chance. But sleep was one of life's necessities, and his would be destroyed if he wasn't totally honest with this man.

"In my business we take risks," Georges said. "We gamble. I believe you are, as they say, a sure thing. I talked with Aaron earlier, and the papers are already drawn up. All we have to do is sign. Do you agree?"

The guy really wanted him to do the work. "Yes...yes, I agree." Excitement sent him pacing before the windows. And each time he turned toward Susan he met her deep frown, her narrowed eyes. Short of making the Duclaux uncomfortable, the reason would have to be explored later.

"Very well. Come into the study and we will sign. Susan, will you witness our signatures?"

"I—" She stood up and wiped her hands on the sides of her shorts. "Perhaps someone else should do it."

Georges smiled disarmingly. "There is no one else, Susan. This should not be done by Libby, I think."

With that, he led the way along the slate-tiled hallway to a room that must once have been a study. The house was always rented out now, and bookshelves lining the walls of the small room were empty.

Papers were produced and spread out on an old, scarred fruitwood desk. And all the time Mike was aware of waves of what felt like anger sweeping in his direction from Susan.

He looked at her sharply. Did she disapprove of her brother-in-law trusting him as much as he obviously did?

"Sign here," Georges was saying, "and here."

Looking at Susan, Mike took the pen Georges held out. She kept her hands behind her back, and her lips formed a hard line.

"This should be an evening for celebration," Georges said as Mike signed where indicated. "I will take Libby for dinner. Both of you will join us?"

"Well—" Mike handed the pen to Susan and kept a finger on the line below his signature.

She wrote rapidly without reading the printed paragraphs above. "I don't think so," she said, dropping the pen and standing back. "It's been a tiring day. I think I'll get to bed early. Don't let me stop the three of you." Her cheeks were pink and she avoided Mike's eyes.

"You and Libby go," he said, a solid knot of disappointment in his throat. "You need time alone. I think I'll go back to *Ma Libby* and make some notes. There's a lot to be done."

"Of course," Georges said, smiling and apparently oblivious to the crackling antagonism in the room.

"If that's all you need?" Susan raised her brows at Georges.

"Yes, thank you, Susan. Rest. Tomorrow you'll feel better."

"I hope so." She didn't close the door as she left.

Susan opened her eyes and looked directly at the moon through thin white draperies.

The sheet was twisted around her body, a sign of how shallow and disturbed her sleep had been.

Something had awakened her.

Her breathing quickened. A noise. A click. She sat up and glanced at the clock on the dresser. Nine. Libby had come at seven to say she and Georges were leaving and that Mike had already set out for Nawiliwili.

An animal must have skittered by outside, or a branch broken. She slipped tentatively down into the bed again. Telling Georges she was tired hadn't been a lie, but it still surprised her that she'd slept so quickly.

She shot up again. This time she knew what she'd heard, or at least where the noise had come from—the little study that shared a common wall behind her bed.

Pausing to pull a robe on over the cotton shift she wore, Susan considered whether she should try to barricade herself into this room and wait for the intruder to leave, or confront him.

Georges's papers were in that room. What if someone involved in the spa deal was trying to steal information?

Her bare feet moved soundlessly over the wooden floors, and the bedroom door opened smoothly beneath her fingers. Several steps took her to the study.

A pale, shifting glow showed beneath the door. Susan

wrapped her robe more tightly around her and calculated the distance to the living room phone and her chances of making it there before she was caught. A rattle sounded, then another. She let out a long sigh and smiled in the darkness. There were French doors off the study. They had been open earlier and must have been left open. They were banging in the breeze, and the light she saw was from the moon.

Scolding herself for being a dolt, she thrust open the door and walked in. Whoever grabbed her was very strong, and there was no light in the room.

The arm around her waist hurt so badly that it knocked the breath from her lungs. Something hard dug into the back of her neck, doubling her over, and in the same instant pressure at the backs of her knees buckled her legs.

Susan dragged in a sobbing breath and flailed. Her mouth was open to scream when her assailant jerked her forehead to the floor.

Words began to pour. French words spoken very rapidly and in a very familiar voice.

"Georges?" Susan managed. She hurt all over.

"Mon Dieu!" A light came on—a flashlight—and she was turned over and hauled to her feet so quickly that she clutched for support. "Susan! I thought… *Mon Dieu!"*

"What are you doing?" she gasped. "Why are you creeping around here? Where's Libby?" Her head pounded.

He wiped a hand across his brow—a hand that held a gun.

Susan recoiled, covering her mouth.

"Libby is at the restaurant." At the little cry that escaped Susan, Georges glanced at her face, then at the gun. "Ah, there is so much, so much. Come, sit down."

Sitting in the living room, she accepted a glass of brandy

and managed two sips before the burning in her nose and throat made her set the drink aside.

"Have I hurt you?" Georges sat beside her, holding her hand while he peered anxiously into her face. "It was reaction. I received a call at the restaurant and I thought it must be them, that they had followed me here."

Susan had begun to calm down. She pushed back her hair and smiled at him. "I'm fine. Probably battered and bruised, but fine."

He shook his head, but she laughed. "I'm not hurt, Georges. But something's very wrong with you. Who are 'they' and why the gun?"

"You should not worry your pretty head."

"Don't use that line on me," she warned him, suddenly tired of the hedging, the suggestions that were never fully explained. "Why is Libby at the restaurant while you're here with a gun?"

"I came to get the gun," he said simply, falling against the back of the couch and lowering his eyelids. "There was a call. Don't ask me how they knew where we were. The same thing. If I don't abandon the spa project…"

She'd never seen him look so tired or so disheveled. His dark hair fell in tangles over his brow, and the white linen shirt he wore was creased and escaping his belt. "If you don't abandon the project? What do they say they will do, then?"

"Make a better job of their next attempt on my life…and take Libby out, too."

Susan heard her own stifled scream.

Georges gathered her into his arms. "I'm sorry. But you asked and I think it's time you knew what's been happening. Libby, too. When I return to the restaurant, I will explain. I've been trying to protect her, but she must now have a chance to say how she thinks I should proceed."

"You said…have they tried?" She knew the answer.

"When I was in Geneva, they attempted to kill me. I forgot something just after I turned the ignition on in my car. When I was a few feet away going back into the apartment, the car exploded. My neck was cut by flying glass. If the bomb hadn't malfunctioned slightly, I'd have died the instant I switched on the car."

Susan pressed her fists into her stomach. She felt close to vomiting. "What do the police say? You did tell them?"

He laughed shortly. "With a car in little pieces all over one of Geneva's main streets, there was no choice. There are no leads and none are expected. These people don't tend to get caught."

"Not even when there are threats made? You know who wants to stop you, surely you can implicate them."

"They are so-called respectable businessmen. They would deny all knowledge of these events." He drank from her glass himself, coughed and pressed the back of his hand to his mouth. "I have many enterprises. Only I am sure this is the one that is responsible for my troubles."

"Then get out of it." Her voice sounded shrill. "It's dangerous and your life is more important. So is Libby's."

A pale line formed around his compressed mouth. "For Libby I may have to. But I detest giving up. Only for her will I back down. Susan—" he turned to her "—I need a promise from you."

"Georges, I can't—"

"Do not argue with me now. I must get back to Libby. It is possible that…that events have been set in motion and that it is too late to change." He inclined his head. "I am, understand, probably being overly dramatic, but still I must say these things. Promise me you will take care of Libby if…if something happens to me."

She couldn't speak. Tears sprang into her eyes, tears of fear.

"Shh," Georges said, ducking his head and smiling. "This will not be necessary, but provisions should always be discussed. Jean-Claude is my executor and would deal with all financial matters. Aaron and Mike also know the possibilities and would be there to support her. Aaron is officially named to advise. But my Libby would need her sister. You promise?"

"Yes." She wanted Libby now, right here where she could be sure she was safe.

Georges stood and slipped the gun into the pocket of his pants.

"Georges!" She leaped up, her heart pounding. "Is something going to happen...here in Hawaii? Should we call the police?"

"No, no." He laughed, and as she saw him relax, her own muscles untensed. "Forgive me for overreacting. I tend to lose my objectivity over only one thing—my dear wife. She is fine and I am fine. The rush to get the gun was a foolish impulse. Go back to bed."

She followed him to the front door. "How long will you be?"

"Not long," he said. His white shirt glimmered in the gloom as he walked away. "I'll see you soon."

The surf was luminous beneath the moon. From the chaise she'd pulled close to the lanai railings, Susan stared down. In the living room a tiny revolving brass clock chimed twelve inside its glass dome.

Where were they?

Fine rain misted. Susan ignored the wet dustings that eluded the dense massing of palm crowns overhead. This place was beautiful, but so isolated. The closest house was several miles away. If she called the police, what could she say? Georges and Libby had probably gone from the restaurant to some club. They were undoubtedly still deep in discussion and trying to unwind at the same time.

"Hi, there."

She jumped. "Mike!" She hadn't heard him come into the house. He would probably hear disappointment in her voice, but she couldn't help it. When Georges had been telling his story, Susan hadn't missed the fact that Mike apparently already knew everything. She resented that, and she resented his not telling her.

"Couldn't you sleep?" He dragged a chair closer to the railing and sat down.

"Something like that." Being touchy with him was pointless when she should be sensible and share her concerns about what had happened tonight.

"Still angry with me?"

She closed her eyes.

"There you go again. Hiding out."

Susan puffed out her cheeks and stared into the night. "I don't know what you're talking about."

"You were angry with Georges's decision about the boat—and investing in my business. Why?"

"It isn't my affair."

"That isn't the issue. Why were you angry?"

"Okay." She gave him her full attention. "I didn't think you should be so quick to let Georges put up so much money."

"Oh." His eyes glinted in the darkness.

"When I first approached you about working for Georges and Libby, you wouldn't give me any kind of answer except that you would only consider dealing with boats you bought yourself."

"I did say that," he said, and Susan didn't miss the dangerous edge in his voice.

"Then you were so relieved when Aaron put more money into the company so that you could keep on being picky about the boats you worked on...one at a time."

"I'm sure you'll get to your point eventually."

Susan plucked at her bathrobe tie. Only hours ago they'd made love and she'd felt closer to him than she ever had to another human being. She still felt close, damn it, but without trust they couldn't have anything together—not even an affair.

"Go on," he prompted.

"Suddenly you're changing all your own rules. Suddenly you can work on a boat you didn't choose, and you can work on two at a time. Why is that?"

He slumped and she saw his shoulders hunch. "Probably because I'm an opportunist, wouldn't you say? I saw Georges Duclaux as an easy mark. I'm going to take his money to make things easier for me, then fiddle around with his commission forever. That must be it, I guess."

"Why did you decide to work for him?"

"You don't trust me." He got up and Susan caught his hand as he started to walk by. "What is it now?"

She'd hurt him. Her impetuousness, her inability to wait and see had made him believe she thought he was dishonest.

He let her hold his hand. "I decided to work for Georges because *Ma Libby* is probably the most beautiful boat I've ever seen. Your brother-in-law has incredible taste."

"I know," she said quietly.

"I'm also glad to have him as a partner. And so is Aaron, evidently."

"I shouldn't have doubted your reasons." She didn't anymore.

"But you did."

And he wasn't going to forget, not yet. "Please don't go away. I need you."

"And I need to walk."

"Please."

He sighed and sat on the edge of his chair again. "What's wrong?"

Hesitantly at first, finishing in a rush, she told him what had happened while he was out. When she finished, he was quiet for a long time.

She couldn't wait any longer. "What do you think?"

"What I've been thinking since the night your boat sank. The Duclaux have big trouble."

Swinging her feet to the ground, Susan scooted closer. "What does my boat sinking have to do with anything?"

"Why do you think she sank?"

"She was holed, I guess."

"How? When was the last time you had her out of the water?" The flat, matter-of-fact way he asked the questions turned her cold.

"She hadn't been out for a while, and I don't know how she was holed. I probably hit a deadhead. What else could have happened?"

"I'm asking you. Wouldn't you have known if you hit something big enough to make the kind of hole it would take to send her down like concrete?"

"Yes," she admitted slowly, starting to feel hot now.

"Libby was supposed to go back for Georges, not you."

"Yes."

"Doesn't that suggest something to you…after what you found out tonight?"

She bowed her head.

"We don't have proof, Susan, and getting any wouldn't be easy, but it could be that the Tolly was deliberately holed. It could have been done just above the waterline so that nothing would happen until the weight of a passenger made her ride lower in the water. Obviously all this was pulled off while you and Libby were at the salon, or the two of you would have gone down on the way from Brown to Friday Harbor. There was enough gas to get you out in the middle of nowhere, then...well, the rest is history. Who knew Libby was supposed to go back alone for Georges?''

"No one...but Georges and me."

"Aaron knew for one, Susan. He told me, and that's why I tried to reach you at the salon. If Aaron knew—and he's obviously not a suspect here—but if he knew and you've forgotten, how many other people might have been aware? How many people know Libby can't swim?''

"I don't know!''

"Couldn't it be that one of Georges's 'friends' decided that getting rid of Libby could throw Georges into enough of a funk to make him drop the spa project? Could it be possible that someone's been watching and waiting for an opportunity to kill her?''

Susan shuddered. She felt sick. "I can't take this in. I won't try.''

"So bury your head. There's probably nothing either of us can do about it, but I'm sure as hell going to try.'' He stood up again. "I'm going to talk to Georges now. Whatever he says, he's got to have some protection, for both of them.''

"He's not here,'' Susan said, utterly miserable.

"Not—'' Mike stood over her. "What the hell do you mean, not here? You said he left to get Libby hours ago. You said he told you they wouldn't be long. When was that?''

The constriction in her throat pulsed. "Around nine-thirty. They haven't gotten back yet."

He tilted his wrist toward the doors. "My God. It's almost one."

"I didn't know what to do."

Mike strode into the house with Susan at his heels—and almost collided with Libby.

"Oh, Libby." Susan rushed to embrace her. "I've been so worried. *We've* been so worried. Are you all right?"

"No," Libby murmured.

When Susan released her, she pushed disheveled hair away from a chalk-white face.

"It's going to be okay," Mike said, holding her arms and easing her to a chair. "We're going to decide what to do. Together we'll work it all through. Wait till Georges gets inside and we'll figure out the next step."

"No."

"Libby, it's all right." Susan knelt beside her, so shaky she could hardly breathe. "Mike's right."

"Georges isn't coming."

"Wait." Mike waved Susan to silence. "Explain that."

"He's gone."

"What do you mean he's gone? You mean he left the restaurant again? You should have waited there for him."

Libby turned anguished eyes up to Mike. "I did wait. He didn't leave again. He got a telephone call at seven-thirty and went into the lobby. He never came back."

12

"Nothing." Mike dropped the telephone receiver back into its cradle. "I only hope the police are taking us seriously."

Susan sent him a warning glare and inclined her head toward Libby, who sat, her eyes closed, in the white wing chair. She'd been there for hours, since the three of them had given up searching for Georges and decided to mount a telephone vigil.

"Why don't you lie down and try to sleep for a while?" Susan said to Libby.

She shook her head. "I want to be awake when he gets back."

Mike automatically put a hand to his stomach. He couldn't shake the conviction that Georges Duclaux wasn't going to walk through that door...ever.

"What time is it?" Susan asked.

He didn't remind her that there was a clock in the room. "Eight."

What she didn't say aloud was conveyed by the message in her troubled eyes. Georges had been missing without trace for almost twenty-four hours. Mike nodded slightly and tried to smile at her. Susan was a gutsy lady. She'd hidden her own fear for Georges's safety and had become a rock of support for her sister.

"Jean-Claude should be here soon," Susan said.

Mike would welcome the nephew's arrival, since he could deal with Georges's affairs until they knew what had happened to him.

Apparently getting over the flu and trying to sleep, Jean-Claude hadn't been reached until early afternoon Washington State time. When Mike finally spoke to him, he'd sounded closer to panic than either Libby or Susan.

"I'm going to lie down," Libby said suddenly. She got up, swayed and caught the arm of her chair.

Susan rushed to her. "I'll take you to your room."

"No, it's okay." Libby straightened. "I've been sitting too long, that's all. I got light-headed. Please stay by the phone. I won't sleep."

Standing behind Susan, Mike watched Libby go. Had she given up on Georges, too?

"I'm going through the grounds again," Susan said. Her hands and arms were already scratched from tearing through dense undergrowth on the old estate.

"You're not going alone." He wasn't plagued by unreasonable fears, but neither was he a fool. If he had his way, Susan would stay where he could see her at all times.

"Someone has to stay by the phone."

"Fine. You stay and I'll go." Although it would be a useless exercise. As Mike had already reminded Susan, the rental car Georges had driven wasn't parked in its space at the gates. She'd insisted it might have been driven away by someone else and Georges left unconscious somewhere nearby.

When he lingered, Susan turned to look at him, the first time she had really looked at him since last night. All the bickering that had passed between them didn't seem to matter anymore.

"Is he dead, Mike?"

"Oh, hell! Come here." He pulled her into his arms and

stroked her hair. Beneath his hands, in the loose cotton shirt and pants she'd been wearing since early morning, she felt small and fragile. "He can't be dead, Susan. He can't."

Her hands stole around him and she held on to his shirt. "So where is he? Mike—" she lifted her face "—I watched him walk away. He said he'd see me soon and—"

"And what?" When he linked his hands around her slender neck, he felt the rapid pulse there. Lying with her, just lying and drawing comfort from each other, would be wonderful.

She rubbed her fingers over his back. "I felt so strange. Not only because of what had just happened and what he'd said, but because there was an atmosphere out there. But maybe I'm only imagining that in retrospect." Her escaping breath was uneven. "There isn't any point looking around outside, is there?"

"I don't think so. But I'll go if you want me to."

"No. I want you here with me." She bit her lip and rested her forehead on his chest. "Yesterday seems so long ago."

"Yes and no." Yesterday was gone but not forgotten, never forgotten. There would, as he'd promised her, be other days for them. "It's too bad we had a misunderstanding last night. We can forget it, can't we?"

She looked at him again, and the slow smile, her own special smile, brought a grin to his lips. "Mike, I do think we've forgotten something."

"Ah." He raised his jaw and laughed. "Oh course. I'm sorry if I did anything to offend you last night."

"You didn't. But I'm sorry I was such a suspicious witch."

He hugged her close, and the instant response in his

loins surprised him. "There we go. Pulled it off again. Boy, are we reasonable."

They stood together for seconds before she said, "I wish something would happen, that Georges would come home, I mean."

A sharp rap on the front door sent them leaping apart. They stared at each other before he strode into the hall and opened the door to be confronted by Jean-Claude Duclaux. The man was pallid with a sheen of perspiration on his brow and upper lip.

"Come in," Mike said, and picked up the single bag that stood on the step. "Libby's lying—"

"I'm here. Jean-Claude. Oh, Jean-Claude." Libby catapulted into his arms, and he staggered but held on. Clearly he wasn't completely recovered from his illness. Mike pitied him.

"Come," Jean-Claude said, and walked, an arm around Libby's shoulders, into the living room. He barely acknowledged Susan as he pressed Libby onto the couch and lifted her feet onto an ottoman. "You will worry about nothing. This has to be a small misunderstanding that will come right. I only wish Georges had listened to me and abandoned the spa. Switzerland needs no more body factories, anyway. These people, they have driven him into hiding. He would go to make sure you are safe, Libby, and that is right. But now we must find him and make sure there is adequate protection for both of you.

He held his mouth open, visibly short of breath. "You will not be concerned. I am here now and I will take care of you, as Georges would wish, until he returns. There is no need for anxiety, I assure you."

If there hadn't been need for concern before, there seemed to be a great deal of need while the man gabbled on, Mike thought. Spineless was the term that came to mind. Spineless but determined to cover up. But Mike was probably being uncharitable.

"Thank you for all you've done," Jean-Claude said, mostly to the air. "Georges will be grateful when I tell him. Ah, such a journey. I was afraid I would not make the connection in Honolulu." He sat down, produced a mangled handkerchief and mopped his good-looking face.

"I'm sorry," Susan said, and caught Mike's eye. The tiny glimmer of mirth that passed between them was irreverent but healing.

"Mrs. Duclaux!"

A voice came from the hall. They'd forgotten to close the door.

Libby raised her face, and the terror in her eyes froze Mike's gut. "Stay put," he said, although only Susan had made a move. She went with him, anyway, ignoring his attempt to wave her behind.

Two policemen stood on the step, both dressed in heavy navy blue uniforms that Mike thought must be unbearably uncomfortable in this climate.

"Mrs. Duclaux?" The older officer, a big handsome man who appeared to be Samoan, looked at Susan. "Are you Mrs. Duclaux?"

"Er, no. Please come in."

The two men took off their caps and went into the living room where Jean-Claude now sat beside Libby and held her hand.

"This is Mrs. Duclaux," Mike said.

Libby seemed to shrink. "You've found him. Where is he?"

"Ma'am, could we ask you some questions?"

"No." Jean-Claude was on his feet, glowering. "Madame Duclaux will answer no questions. She is distraught."

"Yes, sir," the second officer, a thin black man, said. "We understand the pressure the lady's been under. And we wouldn't trouble her if we didn't have to. Did your husband carry his passport with him?"

Libby covered her face and began to cry.

"Damn it," Mike said. "Cut the twenty questions. Come out and say what's on your mind."

"It's okay, Libby," Susan said calmly. "I'll answer what I can. My brother-in-law probably carried his passport with him. Why?"

"We do have a lead," the bigger man said politely. "But it has everyone puzzled and we were hoping you folks could help us decide what steps to take next."

"You will take the necessary steps," Jean-Claude shouted. "I want to see your superior."

"Yes, sir. We'd be glad to take you down to the station with us."

"He can come here."

Mike winced. "We're all a bit overwrought, Officer. I'm sure you understand."

"Of course, sir. We'll make this as short as possible. What we're hoping to determine is where Mr. Duclaux might have gone when he flew out of Kauai last night."

13

Susan had decided that Aaron Conrad's strong, calm presence could be exactly what was needed on Brown Island today. He hopped to the dock, tied up Mike's boat and walked toward her, shading his eyes against the late-afternoon sun.

"Hello." He waved and she waved back.

When the sad and confused company—convinced by the police that there was no point in remaining in Hawaii—had trailed back to the mainland a week ago, Aaron had been there to greet them. Tight-lipped and equally tightly controlled, he'd made it clear that he didn't believe the notion that Georges would find any pressure heavy enough to make him flee his responsibilities. Since that morning—Susan could hardly believe a whole week had passed—Aaron had phoned daily to soothe and encourage Libby.

This afternoon it had been Susan who called Aaron. The incredible tension between Libby and Jean-Claude had become unbearable, and Aaron seemed the logical one to turn to for help.

"So," he said when he stood before her, "perhaps we should talk first."

"Good idea. Let's walk around the point." Susan glanced back at the house. When she left, Jean-Claude had been in the loft and Libby resting. With any luck they'd stay away from each other, at least for a while.

They set off, Aaron with a green windbreaker slung over his shoulder. His lean face showed nothing of what he might be thinking.

He offered her a hand as they climbed over a rock out-cropping above the water. "Mike sends his love."

She was so startled that she almost slipped. "Oh." Just like that he sent his love.

Aaron's expression might have changed a little. She couldn't be certain, but for an instant she thought a gleam lightened his dark eyes. "He said he'll meet you later as planned."

"Yes." She felt herself color. They'd decided, reluc-tantly, not to see each other for a few days after the return from Kauai so that Susan could give all her attention to Libby. But at seven this evening she was to take her new boat to Friday Harbor where Mike would pick her up. They were going to have the much delayed pizza in his office at the boatyard. An assignation. She tipped her heated face up to the breeze. So Aaron knew there must be something more than casual friendship between her and Mike. That shouldn't concern her. They were all grown up enough to handle the truth.

"You and Mike—?" Aaron spread his hands.

"Yes?"

"Nothing, really. I was only going to say you seem very drawn to each other. He's quite a guy."

"I know." Susan hid a smile. Aaron was an unlikely matchmaker. "I hope I didn't call at an inconvenient time."

"Not at all. I'm vacationing in a way—and trying to be useful around the yard while I learn more about the busi-ness. It's fascinating. If I ever wondered why Mike was so keen, I don't anymore."

They were both avoiding the real issue, but Susan didn't

feel ready to jump in. "What made Mike decide to go into boat renovation?" She'd never considered the question before.

"When he was a kid, he spent summers up in Maine with his grandfather. The old man built and maintained fishing boats, and he taught Mike a lot. Ever since then, according to Mike, he's wanted exactly what he's got now."

And he'd tried to walk away from it to please his father. Her heart warmed even more to the man she knew she loved. He'd told her he didn't know what they could have together, but she wasn't willing to give up hoping for a miracle.

Libby must be her only concern for now. "When we go into the house, it would be better if you didn't say I called you."

"Naturally. Can you give me a clearer idea of what's going on?" Aaron held her elbow as they clambered over more rocks. Susan glanced at him. Here was a man who had only one face—the one he presented.

"As you would expect, Libby is distraught. Quietly frantic might be a better description."

Aaron stood still and stared across the water. "I'd do anything to change it all for her. Where the hell is Georges?" He picked up a flat stone and skipped it across the waves. Thrown with too much force, it sank at the first impact. "What are the police doing? What's anyone doing?"

"Searching. Both through official and unofficial channels. Checking airports. Asking thousands of questions. So far the trail ends in San Francisco where he landed. There's no evidence of his having left the United States. Libby thinks he's in Geneva, trying to quietly clear things up there."

"Immigration could trace that."

"Not necessarily if he left with a phony passport, which is Libby's theory. She wants to go to Switzerland herself. So far I've been able to convince her that if Georges is there, he doesn't want her to follow. But every day it gets harder to stop her from rushing after him."

"She can't. If her theory's right, and it could be, she'd be in danger. I won't have that. You'll tell me if she makes definite plans to leave?"

"Immediately." Susan was grateful for his support.

"All right. Now, you hinted at a problem with Jean-Claude."

"We'd better start back." She turned, cramming her hands into the pockets of her baggy gray sweater. "Jean-Claude insists Georges has simply chosen to drop from sight until he can be sure any danger is past. Libby refuses to believe he would worry her like this."

"And what do you believe?" Aaron asked quietly.

Susan looked up into his face. "You and I are with Libby. Georges wouldn't run from anything. And leaving at this point would be running."

"I agree." He whistled tunelessly before adding, "Apart from that, is there any other problem between them?"

"Yes." She nodded emphatically. The house was in view again and her stomach turned over. "Jean-Claude says that in Georges's absence, all business decisions are his."

"Isn't that true?"

"Yes," she agreed unwillingly. "But he's trying to countermand some of Georges's decisions, and Libby's angry. She says Georges will be angry too when he gets back."

"What kind of things is he countermanding?"

"The famous spa project, of course." A wave crashed in and they both jogged farther inland. "He says, and I can't entirely blame him, that he isn't prepared to take Georges's place in the hot seat with this one and he's getting them out."

"And Libby doesn't like that?"

"She hates it. She's a fighter, Aaron, and she's loyal. I'm not sure what's right. How could I be? But while she's under so much other pressure, I just wish she didn't have to be warring with Jean-Claude."

"Let's go in," he said. "Stop worrying. It'll be okay. I'll make sure of that. By the way—" he inclined his head "—why not come back to Friday Harbor with me? Mike can run you home later."

"He won't want to come all the way."

"Yes, he will. He said so. I should have mentioned it as soon as I arrived." He gave one of his rare smiles, a smile that deepened the lines that outdoor living had etched around his eyes and mouth. Aaron Conrad was too good to be on the loose.

"Well..."

"He said he doesn't want you on the water alone at night. Does that convince you?"

They reached the path. "Maybe I should call him and postpone this meeting until we can do it in the daytime."

"No!" He shook his head. "Mike would never forgive me. He'd think I said something to put you off."

Not that she really had any intention of not going. She'd been missing Mike all week and counting the hours since his call of yesterday when he said it was time she got away for a while.

"I'll come with you," she said, opening the door to the house.

A few steps into the living room, Susan halted, holding a finger to her lips. Raised voices came from the kitchen.

Aaron closed the door softly and stood beside her. He crossed his arms and frowned at his shoes.

"We should back out of the Kinnear deal."

Susan flinched at the harsh tone of Jean-Claude's voice.

"Never," Libby said, her voice raised but unsteady. "You're behaving as if Georges were dead."

Susan took a step forward, but Aaron put a hand on her shoulder and shook his head.

"I am a businessman. And I am looking after your estate as Georges asked me to do."

"Stop it. Georges will be back soon and he won't want any changes."

Susan tried to twist away. Aaron pulled her back. His mouth was a grim line.

"Anyway," Libby said with shaky defiance, "the papers Georges drew up have already been sent to our lawyers. And I instructed Mike to go ahead with arrangements to have the boat moved here."

"You—" There was a pause. "You took it upon yourself to interfere?"

"Georges asked me to make sure...if he couldn't. At the restaurant he made me promise. It was important to him and I did it."

There was a sound of something hard hitting another hard surface. "*Sacre bleu!* I will not have interference. These things are not for you to interfere with. Georges would not want it. That was why he made sure I was prepared to take over from him. You...you...this Kinnear will get a very large sum of money. Do you understand? And if he does not complete the work, he will still have that money. Ah, but I should have made sure such a mistake was never made."

"It wasn't a mistake." Libby's voice rose. "Georges wants that boat, for himself and for me."

"Foolishness."

"I think you've said enough. Georges's estate is just that—his. Because you're his brother's son, he treats you as if you were his own. You know how much you mean to Georges. I can't believe you're behaving like this."

The thud came again, and Susan winced, wondering if her tile counters were being destroyed. "Libby, I do not like to resort to this," Jean-Claude said. "I have no alternative. You mention my father. Do you know how he died?"

"We don't have to talk about things that must be painful."

"He was, like Georges, very talented and shrewd. After my grandmother's death, each son had an extensive inheritance. My father was enormously successful. But something went wrong. A few bad deals on a large scale and he was faced with professional ruin."

"Jean-Claude—"

"*Non*. This does not hurt me now. My father could not confront failure. As I am sure Georges has told you, my father, Georges's brother, took his own life."

Susan noted the omitted mention of jealousy on the part of Jean-Claude's father toward his wife. She rubbed her eyes, praying for all this to be over.

"I'm so sorry," Libby said. "I wish I could have met him. Georges always speaks so well of Henri."

"The point is that you cannot continue to hide your head, Libby. Georges and my father were of—how do they say?—the same cloth? This will be painful, but it is my theory that Georges may have gone the way of his brother. He may have committed suicide."

In the silence that followed Susan met Aaron's eyes and

encountered dark rage that shocked her already reeling brain. His hand dropped from her shoulder.

"Jean-Claude!" He strode into the kitchen, bumping furniture as he went. "What the hell do you think you're saying? What are you trying to do to Libby?"

Susan, a step behind, no longer cared whether anyone discovered she had asked Aaron to come. "Don't listen to him, Libby." She gathered her sister into her arms. Libby showed the ravages of little sleep. Her clothes hung loosely on her body.

"Do not intrude here," Jean-Claude said.

"Georges Duclaux has been my friend for many years. He isn't a man who takes shortcuts...out of anything." Aaron went to Libby and stroked back her hair with one hand while he tipped up her chin with the other. "Jean-Claude is worried, too, Libby. He doesn't know what he's saying."

"I know exactly what I am saying. But I am glad you are here, because you might as well hear what I'm thinking. And I intend to act upon it. There will be changes made."

Libby leaned against Aaron, and he rubbed her back.

"Kinnear is your friend," Jean-Claude continued. "Your friend and your partner. His company is your company. It has not been doing too well, eh? But Kinnear knows that my uncle, although shrewd, is also a romantic. I am not."

"What the hell are you implying?" Aaron eased Libby away from him. "Georges spoke to me about what he intended to do. It was his idea, not Mike's, and as far as I'm concerned, the decision is sound. Mike has never failed to deliver on anything he undertook."

"Perhaps he had never been in financial difficulty before."

"Damn you."

"It is unfortunate Georges did not talk to me."

Aaron took a step toward the other man. "He tried to. Evidently you were already nursing your flu and had the phones turned off here."

Jean-Claude shrugged elaborately. "All of this is of no importance. I am in control and, in that capacity, I will make all business decisions."

"On my behalf," Libby said. "And only until Georges gets back."

"As you say." Jean-Claude bowed slightly. "Until Georges...gets back."

Mike stopped his truck at the top of the driveway to his house. "Are you sure you don't want to join us for pizza?" he asked Aaron.

"Even I know the theory of three," Aaron said, jumping from the cramped cab. "Anyway, my buddy Anne and I have a Nintendo date."

"Nintendo?" Susan couldn't visualize Aaron peering at a screen and madly pressing buttons.

"I'm going to save the princess tonight," he replied, chuckling as he walked away.

"He really gets along well with Anne," Mike said, reversing and driving back the way they'd come.

"Sounds like it."

After the showdown, Jean-Claude had gone to his rooms, announcing he wouldn't be down again until morning. Libby had insisted she was going to be fine and that Susan should keep her date with Mike. On the trip over and while they'd waited for Mike to drive into Friday Harbor, Aaron had persuaded Susan to tell Mike nothing of what had been said—at least for a while.

"You're quiet," Mike said.

"I'm thinking," she said honestly.

When he looked at her, the dashlight turned his eyes gleaming green. "Are you okay? It's got to be tough."

"It is. Every time the phone rings Libby almost faints. She won't eat and can't sleep. Mike, I can't take all of this in."

"Neither can I." He dimmed his headlights for an oncoming car. Rain began to slash across the windshield. "But I did have another theory. What if he didn't leave Kauai alone? What if he was kidnapped?"

"Oh, my God!" Susan let her head fall against the seat. "It happens all the time, doesn't it?"

"Yup. And sometimes it takes a while for the kidnappers to make a move."

Kicking off her shoes, she pulled her feet beneath her. "We've all got to hang on, for Libby's sake. If only Jean-Claude—"

He cocked his head. "What about Jean-Claude?"

"Um, if only he wasn't so upset, too. It doesn't help." It also wouldn't help to inflame Mike with the suggestions that had been made this afternoon.

"Hold your hat," Mike said, cranking the wheel hard right and turning onto the bumpy track that led to the yard.

Susan was jiggled from side to side until they drew up in front of the workshop. She felt suddenly and ridiculously awkward. They were coming here to be alone. They both knew as much and so did at least Aaron, since Mike had made a point of telling him where they could be reached in case of an emergency.

"Here we are."

"Yes." She slipped her feet into her shoes.

"Wait in the truck while I turn on some lights."

She remembered something. "Mike, we didn't pick up the pizza. We'd better run into town. Are you hungry?"

"Not especially."

"Me, too. We could eat it there. Then it wouldn't be so bad getting back to Brown afterward."

"I said I *wasn't* particularly hungry." He slid his elbow onto the back of the seat and faced her in the darkness. "And I'm not in any hurry for you to go back to the island. Are you?"

She swallowed. "Libby might need me."

"If she does, she'll call Aaron and he'll call us. That was the reason I gave him for us deciding to come here for the evening. So we'd be easy to reach. Does that make you feel better?"

"I feel fine." She felt like a jumping bean.

"Good. Do you still want to go into town? We could notify Aaron from there." Only the glint of his eyes and teeth were clearly visible. His big body was a dark shadow, and she could smell the faint sea and pine scent of him.

"Go put on some lights. I'm ready for some coffee." And for some of his undivided attention. Please let this be a special time. Please let her manage not to say all the wrong things.

"Great. I've got cheese and crackers and some smoked salmon. We won't starve."

After what felt like scant seconds, he was back and a warm glow showed in the upper-story windows. Mike opened the cab door and helped her down. "Run," he said, rushing her through the rain. When he put an arm around her waist to lead her through the workshop and upstairs, the feel of him was so sweetly familiar her legs began to weaken.

The office, with its comfortable furnishings, was inviting. Susan avoided looking at the bed.

"Is it warm enough in here?" Mike raked back his hair and shook his arms to dislodge raindrops from his blue V-neck sweater. "I can turn up the heat." He wore nothing underneath the sweater, and her eyes were drawn to the gilded hair that showed at his neck.

"I'm not cold, thanks." She wore a heavy black cardigan over a white silk blouse and black pants. "I could make us some coffee, though." Anything to bridge the discomfort of these moments.

Mike rested his weight on one leg and showed no sign of moving. "Okay. If you need water, it's in the bathroom. Through there." He indicated a door behind the railing that ran around the open staircase.

"I...do you want coffee, Mike?"

"No." Slowly he extended a hand and touched her face. With one finger he made an outline from her temple to the point of her chin. "I've missed you. I'm never going to forget that beach...that beach with you." The fingertip continued sweeping down her neck, tracing the lapel of her blouse all the way to the top button between her breasts. He dropped his hand and left her tingling and bereft.

"This seems so calculated," she said, unable to meet his eyes.

"It is, Susan. But that doesn't make it wrong."

"Doesn't it? Not even if we're like two animals driven by instinct and a need for gratification?"

He rubbed a hand around his neck. "Do you think that's all it is with us?"

"Is it?"

"Not for me. But I can't make you believe that."

He could. With a few words he could take away the hint of a grubby feeling that clung to what should be beautiful. "I..." Careful. One wrong word could send him running and leave her feeling like a fool. "You're a special person to me, Mike. You'd have to be, or there could never be anything between us.''

When he didn't answer, she turned away and went to look out the rain-spattered window. But all she could see was a reflection of the room and of the man behind her. She glanced briefly at herself, at her wide dark eyes, her pale face. Mike moved close.

''This has been a hard week for me,'' he said, dropping a kiss on the back of her neck. ''I've got to be honest, Susan. I'm having difficulty confronting what I think I feel for you.''

Her head automatically bent forward, and his mouth brushed over her sensitive skin, nuzzled beneath her collar, trailed to the dip beneath an ear and made her shudder. She dared not speak. If she did, she might ask what he thought he felt, and she wasn't ready for the possible answer.

Mike folded his arms around her and pulled her against him. ''Have you...have you done any thinking about us?''

Her laugh erupted before she could hold it back. ''What do you think? I'm out of my mind with worry about what's happened to Georges, but you're in there, too, Mike, all the time.''

''And what have you been thinking? Apart from that I'm special to you?''

Oh, no, she wasn't walking in where he didn't have the courage to tread. ''Probably the same kind of things as you.'' Very doubtful, but the best she could manage at short notice.

He sighed into her hair and kissed her ear, the side of her face.

Susan rested her head on his shoulder and closed her eyes. She ached inside, trembled with longing.

Mike shifted, spread his hands over her breasts, and Susan moaned. This was the hunger she'd felt, a hunger for what she already knew he could create in her.

He rubbed his palms back and forth over her stiffened nipples. "It frightens me," he said, a break in his voice. "The questions crowd in. And I don't have answers to what's going to happen between us next week or next month."

And neither did she, but she did recognize the basic cause of his agitation: fear of a commitment that could turn sour on him. And she was helpless to convince him that he had nothing to fear from her. He had to make that jump in trust himself. For now, they were reacting to strong physical attraction...but that wasn't all, not for Susan.

Threads of heat shimmered from points beneath his hands to her center. Twisting in his arms, she clasped her hands behind his neck and studied his face. "I love looking at you."

"Ditto," he said, looking at her mouth. Very slowly he bent his head until their lips met and parted. His tongue made a gently intimate foray to meet Susan's. He groaned deep in his throat and twisted his head over hers more and more forcefully. Between the deep thrusting of his tongue he drew back to nip at her lips, sucking, drawing them between his own, moving on to press moist little imprints on every exposed inch of her face and neck and below, into the dip between her breasts. Swiftly he undid her blouse buttons and lavished attention on the pale flesh above her white lawn camisole.

"Oh, Susan," he said against her skin, pushing her breasts up beneath the soft, intricately tucked wisp of fabric. "We have to have each other, don't we?"

She couldn't answer and he didn't seem to notice. He inflamed her, turned her into a primitive thing unable to differentiate between body and mind. Already the dark, tight places of her body were ready for him.

Mike stood back and turned her toward the window once more. "You are very beautiful, and very sexy," he murmured. "I could make love to you forever."

Standing behind her, he pulled his sweater over his head. She watched his tapered body flex with the raising of his arms. Mesmerized, she crossed her arms, unable to look away, not wanting to.

Next, keeping his eyes on hers in the window, he unsnapped his jeans and stepped out of them, taking off his briefs at the same time. A distinct pattern of hair spread wide across his flat nipples and diminished to a darker line at his taut belly, to flare again where his body betrayed his need.

Susan's breathing quickened. He wasn't ready for more than this wild sexual attraction they had for each other, might never be ready for more. But she wasn't strong enough not to take whatever he had to offer. She desired him, but more, she loved him.

He was slipping the cardigan from her shoulders, tossing it aside, pulling off her blouse. It caught at the wrists, and she laughed at his frown of concentration as he lifted her hand to work a button loose from the wrong side.

"Mmm," he said against her ear. "I like to hear you laugh. You're much too serious."

"Life's serious."

"It doesn't have to be all the time." The cuffs undone, he let the blouse fall and ran his hands back and forth over her shoulders, planting kisses on vulnerable skin. Reaching around her, he unbuttoned and unzipped her pants, and she stepped out of them, kicking aside her shoes.

Going to his knees, Mike stripped off her panty hose, kissing ticklish spots all the way from the legs of her

French-cut white lace panties to her ankles, while she wiggled and made useless grabs for him.

When she tried to turn around, Mike stopped her, held her fast with his big hands spread wide over her hips. He pressed his mouth into the dimples at the base of her spine, ran his fingers around to lace over her ribs. "You are lovely."

She began to slip, to buckle. "So are you."

His laugh was hoarse. "I've never been called lovely before."

Susan knelt in front of him, his knees between her thighs, and Mike layered her body to his. Against her bottom she felt his rigid arousal, but he wasn't hurrying, wasn't neglecting a millimeter of her.

"I've never felt…this… Being with you is something," he finally finished. "You're new somehow. Does that make sense?"

"Not really." Unless he was suggesting she seemed inexperienced, which she was by most people's standards. "I never knew… Great sex was only something I'd read about before you."

"Good," he said, sounding supremely satisfied. "We'll keep it that way."

And what did that mean? What was he almost saying but managing to hold back at the last moment?

In a quick move he brushed the camisole straps from her shoulders and bared her breasts, supported their weight. His thumbs worked the magic she longed for, flicking back and forth while she arched her back.

"Yes," Mike whispered. "Yes, Susan. Let yourself go." While he stroked he bent her over his arm to kiss her aching flesh, and she managed to slip the tiny satin buttons undone and wiggle free of the camisole.

She reached for him, and again he turned her firmly

away. Now she sat on his lap, her thighs astride his, separated from his penetration only by a scant piece of lace.

"Let me hold you," she gasped. He had begun to move, lifting his hips, pressing against her until she raged to be free of the final barrier between them.

Finding her hand, he guided it back to encircle him, and his gasp jerked against her neck. Holding him, she gained confidence, caressed him boldly until his breath came in bursts. Mike pressed his palms to her breasts, circled with exquisite slowness, played there with one hand while he sought the pulsing spot that brought a cry to her lips.

Her release was instant and she leaned against him, shuddering, embarrassed. "Mike, I—"

"It's okay." He laughed. "It's great, darling." And he entered her, driving from behind in a way that thrilled and shocked her. "Anything's okay between people who love each other. Let go, Susan."

She moved with him, her breasts tender in his hands, her skin bathed in perspiration, until she fell forward onto her hands, panting, hearing his sobbing triumph at the climax that took them both.

In the seconds that followed they slipped facedown, Mike cradling her beneath him until they lay huddled together on the rug.

"My, God. I..." Mike rolled her over until she rested on top of him. Susan, her eyes wide open, pressed her mouth against his salty skin.

He couldn't say it, couldn't say he loved her. A few minutes earlier he'd told her anything was right between people who loved each other. But he couldn't say the words—not exactly. She squeezed her eyelids together against stinging tears.

"We're going to freeze down here," he said, sitting, then kneeling and getting to his feet with Susan in his arms. He carried her to the bed, threw back the covers and slid her in, stretching himself beside her before pulling blankets and quilt back in place.

"This wasn't meant for two people," Susan managed.

"Depends upon the two people," Mike said. "With you it's plenty big enough." They were crushed, damp skin to damp skin, into the narrow bed. Susan wished they'd never have to move again.

The loving would become as necessary to her as air, Mike had told her. Love or sex? If she wanted him, she'd have to learn not to want more than he could give.

His breathing became regular, and she tried to shift. Being with him like this and knowing she had no right to more made lead of her heart.

"What is it?" he asked, making her jump.

"Nothing."

"Women," he said, sighing. "Nothing means something every time."

"You seem to have a vast experience with women."

"No, not vast. But substantial. I'm not a kid."

She opened and closed her mouth, stunned at his bluntness. "Oh."

"Sorry. I'm not the king of tact. Tell me what's on your mind."

"You'll only be angry."

"Try me."

She tilted back her head to see his face. "I didn't think about pregnancy while we were making love. But it comes back again, Mike. I can't help it. I don't expect you ever to understand how I feel, but that's the way it is. For me the loving would mean so much…it already means so much. I only wish something so beautiful could result in a child."

He didn't sigh or grit his teeth or look angry. "I know

you do. All I can tell you is that I wish it wasn't that way with you." He paused, seemed to consider what to say next. "You haven't mentioned the adoption lately."

And he probably hoped she'd given up. "Things have been so hectic. I have a form at home to fill out and get back, but it's proving a problem for me."

"Why?"

If she told him, what would he say? She swallowed with difficulty. "It's being suggested that I find a cosponsor, someone who would agree to be available for the child if something happens to me."

"I see."

"It would kind of be like cosigning a loan for someone who would never default. Completely risk-free. Only I don't know who to ask. I thought of Libby or Georges, but…"

"Mmm. Not in the near future."

"No."

"A child isn't a loan, Susan. A child is forever, for better or worse." He was on his back, a hand beneath his head, staring at the ceiling. "Maybe you should put the adoption on the back burner until you've got the rest of your life straight."

The suggestion didn't rankle, but it did make her curious. "How would I do that? I thought it was straight."

"Your business is in good shape, and your finances from what you've told me. Libby and Georges's trouble will only be a temporary part of things for you. What you need is to be able to feel like a complete woman. Complete without a child first."

She ran a finger across his mouth, and he gently caught it between his teeth.

"You aren't telling me how to do that." Or was he?

"A man you could count on would be a good start.

Someone who isn't afraid to love you. You deserve that. Then it might be time to consider taking responsibility for another life.'' He moved her hand beneath the covers and trapped it against his chest. "Or it might prove to you that a child isn't what you need in order to feel whole. Aren't you tired?''

"Yes.'' A heavy weight seemed to press in on her chest—disappointment.

"Close your eyes and rest.''

"Yes.'' And within seconds his even breathing let her know he was asleep.

He thought she needed a man who could love her without reservation. But he'd made it clear he couldn't be that man.

14

Molly poked her head around the edge of the mirror where Susan was working. "There's someone here who insists you and only you will do, Susan."

"When I finish Mrs. Abrams, I'm on break." She was aware she sounded belligerent, but her feet ached and she wanted to be alone. "I do have a free appointment in an hour." She smiled at Mrs. Abrams, the wife of a local fisherman, and sprayed the woman's soft gray hair.

"Have it your way." Molly waggled her head. "What the boss wants, the boss gets. Go away little girl. Ms. Ackroyd doesn't talk to children, particularly if they belong to the man she's crazy about."

"Molly!" Susan stopped her incorrigible employee as she turned away. "Are you telling me Anne Kinnear is here?"

"Oh, you are quick. That's why you're the boss."

Susan favored Molly with an exasperated glare. "Tell Anne I'll be right there."

Moments later she found Anne sitting in a chair near the reception desk, leafing through magazines. When Susan approached, the girl promptly dropped the book and stood. "Hi, Susan. I've got to go back to school on Tuesday. D'you suppose you could do something with my hair? And my makeup? D'you do things with makeup, as well?"

She looked around the salon while Susan recovered from the rush of conversation.

"I can," she said cautiously.

"Dad said it was all right if I came." Anne worked a wallet from the back pocket of her jeans...clean jeans with no holes, worn with a too-large but equally clean and cheerful yellow sweatshirt and flat black shoes over yellow socks. Susan entirely approved of the attractive outfit. She concentrated on Anne's hair. Something was definitely afoot here.

"See, I grew it some." Anne presented an accumulation of about three-quarters of an inch of shiny blond hair on the previously shaved side of her head. "Could you do something with it?"

Susan realized her hands were tightly wound together and deliberately dropped them to her sides. Mike had taken her back to Brown Island at two in the morning, and there could have been no question of his not sensing her withdrawal from him. When he asked to see her again—tonight—she'd said she didn't think so, that she wanted time to think. He'd kissed her at the door to her house, but he must have felt her lack of response.

"Can you, Susan?"

She met the girl's eyes and swallowed. So like Mike and so much in need of that thing that scared him to death—unconditional love. "You bet I can. Let's wash it first and I'll tell you an idea I have."

Beneath the harsh salon light, with her face turned up over the washbasin, Anne's skin was translucent, her neck that of a slender, vulnerable child. Susan longed to gather the fragile body into her arms.

"We even it up," Susan said, wrapping a towel around Anne's hair. "Then we cut the top to spike. You could leave it soft, or use gel sometimes. On you, with those great cheekbones, it'll look terrific. But it's up to you," she added. "If that doesn't sound good, say so."

"Could you show me a picture or something?" the girl asked dubiously.

Susan found one.

"That's totally cool!"

Susan almost whooped at Anne's delighted reaction. "Totally cool" was probably the highest compliment Anne could make.

While she worked Anne talked—and Susan got mixed messages.

"So this time Mom's really gonna use the money Dad sent to come and see me. She promised she would. Dad'll get the check for her today, if he remembers."

Which meant the check Susan had seen was one of many.

When Susan didn't answer, Anne continued, "She would have come all those other times, but it's hard trying to be a singer, and she kept needing help with her rent and stuff. You know how it is."

"Sure." She could imagine, even if she hadn't had the experience.

"Dad's really ratty today."

A puddle of silence fell and, as could be anticipated, there was a lull in activity on all sides. Susan's watchdogs were on alert. She swept a narrow-eyed stare around the room, and dryers sprang to life again.

"He was real cheerful when he went to meet you last night." Innocence had never looked this innocent. "Uncle Aaron said the two of you get along, um, swimmingly?"

Susan smothered a smile. "Is that a fact? Was that because you asked him?"

"Well, sort of. I like what you're doing to my hair. I'm getting too old for that other stuff, anyway."

"Yes," Susan said, silently offering a prayer of thanks-giving.

"Anyway. Last night Aaron said Mike was probably going to bring you to our house tonight. He said he was gonna rent a movie I could watch—" she curled her top lip disdainfully "—'cause he still thinks I'm a kid. And one for the two of you. For after I went to bed, Aaron said. Only now Mike says you can't come and he's being awful to everyone."

Another little matchmaker. This one really puzzled Susan. What did Anne want? On the one hand she gave out constant messages that good old mom was still in the picture. But then Anne also seemed to want her father and Susan to be an item. Maybe Anne had really given up on her mother and father getting back together. Of course, if she had, that didn't mean she wouldn't still want to see her mother.

"What do you think?" Susan asked, finishing with the scissors and running gel through the girl's hair.

"Yeah," Anne almost whispered, her eyes wide with awe. "Wait till the others see this. Can you come over tonight, after all?"

Susan made much of sterilizing her comb and scissors. "I'd like to," she told Anne. "But I'm needed at home." That wasn't a lie. Libby was falling deeper and deeper into depression with each passing day.

"Sure." Anne's mouth turned down at the corners.

Susan went to the drawer of cosmetics Molly sold as a sideline to her nail business. "I'll pay you back, okay?"

Molly nodded, looking serious. Clearly she was over-hearing and analyzing every word that passed between Anne and Susan.

"You have perfect skin," Susan said, applying the light-est coat of pink blush. "Best not to clog it up with heavy makeup. A little eye shadow, some mascara and lip gloss and you'll be a stunner.''

"A stunner?'' Anne frowned, wrinkling her nose.

Current lingo was beyond Susan. "You'll like the way you look,'' she said, and proceeded to use soft brown shading above the eye and a thin coat of glossy mascara. She finished with a touch of peachy pink lip gloss and stood back to assess the result.

Jeff came behind the chair and whistled. "You're something,'' he said, and Anne turned a bright shade of pink.

When Anne got up from the chair, she opened the wallet and slid out a fat wad of bills. Susan winced. Mike couldn't get the hang of when enough was enough.

"Put that away,'' she told Anne. "This is my going-back-to-school treat.''

"No. I've got to pay. Dad said so.''

"And I'm telling 'Dad' that looking at you today is all the payment I need. Can you remember that?''

"Of course.'' For an instant Anne looked offended, but only for an instant. "Susan, is it your break now?''

The plaintive, tentative approach twisted Susan's heart. She glanced at Molly, who nodded. Molly would pinch-hit if Susan were to be a few minutes late for her next appointment. "Sure it's my break. How about an ice cream downstairs?''

"Okay. My treat,'' Anne agreed with old-fashioned politeness that tightened Susan's stomach a little more.

Seated close to the café windows because the wind was chill, they licked gigantic strawberry cones in companionable silence until Anne ran her tongue all the way around hers and propped it between both hands. "I wanted to ask what you think.''

"Shoot." Susan wasn't hungry, but she was loving this moment of closeness with the child.

"I've noticed something about Mike. I think it means he really likes you. See, when he's gonna meet you or something—like when he knew you were going to Hawaii, too—he's really happy and that makes it pretty good at home." She scrunched her face conspiratorially. "Connie's been trying real hard to do things right and everything, and if Mike's in a good mood, he says nice things to her and she's happy, too. But when Mike doesn't see you for a while or something goes wrong—I mean when you have to change a date, like tonight—Mike stops talking and everything gets like it used to be when Mom... It gets quiet and kind of scary."

"What makes it scary?" Susan asked gently. She pointed to drips down the sides of Anne's cone, and the girl licked at them disinterestedly. "What, Anne?"

She shrugged and kept her shoulders drawn up. "I don't know. Like Mike might go away, too, I guess. I don't know."

To Susan's horror tears gathered along the girl's lids and her pale blue eyes shimmered. "Oh, Anne, your dad would never leave you. He loves you too much."

Anne half turned her face away, and huge tears overflowed to course down her cheeks. She licked one from the corner of her mouth. "Mom loves me, too."

Bright pink ice cream drizzled over her fingers.

The footsteps Mike heard on the office stairs were unmistakable. His spirits leapt. Even when he had a seemingly insurmountable problem, as he definitely had this afternoon, the thought of seeing Susan sent his pulse thrumming into his ears. Perhaps if he talked to her about what he'd discovered, she'd say something—anything—to help him find a solution.

He got up and went to meet her at the top of the stairs. She evaded his arms and went to take up a position by the couch. In the red jumpsuit he liked so much, she looked irresistible—as long as he avoided the combative glare she aimed in his direction.

"I'm glad to see you," he said while his hopes sank. "You'll never know how glad."

"I'm not here to talk about that. Anne came to see me."

"She said she'd like to have you do her hair, not that I know what you could do at this point."

Susan came toward him, and he kept his hands at his sides with difficulty. Last night, only hours ago, they'd made love in this room. He wasn't ever going to forget it, and neither was she, regardless of what was on her mind today.

"Anne looks wonderful. She's very pretty, now that she's figured out that looking like a wild mess isn't going to get her any more of the attention she needs than making the best of herself will."

He sat on the edge of his desk. "Susan, I'm not following you. What's wrong?"

"How often do you send Frances money?"

He blinked. So that was it. "Frances isn't important to me anymore, not the way you think." The idea of Susan feeling jealous of Frances wasn't without appeal.

"I don't care how important she is to you. I just want to figure out how often Anne gets her hopes up that her mother will come and see her, only to be disappointed—and be made more frightened."

"I don't get this." Pain gnawed between his shoulders. He went to a love seat and sank down. "And I've got enough trouble for one day.'' His father had admitted to being deep in debt from gambling losses.

''Too much trouble to care that a wonderful little girl who's your responsibility is miserable?''

What was it now? Was Susan nagging him about Connie's shortcomings, or suggesting he didn't spend enough time with his daughter? Well, he was doing his best and he couldn't do any more, not in the foreseeable future.

''Are you listening to me?''

He rocked his head from side to side. ''Come sit with me. I need you.''

Susan sat...on the couch opposite. ''Anne misses her mother. Do you know that?''

He nodded. ''That's natural.''

''You aren't listening to me. Think about Anne. If you want to help Frances, do it without giving Anne reason to hope her mother's coming home. And why don't you send Frances a ticket to get here, for God's sake?''

''I have.'' He was so weary. ''She sold it.''

''Oh, no.'' Susan tilted her face up to the ceiling. ''I want you to listen to me and then think about what I say. Anne is trying to find ways to make you happy. How does that make you feel?''

''Glad someone is. She's a sweet kid.''

She got up. ''You don't get it at all. She's trying to make you happy, and if being nice to me will help, she's willing to give it a try, even though she adores her mother.''

Mike shook his head. ''Anne does like you. She isn't pretending.'' Even as he spoke his jaw tightened with apprehension. ''Anne's fine. We talked this morning and she was absolutely fine.''

''That's what she wants you to believe.'' Susan's mouth turned down sharply and quivered. ''Your daughter is afraid of rocking the proverbial boat and doing something that'll make you mad. Her mother supposedly loved her, but when Frances got unhappy she went away and left her little girl. Anne says she can see you're unhappy. Are you getting the message now?''

Mutely he shook his head again. He did get the message. He just wished Susan was wrong.

"Anne's scared, Mike. Scared you'll leave her, too."

An aching in his chest reminded him to breathe. "I'd never do that. She knows I wouldn't."

"No, she doesn't. Experience has taught her that you can't trust people who say they love you not to change their minds."

"But I never would." Could he have been so preoccupied with his own problems that Anne thought he didn't care about her?

Susan wrapped her arms around her middle and leveled a stare at him. "You of all people should understand why she's afraid to trust. She had the best teacher in the world—her father."

"You're not being fair. I've never given Anne any reason to doubt me. She's the center of my life." And so was Susan. Mike stared at her. It was happening. No, it already had. Regardless of his resolutions, he'd lost the fight not to love this woman. A sheen glittered in her eyes. "What is it, Susan?" She was going to cry.

"Nothing. Not a thing. I'm glad to hear that at least one person means something to you. Make sure she knows it, Mike, before it's too late." She jumped up. "People need to know they matter—really matter."

By the time he could make his legs move, she'd already run downstairs. He reached the bottom himself in time to see her yellow Volkswagen, its top down, swing wildly in reverse and head for the gates. Susan's black curls, whipped by the wind, shone in the pale sunlight.

"Everything okay, boss?" Rudy called from behind him.

"Everything's wrong," he responded.

Back in his office Mike stretched out on the bed. He turned onto his side, pulled down the quilt and smoothed the spot where Susan's head had rested.

He'd figure out what to do about Lester. And he'd be fully there for Anne, make sure she understood that he was the one person in her life who would never willingly disappoint her. What he couldn't figure out was what to do about Susan. She wanted things he didn't want—or was pretty sure he didn't—and she chided him, criticized him regularly.

Anne's teacher in the no-trust department was an expert, Susan had reminded him. And she'd been right. He wasn't sure he could trust enough to make another commitment.

But he was sure of one thing: whether he wanted to be or not, he was in love with Susan Ackroyd.

"I'm going. You can't stop me."

Susan looked helplessly at Aaron, who held Libby's arm while she railed at him. This scene had been in progress when Susan returned home after leaving Mike.

"Libby," Aaron said very gently, "don't you want to do whatever Georges would want?"

"Yes." She wiped tears from her cheeks and sniffed. "He's in trouble, I tell you, and I'm going to help him."

"Where exactly are you going?" Jean-Claude asked coolly from his perch on the window ledge in Susan's living room.

Susan tried to remind herself that he was only trying to

be logical, but his manner, the quick way he'd slipped into Georges's shoes, irked her.

Libby approached him, her face set. "I'm going home— to Geneva. That's where he is."

"I think you are not," Jean-Claude said. "I would be failing Georges if I did not make sure you were safe. If I did not believe it important to stay here and protect certain...interests—" he cast a significant glance at Aaron "—I would go. Whatever happens, I will not be able to put off being there much longer. Someone in authority must be present in Geneva."

"I must go, I tell you," Libby said. She twisted away from Aaron's restraining hand. "The police are doing nothing. Nor are the private investigators we hired."

"Libby," Aaron said, "they're doing far more than you could. Would it make you feel better if I flew over and checked out the apartment? I could go to Madonna di Lago and look there, too."

"This is not your affair," Jean-Claude snapped.

"On the contrary, as we both know, Georges named me as an adviser to Libby, should that become necessary."

"Please, let's not argue," Susan said, unable to bear the dissension a moment longer. "It's Georges that matters here. Georges and Libby."

"Agreed," Jean-Claude said.

Aaron reddened and went to cross his arms on the mantel. "This is hell," he muttered, and rested his brow on his hands.

Susan caught sight of a white launch approaching the dock. A uniformed man stood on the foredeck. Her heart stopped, then bounded. Sheriff. She tapped Aaron's shoulder. He looked through the window and his mouth tightened. "What the hell...they're coming here."

Libby was the last to notice the launch. Jean-Claude was already opening the door and hurrying outside.

"Aaron" was all Susan could manage, and he clamped a hand on the back of her neck.

"They've found him," Libby said, but she frowned and held a fist to her mouth. "He's all right. I told you he'd be all right."

Through the window they watched Jean-Claude confront a stocky uniformed man who walked with long, deliberate strides toward the house. When he neared Jean-Claude, he stopped, and Jean-Claude took something from his back pocket. His wallet. He removed a card and offered it. Identification.

Susan felt Aaron's fingers convulse. "Stand close to Libby," she whispered.

The two men outside talked, and when Jean-Claude nodded and stood aside, waving the officer ahead of him, Susan felt a rush of relief. The man's face was calm. The news might be bad, but surely not too bad.

"Officer Morgan," the man said as he entered the room. "Which of you ladies is Mrs. Duclaux?"

"I am." Libby glanced back at Aaron, who smiled at her.

"This is difficult, ma'am. I'm glad you've got your family with you."

Jean-Claude had come in, and he stood close to the door, a hand over his mouth and nose. His skin seemed pale and he held himself rigidly.

"Where is he?" Libby asked faintly.

"Still in Hawaii, ma'am," Morgan said. "The authorities there wanted you contacted before they take any more steps."

A roar started in Susan's head. Libby's face was still blank with a vacant smile in place.

"Morgan," Aaron said, "what's happened to Georges Duclaux?"

Morgan removed a notebook from his breast pocket. "The report we received states that Mr. Duclaux was last seen at a restaurant in the Waioli area of Kauai on the evening of August 21. He was called to the telephone. Afterward he left and didn't return."

"He came back to the house where we were staying," Susan said. "To…get something."

Morgan gave her a hard look. "You're likely to be asked more questions about that."

"I already have been."

"Yes." He bent over his notes again. "Evidently Mr. Duclaux decided to go to Nawiliwili Harbor to visit a boat he owned there. Were you aware of the boat?"

"Yes, yes," Jean-Claude said. He pressed the heels of his hands to his temples. "Finish."

"Yes, sir. Mr. Duclaux is thought to have decided to go for a swim from the deck of his boat. Unfortunately he drowned."

15

"**I** appreciate this," Susan told Mike. "The doctor felt she should be where medical attention was more readily available."

"Damn," Mike said. "All I can do is offer a place for Georges's wife...his widow to rest. Do you know how helpless that makes me feel?" He jerked upright from a black leather chair and stuffed a block of wood into a circular stove in the middle of the room.

Aaron, cross-legged on the floor of Mike's den, took a deep swallow from a glass of bourbon. "We're all helpless," he said, and coughed. "There's nothing you can do for the dead."

Susan felt tears threaten again and blinked rapidly. "She wants to bury him at their place in Italy—at Madonna di Lago. I'm going with her."

"So am I," Aaron said.

Mike said nothing. The rift between Susan and him hadn't miraculously mended, not that he'd expected it to.

"Jean-Claude took it badly," Aaron said.

"He seems like a tough nut, but he loved Georges," Susan said. Jean-Claude had accompanied them to Mike's, then left to go walking, saying he couldn't be indoors.

A light tap on the door preceded Connie's entrance. Dressed in a loose but conservative gray dress, she was visibly subdued. "Would you like me to bring coffee or tea, Mike?" she asked, her hands clasped.

He looked around, but Susan and Aaron shook their heads. Susan had noted that, although not perfect, the Kinnear house had undergone an agreeable transformation.

"Should I take something up to your sister?" Connie asked Susan. "Poor thing."

"She's sleeping," Susan said. "But thanks. Maybe later."

"You can leave it to me to take care of her if you have to go somewhere," Connie continued, and Susan managed a smile of thanks. Like most people, Connie improved when she felt needed.

When they were alone again, Mike poured himself a drink and stayed by the bar. "What happens to Libby now?"

"I wish to God I knew," Aaron said.

Susan looked sightlessly at trees beyond the window. "If I can, I'm going to get her to stay with me."

"Her place is in Geneva."

Jean-Claude had come silently into the room. He headed directly to get a drink.

"In Geneva she'll be alone," Aaron said, his dark eyes hooded. Aaron Conrad seemed an even-tempered man, but his antipathy toward Jean-Claude was very evident.

"She will have me and my mother. We will care for her as is appropriate. We are her husband's only remaining family."

"And I'm her sister," Susan retorted, unable to contain herself.

"She cannot be smothered," Jean-Claude insisted. "We will ensure she becomes whole again. She agrees with me."

Susan sat straighter. "Really. Since when?"

"We talked a little while ago. She was not sleeping, and I decided the sooner we get this funeral over and get on with life, the better."

Aaron muttered something Susan couldn't hear, and Mike turned his back on the room, apparently deciding to straighten a pen-and-ink sketch of a clipper under full sail.

"I'll go up and talk to her myself," Susan said.

"Do not bother," Jean-Claude said. "She has gone out for a while to think."

Mike turned around and Aaron stood up. "Gone out?" they said in unison.

"You do not understand, do you?" Jean-Claude looked at the ceiling, and Susan couldn't fail to notice how tired he appeared. "We are hurting deeply, Libby and I. The only way I know to help us both is to carry on, shut it out. Do you think this does not take everything from us? Georges has been the...the substitute father in my life. He was much younger than my own father, only eleven years my senior, but he gave me back what I had lost. For that, and because it is right, I will do for him now what he cannot do himself—I will look after his Libby."

There was a momentary pause. "Forgive me," Susan said. "I'm so tied up with my own grief I'm not thinking straight."

"Where is Libby?" Aaron had put down his glass. "Is she in the garden?"

"Probably," Jean-Claude said. "Please, allow her to be alone. She needs to think."

"I don't...how long has she been out there?"

"Not long. Perhaps an hour."

"An hour!" Mike smacked down his own glass and rushed for the door. "Good Lord, man. Are you mad? She was under sedation less than two hours ago."

Before he could leave the phone rang and he snatched

it up. "Kinnear. Yeah…yes." He leaned against the wall and pushed his fingers into his hair. "Yes. Thank you."

"What is it?" Susan, with Aaron at her shoulder, arrived at Mike's side as he hung up.

"That was the sheriff, calling from the medical center. Libby's in the emergency room." He went to touch Susan's arm but waved broadly instead. "There's no need to panic. She'll be okay."

"What happened?" Aaron asked. "How did she get from the garden to the medical center?"

"In Susan's car," Mike said, not meeting her eyes. "Evidently she took a drive…right off the road. She's okay, apart from a bump on the head and a few scratches. They've got a guard with her."

"Why?" Susan whispered.

"In case she comes up with another way to join Georges."

Susan checked the clock in Mike's truck and tried to find a comfortable place to rest her head. He was in the garage, talking with the mechanic about her battered Volkswagen—the car Libby had tried to kill herself in. At first she'd stayed with Mike, trying to understand what was said. He'd ignored her while he talked to the mechanic and the sheriff, who was also present. Eventually she excused herself and went outside to wait.

Suffering from a mild concussion, Libby had been kept at the medical center for several hours, then allowed to return to Mike's where she'd rested all day, closely watched over by Connie and Aaron.

The driver's door opened without her hearing approaching footsteps. "That proves that," Mike said, climbing in beside her. "Next stop, the harbor."

"What's been proved?" He'd agreed to her coming

with him, but had shown no enthusiasm and no inclination to communicate.

"Libby didn't try to kill herself. She didn't deliberately drive off the road. The brake lines on your car were cut."

"No!"

He paused in the act of putting the truck into gear. "Yes."

She couldn't help the tears that came. "But I don't understand this. You mean someone—" Her mind became clear and cold. "Why would someone try to hurt me?"

Mike averted his face. "Not you, Susan. At least I don't think so. Soon we may know for sure. They've managed to recover your boat. We should know in an hour or two whether it really did sink by accident."

She put her hand on his arm. "You mean cutting the brake line could have been a second attempt to kill Libby? Why?"

"I don't know and I could be wrong." He patted her hand and set it on the seat between them. His own remained there for an instant, warm and strong. Then he put the truck into gear and they headed toward the harbor.

Soon, Susan thought, when this hell was over, there would be no reason at all for them to see each other.

Two hours later Susan and Mike were met at his front door by Aaron. "Well?"

"Could we come in first?" Mike asked, pushing past and going directly to the den with Aaron and Susan in his wake. "You tell them," he told Susan. She'd never seen him look so exhausted.

Jean-Claude came closer. "Tell us what?"

"Ever since my Tollycraft sank Mike's had a theory that someone was trying to kill Libby."

Aaron scrubbed at his jaw and looked at Jean-Claude,

who shook his head slowly. "Why? Why does he think that and why would anyone want to kill Libby?"

"Because Libby should have been the one in the boat that night and she can't swim. Neither of us can figure out why someone would want to do it."

"But the sinking was an accident," Aaron said.

"No. Divers brought it up today. A hole was deliberately made at the waterline. As Mike suspected, the plan was that when Libby got in, her weight would push the hole under the water so that the boat would start slowly sinking. The job would be finished after the gas ran out."

"And Libby didn't deliberately drive the car off the road," Mike added. "The brake lines were cut."

"That is it. All." Waving his hands in the air, Jean-Claude marched back and forth across the living room. "They have done as much as we can take. If only Georges had listened to me and let them have their spa to themselves. He would be alive today. Do you hear me?"

Susan met his glittering eyes and quickly looked away. "Yes."

"We must delay no longer. Immediately it must be announced that Duclaux is withdrawing from the project...before anything else happens."

"You think these people know Libby has been insisting that none of Georges's wishes be countered?" Aaron asked slowly.

"What else can I think?" Jean-Claude asked, his voice rising. "Georges is dead. Now they will get everything they want. Libby was all that stood in their way."

"Because they, whoever 'they' are, know you wouldn't be the one to hold out," Mike remarked tonelessly.

Jean-Claude shrugged. "If you think that is an act of cowardice, then you are entitled to your opinion. I am not a fool. Duclaux will continue to do well without this."

Without thinking, Susan had crossed to stand close to Mike, who put his arm around her. She glanced up and he smiled, but it was a wistful smile. He gave her shoulder a quick squeeze and released her.

Connie came in without knocking this time. Susan immediately made a move toward the door. "Who's with Libby?"

"It's all right," Connie said, sounding nervous. "Anne's with her. She's a good girl. She'll let us know if Libby wakes up. Mike, could you come and talk to someone?"

He went without question and Susan was left with Aaron and a clearly irate Jean-Claude.

"You do agree with my decision?" Jean-Claude asked Aaron, and Susan remembered that Aaron also held some responsibility in guiding Libby's fate.

"I don't know what to think."

"Whatever happens," Susan said, "I want my sister here with me for as long as she wants to stay." And she wanted to put distance between herself and Mike. They both needed space—and a chance to really think.

He walked into the room again, and Susan jumped when she saw Officer Morgan at his heels.

"I've said we're all strong enough to hear what the man has to say," Mike said.

"We already know." Jean-Claude's dismissive gesture could be excused. Like the rest of them, he'd suffered too much. "Unless you have come to tell us you have caught the bastards."

Aaron held up a hand. "Let him talk. There's something else, isn't there, Officer?"

"You might say so. I understand Mrs. Duclaux is under sedation?" He fished for the notebook again, and Susan felt her stomach rise. "As we understand it, the only change as far as she's concerned is that the transportation of the body will have to be postponed until investigations are completed.''

The groan Susan heard was Jean-Claude's.

"Yes, well." Morgan gave him a sympathetic look. "Evidently there were some marks on Mr. Duclaux's body that raised questions. They tell us they decided not to mention this until they were sure."

Susan held her breath.

"According to the dispatch from Honolulu," Morgan said, flipping shut his book, "Duclaux was dead before he entered the water. I'm not authorized to say any more."

16

A few more days and she would leave for Italy with Libby, Jean-Claude and Aaron. The Hawaiian authorities were releasing Georges's body. The coroner had brought in a verdict of death by unnatural causes; Georges had been killed by a blow to the skull. So far no progress had been made with the case. Someone, probably the murderer, had left Kauai using Georges's name, then simply disappeared. Now the people who had loved Georges best would travel to the place where he'd been happiest and bury him.

Scrambling to the dock at Friday Harbor, Susan tied up the Boston whaler that had been Georges's gift to her and climbed the ramp toward the pier. Connie was on Brown Island with Libby—Connie's own idea—and Susan wanted to check in at the salon. Later, when the rest of the nightmare was over, she'd make sure her staff knew how much she'd appreciated their support in the past weeks.

"Susan."

She raised her head to see Anne Kinnear waiting for her. September was proving a cold month this year, and the girl wore a bright blue down parka over a black skirt.

"Hi, Anne. How come you aren't in school?"

"It's *three-fifteen*," Anne said in a tone that suggested Susan should know the school schedule.

"Ah, of course. I didn't realize." When she drew level, Anne surprised her by slipping a hand through her elbow and smiling. The smile wobbled a little.

"I went to the salon. I was going to ask if it's time my hair was trimmed again."

Susan pursed her lips. They both knew the answer to that question. Only three weeks had passed since the cut. "Not yet," she said. "About the second week in October should be soon enough."

"Oh." They turned from the pier to the waterfront. "Do you have a break now?"

"I haven't gone to work yet."

"Oh."

The small hand sandwiched between her arm and her side felt so good. "I could take a break before I go in." She shouldn't, but Anne needed her or she wouldn't be here.

"You could?" The smile became brilliant. "Good. We could, er, have some lunch?"

"Didn't you have lunch at school?"

"I wasn't hungry today."

"Neither was I." Or yesterday or the day before. Where was Mike—right now? What was he doing, thinking? Did he ever wonder the same things about her? She had a hunch he did, but she doubted he was having as hard a time coping as she was.

At Anne's suggestion they bought sandwiches and went to sit in the shelter above the yacht basin. Recently she'd avoided being inside more than absolutely necessary.

"It's sad about Mr. Duclaux," Anne said, turning a plastic-wrapped hero sandwich around and around. She'd insisted she was hungry enough to eat it—and she'd added potato chips, a huge pickle and a carton of potato salad to her order. She hadn't touched a bite of anything.

"We still aren't used to it. I don't think we ever will be. he was so...special." Remembering the days when he'd been carefree, she smiled. "He could be so funny."

"That's what my dad said. He liked him a lot."

Susan studied the yachts bobbing at their moorings. Already some owners were beginning preparations for winter lay-up. Windbreakers and jeans had taken the place of T-shirts and shorts. The picture that came into her mind was of Mike, bearded and shaggy, in a tattered orange tank top and impossibly short cutoffs. Tanned, relaxed, holding out a muddy hand...and smiling his wonderful smile.

"Georges liked Mike. He's easy to like." Why shouldn't she say what was true?

"You like him, too, don't you?"

"Yes, very much." So Mike did think about her, or at least he wasn't his usual ebullient self and Anne had decided his mind was on Susan. "Eat, Anne. Some of it, anyway."

"I think Mike needs you."

The bite of croissant Susan had taken stuck in her throat, and she swallowed with difficulty. "Your dad will be fine. He's got a lot of business worries at the moment, and they keep him preoccupied." She didn't completely believe it, but neither was she ready to approach Mike.

Anne was carefully packing her food back into its brown bag.

"Aren't you going to have any of that?" Susan asked, feeling guilty that her lack of response had probably ruined the girl's appetite.

"Yes. I need to go to the bathroom." She left her school bag with the lunch and ran off on thin legs in the direction of the public rest rooms.

How ironic that she and Anne seemed ripe to become best friends when the relationship with Mike was at an impasse. He'd kept his distance and so had she. Evidently he'd decided that as much as he wanted her physically, and emotionally, too, at some level, they were too different.

Susan heard Mike's voice before she saw him. "Why didn't you bring your bag with you, pumpkin?"

"I thought you'd like to sit down here for a while, so I saved a place."

Little manipulator. Susan hugged her middle, trying to settle her jumpy nerves.

"I've been waiting up there for half an hour," Mike continued. "I get worried about you, Anne, that's all. I'm not mad because you're late, just worried. Try not to dawdle when you know I'm picking you up."

"Okay. Sorry."

So she'd rushed from school to the salon, discovered Susan was due in and decided to pull off a meeting somehow.

He saw her.

"Hi, Mike. Anne and I ran into each other and I was keeping her company."

"Hi." An old brown leather bomber jacket sat well on his big shoulders. The navy blue turtleneck he wore didn't look bad, either.

"I bet you didn't have lunch again," Anne said to her father. Her hands were tight fists at her sides. "I saved you some."

Anne hurried into the shelter, and Mike looked past her at Susan. His smile was wry, and it didn't disguise that he bore the signs of not having slept well…for some time. Stubble darkened his jaw. A fledgling beard? Susan bit the inside of her lip, swallowing acid regret. Had he completely given up on them and decided to go back where he was when they met? She wasn't ready to give up, not yet.

"There's a hero," Anne said, pulling it from the bag. "The kind you like with everything on it. And potato salad and pickles and chips."

Mike frowned and walked slowly toward the bench. "They served that at school, pumpkin?"

"Er, no." Anne's cheeks reddened and her eyes slid past Susan's. "I, er, well—"

"I invited Anne to have a sandwich with me," Susan said quickly. "We both suffered from the same problem. Our eyes were bigger than our stomachs. There really is plenty if you want something."

His lips parted, and she was certain he intended to refuse...and leave. "Anne and I aren't quite ready to give up the effort." She raised her brows significantly at him, and he nodded slightly before sitting beside her.

"How are things?" Their shoulders touched, and when he turned his face to hers, she wanted to hold him. "How are *you*, Susan?"

"Not great. On either front." Their eyes met and held, and she knew he understood she was admitting she'd missed him.

"Same for me." He drew in a slow breath and Susan sighed.

The silence around them was absolute, noises from the harbor remote—a busy frame around a dramatic painting with stark lines.

"Wasn't it lucky that I ran into Anne?" Susan wished this moment need never end, but the child was there and she needed to be included. "If I hadn't, I probably wouldn't have eaten all day." All this talk about food. Maybe it was better than using the weather.

"Very fortunate," Mike agreed, smiling faintly while

his glance moved over her rapidly. "We wouldn't want you fading away."

"That's what I thought," Anne said, leaning around him. "Susan looks thin, don't you think, Dad? She probably spends too much time on her own and doesn't eat enough."

Susan planted her fingertips firmly over her mouth to hold in her laughter and saw that Mike also had to struggle not to laugh at his offspring's efforts.

"You could be right, pumpkin."

"Connie's been teaching me to cook." Her high voice slowed, then lowered a pitch. "I can make this awesome casserole thing. It's got tuna in it. And it's easy. I could do it tonight."

And so the child would force them to confront what they hadn't managed to approach alone. Susan watched Mike's eyes change to a darker, more reflective green, his mouth turn down. This might be uncomfortable, but at least he was getting a firsthand demonstration of the lengths to which insecurity might drive a worried girl.

"Do you like tuna, Susan? All I have to do is make up some boxes of macaroni and cheese, then use a can of mushroom soup and some frozen peas and those dried onion things. You mix it all up together."

Susan managed not to wince. "Sounds like it's quite something."

"Would you like—?"

"Anne, sweetie. Are you going to eat any of this, or shall I have it all?" He spoke through a fixed smile and unwrapped the hero.

"You have it, Dad." She stood up. "I just remembered. I need binder paper for school. Could I run up to Spring Street and buy some? And pencils?"

"I'll take you."

"No. You don't need to. You don't wanna move the truck and I might go into the cookie place to get desert for after the casserole. What kind of cookies do you like, Susan?"

"Um. Oatmeal-raisin is my favorite, I guess, but—"

"Great. See ya." The black skirt flew behind her as she ran out of sight.

"Good grief." Mike put his head in his hands. "Kids."

"You're getting mayonnaise on your face."

He started, remembering the sandwich. "Hell. When she grows up, she could be dangerous."

"Are you sure she isn't already?" Unthinking, she brushed crumbs from his cheek.

His large hard hand closed on her wrist. "I miss you, you know." He pursed his lips and looked at her palm, sweeping a thumb along the lines. "Staying away has been tough."

"Ditto."

"There aren't any easy answers, love, are there?"

"No." And she couldn't even verbalize the difficult ones while he touched her.

With her hand in his and resting on his knee, he fumbled to put the sandwich back into the bag and toss it into a garbage can. "I love that kid. She does know that, doesn't she?"

"Of course she does. But Anne's bright. Busy minds come up with a lot of what-ifs, and she equates your happiness with security—for both of you."

His laugh startled her. "Can you believe the stunts she pulls? She's got guts. I'll give her that."

Susan smiled, enjoying seeing him relax. "She's great. After the way she reacted when we first met, I'd never have expected us to be friends, but I think we are."

"So do I." His grip tightened.

Uncertain what it all meant, equally uncertain what to do next, Susan glanced at her watch. "I should get up to the salon. I've got a fantastic staff. They probably don't need me at all, but I like to think someone does sometimes."

"I need you."

Her heart seemed to stop, then thunder. Mike released her hand.

"Mike—"

"So does Libby," Mike said, cutting her off.

When she made a move to get up, he held her elbow. "Don't go."

"I don't want to."

"Then stay. At least talk to me for a while. I've tried not to think about you, but it doesn't work."

"It doesn't work for me, either."

Hesitantly he cupped her cheek, stroked her ear and neck and rested his forehead on hers. "I've got to tell you something. Several things. If I don't tell someone, I'm going to go crazy, and I don't trust anyone else."

The weary desperation in his voice constricted her throat. "What is it? Something's wrong, isn't it? Really wrong?"

"You aren't going to believe how wrong." Putting his arm around her shoulders, he leaned on the wall and settled her head against him. "My father's in trouble. He's been gambling heavily, mostly at the track, and he's in legal difficulties for writing bad checks. I have to find a way to get him out of hot water without ruining what's left of his pride."

"You shouldn't have too much difficulty covering his debts now."

"Because of my ill-gotten gains from Georges?" He sounded bitter.

"No!" Susan pulled away. "I didn't mean it that way."

"Okay, okay. I'm supersensitive, that's all. I've got to cover for him, Susan, and make him feel worthwhile again. He's my father."

"Yes." Anything she said would be useless.

"He won't come out of the cottage. And all he says when I make him let me in is that he's no good and never has been. Damn, I've got to help him. Aaron knows and agrees—as you'd expect him to. But I feel as if I've been kicked."

"I wish I could help."

"You can. Don't give up on us—you and me. Not yet."

Not yet? "I don't want to. But I haven't changed, Mike. I still want the same things I wanted before."

"Yeah, I figured you would." His throat moved as he swallowed. "Want to hear another Kinnear problem?"

"I want to hear anything about you."

"Could I get another of those kisses?"

"No. Talk."

"Figures. Your friend Jean-Claude gave me a call."

Susan traced the tendons up his wrist. "He's Libby's nephew by marriage. Nothing to me, really."

"He hates my guts. But he's swift. I'll give him that. Did you tell him I went back to the boat the night Georges died?"

"I...the boat?" The impact dawned slowly. "Oh."

"Right. Oh. Anyway, good old Jean-Claude fixed on that like a limpet. He didn't, of course, want to make any objectionable suggestions, but I might want to consider how the police were likely to view the fact that I returned to *Ma Libby* a few hours before Georges was killed on board."

Susan couldn't quite catch her breath. "I didn't tell

him.... Or I don't...I don't remember telling him. I never thought anything of it. What is he suggesting? Why?"

"He hates the idea of any Duclaux money being removed from his control. At least that's the way it looks to me. His not-very-subtle suggestion was that I should opt out of my agreement with Georges."

"Well, you won't." Susan stood up and pushed her fists into the pockets of her slacks. "He's out of his mind. Oh, really, this is the end."

"Is that a vote of confidence?"

"What?" So agitated she couldn't stand still, she marched back and forth in front of him. "If you're asking me if I think—if I could possibly think even for a second— that you crept aboard that boat and hit Georges over the head to be sure of getting the money he'd promised you for your business without having to do the work on his boat, forget it. For one thing, how could you be sure Libby would bypass Jean-Claude and file the papers? More to the point, I know you, Mike. I really know the man who's made—" She clamped her teeth together and turned away.

"The man who's made what, Susan?" He stood behind her now, close but not quite touching. "What?"

"Love to me." There, she'd said it. "I've got to go."

He spun her around so quickly that she stumbled over his feet. Locking his wrists behind her neck, he looked hard into her eyes. "We're in a fix, my girl. We believe in each other, and that's pretty rare, huh? Do you suppose we ought to keep the lines of communication open? No promises, no declarations. An agreement to consider how to proceed—if we proceed at all?"

"I'd like that." But she was almost afraid to let hope live. "What did you say to Jean-Claude?"

"That I didn't go back to the boat that night. I didn't.

When I left you, I felt like hell and ended up driving to Hanelei and sitting on the beach for hours.''

"Will he let it rest?"

"He can't prove anything else, but it would be messy if he went to the police with his little theory. I told him I'm doing business with Libby and hung up. We'll see if that's the last I hear on the subject."

"I think it will be." She put her hands on his sweater beneath the jacket. His chest was warm. "He's fighting with Libby again now."

"Hell. Why doesn't he leave her alone!"

"Hey, look what I've got." Anne stood, a brown bag hugged to her chest, grinning at them. "All the stuff for my casserole. And fresh oatmeal-raisin cookies. So you can come to dinner, huh?"

Mike, standing with his back to his daughter, smiled wickedly and wiggled his eyebrows.

Trapped. "All right. But I'll have to spend an hour or so at the shop. Oh, no, I guess I can't come. I forgot. I don't have a car."

"No sweat." Mike's beautiful teeth were much in evidence. "We'll come and get you, won't we, Anne?"

"You bet!"

There could be worse traps.

Mike added wood to the stove in the den. "That was a first. I've never seen Anne go to bed without being told."

"I really enjoy her," Susan said. She'd stretched out in his favorite swivel chair with her feet on an ottoman. Seeing her there gave him an overwhelming sense of rightness, even as he thrust aside the notion that she could disappear at any moment.

"Drink?"

She shook her head and stared into the flames. "Summer's okay, but I think I'm a winter person. I love fires."

"Me, too. Fires and good company." They were comfortable together at times like these—when the big issues weren't raised.

"That was Aaron who came in a while ago, wasn't it? He flitted through so quickly that I barely got a glimpse of him."

"Yeah, Aaron's staying the night in my spare room. He often does that when it gets too late for him to return to Seattle. But I think he's got the same idea as Anne—let's throw Mike and Susan together."

"Yes." With her chin tilted up, firelight played over her throat and the smooth skin visible at the neck of the blouse she wore beneath a fluffy pink sweater. She was definitely a woman who made brotherly thoughts impossible.

He poured himself a small brandy and sat on the floor beside her, his shoulder resting lightly against her thigh. She'd kicked off her shoes, and he noted how slender and graceful her feet and ankles were. No matter how often he looked at Susan, he always discovered some newly fascinating feature.

"What did you think of casserole à la Anne?"

Susan laughed and tangled her fingers in the curly hair at his nape. "I'll have to get her recipe. You were right when you kept insisting Connie's good for her. She's obviously relaxed and warm around children—and now that Connie's figured out she really is needed around here, she's a gem. I'm sorry I was so harsh on her at first. In the past couple of weeks I don't know what I would have done without her."

"I think she responds to needy people. When I talk to her, she's fiercely protective of Libby."

"I know. She was furious with Jean-Claude today, and

so was I, but poor Connie looks at him as if he were an alien.''

"Smart woman." Those ankles were irresistible. Her fingers stilled a moment when he slipped a hand inside her calf and stroked all the way to her instep. ''That guy needs a charm school." Hoping she didn't sense his excitement, Mike rubbed the top of her foot and tried to keep his breathing even.

''I'm not too thrilled with what he did today, either. He more or less told Libby she was losing her mind.''

"You're kidding."

"Nope. Jean-Claude doesn't understand that Libby's trying to pull herself together. At first she's bound to make some wild decisions that she'll put aside later, but Jean-Claude doesn't want to give her time for that.'' The gentle pressure on his neck resumed. ''Libby's decided she should try to take an active part in the business. Not take it over, because she doesn't have the expertise, but she'd like to learn something about it."

"And Jean-Claude hates the idea?''

"You've got it. And when Libby talked about getting involved with charity organizations, he really lost it. First he yelled about her needing a doctor—a psychiatrist, then he said she'd probably be better off in a spa! She should rest, he says, coddle herself. Can you believe that, after what we've just been through?''

"No. But in his defense, he is responsible for a powerful operation, and that kind of talk would be enough to rattle anyone."

"Well, he handled it all wrong. Libby got mad and said it was within her power to appoint someone else in his place any time she felt like it. She reminded him that she's Georges's heir and she's not mentally unsound. Jean-

Claude cooled off a bit then, but Libby didn't. She was still fuming—quietly, of course—when I left."

"I don't blame her." There was another subject to be explored. "Susan, I've been thinking a lot about us."

The hand stilled. "So have I."

"Did you decide anything?" But how could she when she didn't know what he'd been thinking?

"Mike—" she gripped his shoulders "—there's someone standing outside the door."

The door stood open a few inches and a shadow wavered in the slice of light from the hall across the polished wooden floor in the den.

He gave her a rueful grin. "Okay, Anne, come on in."

The shadow receded slightly and Mike frowned. "You don't have to creep around. Come in, I said."

"It's not Anne." Gray-faced and disheveled, Lester edged into the room. "Can we talk, Mike?"

The sight of his father, broken and ashamed, hit Mike like a blow. He knew that what his father had done was a criminal offense—something he would go to jail for if anyone ever found out. But Mike knew his father wasn't really a criminal. He had a disease—an addiction to gambling. What he needed was close supervision and as much understanding as it took to heal him.

"I should be leaving," Susan said.

"Don't," Lester told her. "Maybe what I've got to say doesn't mean anything, but if it does, you need to hear it, too, Susan." He glanced down, seeming to realize that his clothes were rumpled. Hitching self-consciously at his belt, he perched on the edge of a chair. Tonight, with his gray hair awry, and white stubble in evidence on his jaw, he looked every one of his seventy-three years.

"Do you want a drink, Lester?"

"No thanks." He tented his fingers and tapped them

together. "While you were both in Hawaii, I made...I went to the track." A flush swept over his pallid cheeks, and he glanced at Susan.

"She knows."

"Yes, I thought you'd tell her. Well, I've always gone on the ferry. Usually I said I was going to be busy at the cottage or made some other excuse. It was easy with you gone." He bowed his head. "I saw someone I didn't expect to see on the ferry."

Mike held his tongue and waited.

"That Duclaux fellow. Libby's nephew or whatever he is. The man Aaron introduced me to once."

"Jean-Claude?" Mike felt Susan stiffen. "He probably had business in Seattle."

"He had a grip. Not a briefcase, a grip, the small kind you carry on a plane. I made sure he didn't see me."

"Why? Oh...sure. I get it. You were afraid he might tell us he'd seen *you*."

"Yes, but I should have mentioned it, just in case."

"Just in case of what, Lester? What are you suggesting?" Susan asked. She found Mike's hand and held it so tightly that she ground their bones together.

"Well, I didn't think too much about it till the next day. That was the day you were calling here looking for Aaron. Remember? You couldn't reach Jean-Claude and you wanted Aaron to go over and check up to see if he was okay. Georges Duclaux was missing and you needed Jean-Claude in Hawaii."

"Yes," Mike said slowly, trying to put together what his father was saying. "And when Aaron went over, Jean-Claude had been in bed with the flu...for two days...with the phones turned off."

"But he was on the ferry the previous morning. And he didn't look sick."

"Carrying a grip," Susan said quietly. "As if he was going on a trip...a short trip."

Mike twisted to see her face.

"Mike," Lester said, "on the morning of the day Georges died Jean-Claude wasn't in bed with the flu. He was headed for Seattle, looking like a man going on a journey."

"Jean-Claude wouldn't... It wouldn't be possible," Susan muttered.

Mike got to his feet and pulled her up. "Wouldn't it? It would be grueling, I'll give you that, but possible, given the time difference. He could have flown to Kauai and...and killed Georges. Then he could have returned to Seattle via Honolulu and San Francisco, using Georges's name to buy his tickets. And that way he made sure there'd be a lot of confusion later. He probably hoped Georges's body would never be found and we'd think that Georges had just disappeared. All Jean-Claude had to do once he hit the mainland was get back to Brown Island—where there was no one to know when he came and went—and lie low until he was contacted."

"I can't believe he would—"

"Can't you? He isn't even subtle about wanting control of Georges's business."

She stared at him for a moment. "Jean-Claude's own father managed to lose the fortune that should have come to Jean-Claude. I suppose that could make him jealous enough...."

"I think Aaron should be brought in on this. We need to decide what to do next—if anything. This is probably all a wild theory." He sprinted from the room and upstairs to return with Aaron who'd been lounging on his bed, still damp from the shower.

"What's up?" Aaron's face popped from the neck of

the sweater he pulled on. He'd struggled into jeans, but his feet were still bare. "Susan, can you give me a précis of what this man's gabbling about?"

She did, and Mike watched Aaron's expression change. "My God…Mike…oh, my God!" He started for the door.

"Whoa!" Mike managed to catch a handful of one sleeve and hold on. "Where are you going?"

"To get Libby, of course. She's over there on Brown, isn't she?"

"Yes."

"And so is Jean-Claude?"

"Yes," Susan said, her voice rising. "But he wouldn't do anything to hurt her."

In that instant Mike's skin, his flesh, his bones turned cold. The three of them stood immobile while their thoughts seemed to shout out loud.

"Susan," Mike said, his throat closing. "Who would inherit after Libby?"

She opened her mouth and drew in a breath. "Oh…it would be Jean-Claude, wouldn't it?"

"Where was he the night your boat sank?" Aaron asked.

"I don't…yes, I do know. He went to his rooms early."

"Did he know your plans?"

"No…yes, yes! Libby offered to pick him up when she came back for Georges. He refused."

"But he knew," Aaron said flatly.

Susan turned horrified eyes on Mike. "Yes, Libby invited Jean-Claude to dinner, too, but he said he had to call a friend in Switzerland—the woman he's going to marry. Then he went upstairs. Yes, he knew."

Before Mike could respond Aaron said, "And he was the one who went walking outside before he suggested Libby should take a drive."

"And he must have cut my brake lines." Susan snatched up the phone. "I've got to talk to Libby."

"This is probably all conjecture," Lester muttered from his chair. "I've probably sent you all on a wild-goose chase."

Mike wished he thought so, too.

"Come on, come on," Susan said into the phone. "Answer. Yes, hi, Connie. Let me talk to Libby, please."

Aaron reached Susan a second before Mike did—the second after she dropped the phone. "What is it?"

"She's not there. She went out with Jean-Claude."

17

"Probably the same way he got to Friday Harbor when he holed your boat," Mike said, peering through the truck windshield into the stormy darkness. "He must have taken someone else's boat to get off Brown that night and repeated the process tonight. Damn this rain. Feels like November."

Susan was grateful to be scrunched between Mike and Aaron's solid bodies. "We don't know how long ago they left Brown. I forgot to ask Connie."

"The sheriff's people will do that. And they'll already be searching."

Mike drove directly to the waterfront, and Susan realized they had no idea where to start looking. "Connie said Jean-Claude told her he and Libby needed to get away. How can we be sure they left Brown Island?"

Aaron hopped from the cab and offered her a hand. When she was beside him, he said, "The sheriff thought of that. He said he was calling the fire chief over there. He'll mount a search."

"So where are we going?" She turned to Mike. "We can't just stand here and wait."

He slowly zipped up his bomber jacket, narrowing his eyes against the rain. "We could check the short-stay dock for any boat he might have stolen."

"I wouldn't know what I was looking for," she told

him. The ferry horn, blaring in the night, startled her. "All we can do is start—Mike, the ferry! What if he's taken her on the ferry?"

He glanced past her. "The thing's about ready to pull out."

"Come on." Aaron was already running. Mike took off after him, but Susan followed more slowly. "Come on!" Aaron yelled back at her.

Susan ran, too, panting as the moisture-laden air hissed past her tight throat. "But we don't know they'll be there."

"The sheriff probably hasn't sent anyone aboard," Mike called. "Leave the islands to the authorities. At least we won't have missed an opportunity to do something."

On the creaking, shiny timbers of the dock ferry personnel were unhitching lines. The ferry's horn blasted again. Mist and rain swirled through the dimmed yellow beams cast by dock lights.

"I can't make it," Susan gasped, sobbing for breath.

Mike glanced back, turned and made a dash to grab her. "Yes, you can. We're going to have to spread out all over the boat." He drew back his lips from his clenched teeth and broke into a sprint, dragging Susan with him.

"Hey, you!" a man handling lines shouted as Aaron whipped past him.

Susan felt her feet leave the slippery pavement and closed her eyes. She landed on the car deck of the ferry a second behind Mike, and they both staggered against Aaron.

"Separate," Mike ordered before her heart had a chance to slow down. "The darkness makes it harder. Check everywhere. I'll take the outside passenger decks. Aaron, you do the starboard inside compartments, Libby the port."

"Where do we meet?"

"Go," Mike said, already in motion. "We'll find each other. Don't directly approach them unless you're seen. He won't risk doing anything in a crowded place. At least I hope to God he won't."

Susan rushed around the lines of parked cars. Aaron sprinted toward the opposite side of the deck. On a cold night most drive-on passengers took shelter on the passenger decks above, and the vehicles stood in gloomy abandoned rows.

Two flights of muddy metal stairs, separated by a heavy steel door, led to the upper decks. By the time Susan dragged open the door to scramble up the second flight, Mike was nowhere in sight.

At the top she bumped into a man carrying plastic cups of coffee and raised her hands. "I'm sorry. I'm sorry."

"Geez." He shook his head, glaring as he made a wide circle around her.

Bench seats. Dozens of bench seats covered in dun-yellow plastic held the kind of tired travelers a late ferry was bound to carry. Susan hesitated, then started walking, looking from side to side. Some people slept, but here and there eyes met hers: challenging, indifferent, wary, shifting away. She moved more rapidly. Where there were tables between benches, card games were in progress, or letters being written, or babies balanced in infant seats amid piles of belongings.

Susan felt sweat on her brow, stinging the corners of her eyes. They weren't here. Her stomach rose, and she swallowed against a rush of sickness.

The swinging doors to the upper foredeck slammed open, and Mike scooted to a halt in front of her. "Nothing?" Rain dripped from his hair and face and ran down his leather jacket.

"No," Susan answered, turning away from him. The

ferry listed and they grabbed each other. "We shouldn't have come aboard."

"Hell. I still feel this was the obvious thing for him to do. Get her farther away, maybe take a long car ride and lose her."

Susan shook her head. She didn't want to hear this. "But what excuse could he have made when he got back without Libby?"

"You don't think he had that worked out?" Mike's laugh chilled Susan.

"Did you check the coffee shop?" Aaron, his green windbreaker tied around his neck by the sleeves, strode from the starboard aisle.

"No," Mike said, and they hurried toward the coffee counter.

Susan ran her eyes over the whole crowded area. Nothing.

"Damn." Aaron shoved his hands into his hair and hung on. "This is dumb. Dumb! Why didn't one of us stay behind? We're trapped and we can't do a damn thing."

"We can look again," Mike said through barely parted lips. "Go over every inch... Wait! Did anyone check the car deck?"

A second clicked by—another. "No." Susan whirled around, reached the stairs first and clattered down, with the pounding footsteps of the others behind her. Her hands slipped on the sweating painted surface of the railings, jerking her forward, but she kept her feet.

At the bottom Mike's hand descended on her shoulder. "Go back up," he said in a low voice. "Wait for us there."

"Nothing doing." She shrugged away and stepped to the catwalk that ran beside the nearest row of vehicles.

"Mike's right," Aaron said. He looked toward the stern and Susan followed his glance. The sea roiled behind, fluorescent spume the color of frothy crème de menthe flying above the troughs of black waves.

"I'm not leaving," Susan said, edging farther along. "You think something's happened to Libby, don't you? You think Jean-Claude's mad."

"Don't you?" Mike hissed through his teeth, and pulled her against him. "Go up top."

Susan twisted away and dodged between a pickup and a battered white Cadillac. Crouching, she moved forward, peering left and right through each pair of vehicles. If her sister was down here in the hands of a crazy man, there was no way Susan could wait up top.

At the next pause she turned her head and jumped so hard that she flinched. Aaron, bent low, was creeping along the next row of cars. Glancing the other way, she saw Mike. He spared her an angry stare and crept on.

Another pointless exercise. Nothing moved in the ghastly tableau.

Then she saw them.

Sidestepping, she came up behind Mike, who swung a fist at her touch, stopping inches from her face. "Damn it. You scared the hell out of me."

"Come on," she said. "I see them. We've got to stop Aaron."

The grinding of the ferry's engine and the wild sea shielded any sound their feet made as they ran headlong to pull Aaron back. He raised his brows, and Susan pointed to where Libby and Jean-Claude stood...at the exposed opening at the front of the boat—an opening that led nowhere but into the deep.

"What?"

Susan put her hand over Aaron's mouth. "Think," she

said urgently. "Whatever we do could send them overboard. Look at him. He's talking to her—talking and talking."

"Go forward," Mike said. "Slowly. Don't make any sudden moves."

Jean-Claude put his arm around Libby's shoulders and kept on talking, his mouth close to her ear. "What's he saying?" Susan clutched the neck of her sweater. "What's he telling her?"

"We don't have any idea."

Aaron stopped. With Libby held against his side, Jean-Claude walked over to unhook the guard rope, the last barrier between them and almost certain death.

"Aaron," Mike whispered, "get on the other side of the divider." He pointed to a bulkhead that separated the central car hold from an overflow ramp. "I'll come from the other side."

"What are you going to do?" Susan caught a handful of his leather sleeve. "He's trying to get her to jump, I know he is. Don't scare him into anything."

"We don't have any choice. We've got to try. Please, Susan, go above."

"I'll take the middle," she said grimly, and he didn't argue.

The snail's pace of her forward progress felt as if she wasn't moving at all. They'd be too late, or Jean-Claude would notice them and... *Move. Don't think,* she commanded herself.

A scream rose in her throat, and she clamped a hand over her mouth. Jean-Claude had inched Libby even closer to the edge. To the side Susan glimpsed movement, and knew Aaron had seen what was happening and had hastened his progress.

"No!" Libby's voice rang out. "No! It's not what he'd want. It's not what I want."

"Libby!" Susan stood up and ran at Jean-Claude.

"Stay away." He locked his arms around Libby and swung her feet from the ground. "Get over there. Stand against the car, or I throw her in."

"He'll do it," Libby cried. "Please, Sue, stay away!"

Susan straightened and did as she was told, sliding along the side of the end car to stand with her hands braced behind her on the cold, damp hood. "Jean-Claude, let Libby go. We can work something out." Whatever she did, she mustn't look left or right, as if she expected help.

"Don't try to talk to him," Libby moaned.

"Work something out?" He frowned. "Why should we have to do that. I am merely helping Libby. Your sister is very unhappy and wants to join Georges. I believe people should be helped to do what they want."

Susan started forward.

"No closer!" he barked, and he fastened a hand on Libby's neck, forcing her face over the sea. "You must not interfere."

"But I'm here, Jean-Claude." She could scarcely form the words. "And I'll tell everyone what you've done."

"Will you?"

Libby began to sob.

"Yes," Susan said. "You killed Georges, didn't you? I know all about it."

"Really?" He took his hand from Libby's neck and walked slowly toward Susan. "You are a very clever woman, Susan, to work out such things."

She saw death in his eyes—her death as well as Libby's. But the gamble was all that was left. Now he needed to dispose of her, too, and to do that he had to make sure she didn't escape him.

"You didn't have the flu," she gasped out, backing away, drawing him with her. "You went to Kauai, killed Georges and came back. Did you pay someone to make threatening calls? Did you try to have him blown up in Geneva? You did, and it went wrong, so you had to kill him yourself."

He stopped, his eyes almost black. Slowly he drew a gun from his pocket.

Susan's eyes fastened on the small gleaming weapon. Not screaming for Mike and Aaron, not searching for them, was the hardest thing she'd ever done.

"Chatter on, *madame*. Even if all you say is true, who will ever know but us? Your talk will not stop me. You will both die. What you know will be gone. Why not make this simple? Come to me and I will help you both."

"No!" Libby twisted, and Jean-Claude shifted his grip to ram his wrist against her neck. Her gurgling cry ripped through Susan.

She knew he would shoot her and throw her and Libby into the sea. Mike and Aaron must be afraid to make a move. There were no more choices.

"Kick, Libby, kick!"

Susan dropped to the deck and rolled. Shots rang out, then a hissing noise—a tire deflating.

A cry of pain jarred her nerves. Jean-Claude's. Libby had driven her heel into his shin.

Susan crawled forward, swung over and crawled some more. Around her, bullets exploded on metal, ricocheting from bulkheads.

"Agh!"

Libby had landed another kick, sending Jean-Claude to his knees.

He put the gun to her head.

Susan's brain froze. She threw herself forward, thinking

nothing, only seeing her sister's slender body beneath the man's tall, sinuous frame. Landing on his back, she wrapped her legs around him and grappled with his wrist, raking it on a metal grating. Blood—his blood—seeped beneath her fingers.

Then there was weight and color and movement. And the shouts of familiar voices. Someone tossed her aside and she scrambled back. Libby lay alone now and Susan covered her, drew her close before she dared to look up.

"Give it to me, Duclaux." With his hand outstretched Mike confronted the disheveled Swiss. "Here. It's all over. We just have to keep calm now."

"Ha!" Jean-Claude's laugh scaled to a hysterical pitch. "Calm so that you can turn me over to your police? I am not a man meant to be ridiculed. I will *not* be ridiculed. But there is no need, hmm, no question? I have the gun."

"No one will find out a thing," Mike said, his voice very soft. "It will be between us. Whatever you say goes. But kill us and you'll have every policeman in the country on your tail."

Jean-Claude laughed again. "Why? You will all be dead. I will be distraught, help search for you. And it will become obvious that you talked Libby into agreeing to the plot that will be disclosed—by me. Your plot to take over Duclaux. I will make you and Libby secret lovers." He waved the gun. "And when this is public, of course it will seem obvious that you have all chosen to disappear and to remain lost to the world. Convenient, eh?"

"Shh," Susan whispered against Libby's ear, trying to quiet her sobs. From the corner of her eye she saw another movement and stopped breathing. Jean-Claude stood level with them, facing Mike. Crouching, ready to spring, Aaron approached from the side.

"Jean-Claude," Susan said, "why did you do all this?"

His lips drew back from his teeth in a catlike grimace. Alternating his attention between her and Mike, the gun moved, pointing at one, then the other. "She should have died," he said, indicating Libby. "I became like Georges's son. All would have been mine in the end. You see that, do you not? It would have been right. But they wanted a child. Even without a child from her own body, she would have insisted they take a stranger's bastard and make it their own."

Susan closed her eyes, certain she would vomit.

"Some illegitimate nothing would have taken what was mine."

"Children cannot be illegitimate," Susan cried out, unable to hold back her fury.

"I was the eldest son of the eldest son." Jean-Claude ranted as if he hadn't heard her. "Through my father's mistake I was left to take his brother's charity, but I earned it and it is mine. Do you understand, you fools? Mine!"

"No!"

But Susan's cry was too late to stop Aaron. He lunged at Jean-Claude's legs. A shot blasted. Mike reeled away, clutching his shoulder.

On the deck Aaron grappled with Jean-Claude. Together they rolled toward the edge.

"Mike!" Susan screamed, and jumped up, running toward the clawing figures. "Mike, he's going to—"

Suddenly still, Aaron, his left arm trapped beneath his body by Jean-Claude's weight, stared up at his opponent. He splayed his right hand over the other's face and pushed, and Susan closed her eyes.

Jean-Claude held the gun to Aaron's temple.

"He's going to kill him," Libby said. She scrambled beside Susan.

Mike, blood running through his fingers from his shoulder, shook his head. "Don't move," he ordered them. "You can't do anything."

"You are correct." Jean-Claude's high voice split the air and he pulled the trigger.

A flat click sounded—and another.

"It's empty." Susan took a step and crumpled to her knees. "It's empty."

"Get him." Libby pulled Susan up again. "We've got to get him."

"Oh, my God." Mike lunged forward. But with a mighty shove Aaron had already heaved Jean-Claude off him.

The last Susan saw of Jean-Claude was his white face, his wide open mouth issuing a scream she couldn't hear. He rolled off the deck and into the water, then beneath the hull as the ferry churned over him.

18

Susan walked along the pier. In the past week she'd become no more than a visitor to her own salon, but that would soon change. Before long the formalities here and in Hawaii would be over, and Libby had made it clear that she would return, first to Geneva, then to Madonna di Lago in Italy, where she planned to set up her permanent home.

A thin and vaguely wintry sunshine was welcome. Its pallid gleam gilded the beautiful landscape.

When Libby left, there would be a void for a while, but Susan was glad her sister was making plans for her life.

"Susan."

She halted, her stomach making its predictable turn at the sound of Mike's voice. He lounged against a railing, noticeably paler after several days in a Seattle hospital. He wore his bomber jacket draped over his shoulders to accommodate a sling on his left arm. "Hi, Mike."

She'd seen him only once, briefly, since the night neither of them would forget. He'd been waiting his turn for police questioning. When she'd had her own session, he'd no longer been in the waiting room, and a clerk informed her that Mr. Kinnear had left, and, no, there wasn't any message for her.

"How are you?" he asked.

"Not so bad." It was true. She was alive, so were

Libby, Aaron…and Mike. How could she be other than grateful? "Is the shoulder healing?"

"Yup." He smiled and her heart squeezed. "Takes more than a bullet to stop me."

She looked away. "I try not to think about that. A few more inches and it would have stopped you."

"And that would have mattered to you?"

"Damn it!" She moved to pass him, but he still had one good arm and he used it. Caught against him, Susan turned her face up to his. "How many ways are there to tell someone you care? It's odd, Mike, but I don't doubt for one moment that you'd have shed a tear for me if I'd died on that ferry."

"Really?"

"Really."

"Maybe you're right. Can you drive a truck?"

She frowned, then nodded. "Why not? Where do you need to go?"

"Anywhere with you. My house would be nice. Just getting here knocked out some of my stuffing. I'm not the man I used to be."

The unyielding pressure of his arm around her belied that statement. "Okay. Sure, I'll take you. I'm sure Aaron will bring me back."

"Aaron's not there. He had to get back to the ski resort. This is the busiest time of the year—when they're getting ready to open." He released her, only to place a heavy hand on her shoulder and point them in the direction of the waterfront. "We'll get you back."

She considered and discarded the notion to ask how. Maybe she didn't care.

Seated high in the truck cab with Mike beside her, she steered the large vehicle up Warbass Way and turned left on Harrison.

"Aaron told me Libby's going to move to Madonna di Lago."

"Yes. She's sad but very sensible. She thinks she can make some decisions there."

"I hope she doesn't spend the rest of her life in mourning."

Susan let out a whistling breath. "So do I." But it was something she feared. "I'm going to miss her."

"Sure you will, but after a while you'll be glad to have the house to yourself again."

The tears that sprang into her eyes infuriated Susan. "You're probably right." But more probably wrong. What was this all about? Was he trying to let her know that although their reasons for being together, the official reasons, were gone, he'd like them to part on friendly terms? Her jaw contracted and she choked back her tears. She wouldn't cry.

"What's happening with the adoption plans?"

The question shocked her. She blinked. "Not much. But I'll get going on it again soon. I was contacted by the caseworker, Mrs. Brock. She saw the account of…she read the paper. At least she's got some human instincts. She wanted to tell me how glad she is I'm safe and to let me know that I should take my time filling in the papers she sent."

He was quiet for a moment. When he stirred, he turned his face away. "I guess that makes you feel better."

"Yes." Susan wasn't sure how she felt—about anything—except Mike. "As soon as I'm back in a routine, I'll go to the agency again. I'm not giving up," she added. And she wouldn't. No matter what, someday soon she would have a child.

They arrived at his house, and Susan parked in front of the garage. "Wait," she told Mike. "I'll come around and help you.'' But he was already out and closing the door by the time she reached his side of the truck.

"You'd be surprised what I can do with one arm." His smile lacked some of the old wickedness, but it still showed his spirit. "Susan, could we walk on the beach?"

"I'd like to get back and check on Libby. I'm uncomfortable leaving her alone."

"Naturally. But Connie wanted to run over and visit her, so I told her to go ahead."

She raised her brows. "Connie's over there now?"

"Yes." He colored slightly. "She took my boat. I did speak to Libby first, and she said she'd be glad to see Connie. The two of them get along for some reason."

Susan smiled. "The same reason Connie gets along with Anne, probably. As you once said, she blossoms when she feels she's needed." Susan pulled his hand out of his pocket, laced their fingers together and set off down the path to the house. "I know where Anne gets her manipulative skills. We'll go to the beach because *I* feel like it. And I'm holding your hand because your balance is probably off and I don't want you falling on your face."

He laughed. "Thanks."

At the steep slope to the beach she slowed down and picked a careful path.

"I'm not a cripple," Mike protested.

"If you fall on that shoulder, you may be. Just take the attention while you can get it." What was this leading to?

"I like that spot over there, don't you?" Mike asked, nodding to the gray mast they'd sat on when she'd come for that first meal with him.

She liked almost every memory they shared. "Yes."

When she was seated, he stood in front of her, looking over the water toward Vancouver Island. "I'm crazy about this place."

"Me, too. It's a great big beautiful world, but none of it competes with the San Juans for me."

"We have a lot in common, Susan."

But not enough, he seemed to say. "Yes we do."

"I've thought about that. All the time lately."

There was no appropriate answer.

"What do you call someone who can't take a risk?" He came to sit beside her. "Someone who can't grab a chance for something wonderful because it could turn sour?"

"I don't know." But she did know what he was saying. If he *could,* he'd throw in his lot with hers. But he couldn't. Deep down he was convinced that, like the other women in his life, she'd only be temporary.

"I'd call a man who won't take a risk a coward," Mike said.

Susan looked at him and their eyes met. "In that case you can't possibly be talking about yourself."

"Why did you lose your two babies?"

She sat straighter and began to tremble. "Mike—!"

"Sorry, I didn't mean to be so abrupt. But I want to know."

For an instant she wanted to flee. The back of Mike's fingers, stroking her cheek, calmed her. He smiled gently and touched her hair.

"It was something about...I'm not sure. I got very high blood pressure and..." She couldn't do this.

"Did the doctors think it would be okay for you to try to have another baby?"

She hunched her shoulders. "I don't remember."

"Yes, you do. Susan, look at me." He lifted her chin until she couldn't avoid doing as he asked. "They said you shouldn't, didn't they?"

"They said I might never be able to carry a baby to

term. That's all it was. But they weren't sure.'' But they were certain that another pregnancy would be a bad idea.

''Okay. We'll let it go at that—for now. I've considered what I'm going to say for weeks. If you aren't interested or you think it would be a liability rather than an asset, just say so.''

He sounded...nervous?

''I'd be very pleased and proud to be your cosponsor for the adoption. There.'' He dropped his hand and stared straight ahead.

Susan didn't move, couldn't move. She narrowed her eyes, watching his profile while she digested what he'd said. He'd be pleased and proud to act as an adoption cosponsor for her. ''Why?''

''Because it's important to you and I'd feel better, safer, if you didn't try to have another baby yourself. I don't want anything to happen to you.''

She glanced at his hand, a tight fist on his knee. ''Why don't you want anything to happen to me?''

''Because—'' he made an airy, extravagant gesture ''—because...I love you, Susan.''

''Yeah!'' A whoop came from behind them.

Susan, blinking against tears of happiness, twisted to see Anne, slithering and sliding, stumbling forward down the slope. She held a long box in her arms.

''Oh, no.'' Mike groaned and turned his face up to the sky.

''Hello, Anne,'' Susan said, smiling through blurred vision. ''Come and join us.''

''I'm coming. Here I am, Dad. I watched like you said.'' Susan tapped his arm. ''Want to explain that?''

''No.''

''Oh, I was getting tired of waiting.'' Anne marched

around and dumped the very familiar-looking box on Mike's lap.

"What were you waiting for?" Susan asked.

"For Dad's signal," Anne said. "I could only come if he made a big wave. So it's gonna be okay, huh? I'll do for a while?"

"Do? Oh, I see. Yes, of course you'll do, Anne. You'll do very well."

"Dad thought you'd probably say that. He told me all about the adoption and how you have to wait for a couple of years before they'll let you have a baby. After you get married, I mean." She put her arm through Susan's. "Give them to her, Dad."

Mike's bottom lip was sucked between his teeth.

"Anne," Susan said, carefully disentangling their arms, "would you sit here for a minute, sweetheart? Just while your dad and I go over there and say a few more things?"

Anne nodded, clearly ecstatic with her lot.

When Susan got up, Mike was already several steps ahead of her. He stopped at the water's edge and waited for her to reach him. He'd left the box behind.

"You changed your mind, didn't you?" Susan asked, close to tears. She'd so wanted for Mike to be strong. "But when it came right down to it, you couldn't take that risk you talked about, so you came up with a compromise."

"You are so wrong, my love," he said, very low. "I will risk anything for you. But I know you still want a child of your own. If we married, I'd be asking you to give up on adopting a baby. You'd have to make do with my child, for two years at least. I couldn't do that. All I could come up with was helping you to get what you want."

"Is there anything else you want to say to me?" She was angry now. How could an intelligent man be such an idiot sometimes?

"Only one thing." He looked into her eyes. "One thing, Susan." With his hand cupping her neck, his thumb stroking her jaw, he kissed her—a long, gently intimate kiss that brought her against him. She softened, weakened, wrapped her arms around him. Their lips hardened and the kiss became possessive, demanding.

"Anne," Susan whispered as his mouth brushed her ear.

"One thing in case you didn't hear just now." His deep voice was hoarse. "I love you very much, my darling."

"That's good." She smiled against his cheek. "Because I love you, too. *And* I love Anne. What does that suggest to you?"

"That I may be about to become one lucky man?"

"What are the roses for?"

"Anne was supposed to bring them for me to give to you…if you…if you agreed…if you said you'd marry me." He breathed in deeply and drew back to see her face. "I love you. I want you. If you decide you want me, too— and you can take as long as you like to make up your mind—but if you do, I'll make you happy. That's a promise."

Susan felt her mouth tremble, her eyes fill. She swallowed. "Tell Anne to bring on the roses."

From the critically acclaimed author of
Iron Lace and *Rising Tides*

EMILIE RICHARDS

**Comes an unforgettable novel about
two families ruled for generations by a
flawless but deadly treasure.**

Beautiful Lies

It's a pearl so flawless, it has no price, but those who
possess it pay dearly. For generations it has cursed the
Robeson and Llewellyn families, unleashing a legacy of
rivalry, greed and murder.

Now Liana Robeson and Cullen Llewellyn embark on a
heart-pounding odyssey to find their son and the
missing pearl. Swept into the wild beauty of Australia,
they are plunged into a deadly game with a rival who
will go to any lengths to possess a treasure as fatal as it
is flawless.

**On sale mid-March 1999
where paperbacks are sold!**

MIRA

MER492

New York Times bestselling author

LINDA LAEL MILLER
Escape from Cabriz

Kristen Meyers's impulsive decision to marry the exotic
prince of Cabriz is beginning to seem like a very bad idea.
On the eve of their wedding, the palace is under attack by
angry rebels, and her fiancé has suddenly become a
coldhearted stranger. There doesn't appear to be any
escape from the complicated mess.

Then Zachary Harmon arrives. Kristen and the secret
agent were once lovers. Now he's risking his life to rescue
her. All the old chemistry is still there, but now they must
survive something even more explosive—escaping from
Cabriz alive.

> "Linda Lael Miller is one of the hottest romance
> authors writing today."
> —*Romantic Times*

On sale in mid-March 1999 wherever paperbacks are sold!

MIRA

Would Rhy Baines
recognize his wife?

New York Times Bestselling Author

LINDA HOWARD

Sallie Jerome, a.k.a. Mrs. Baines, had picked up the
pieces of shattered dreams after Rhy walked out seven
years ago. A news reporter for one of the nation's
leading magazines, she'd become the independent,
self-possessed woman Rhy had always wanted. Only,
now *she* didn't want him. Or did she?

An Independent Wife

"Howard's writing is compelling."
—Publishers Weekly

On sale mid-April 1999
wherever paperbacks are sold!

MIRA®

Look us up on-line at: http://www.romance.net   MLH500